The Smallest Angel

THE Smallest ANGEL

Richard Seib

ARCHWAY PUBLISHING

Copyright © 2016 Richard Seib.

All rights reserved. No part of this book may be used or reproduced by any means, graphic, electronic, or mechanical, including photocopying, recording, taping or by any information storage retrieval system without the written permission of the author except in the case of brief quotations embodied in critical articles and reviews.

Archway Publishing books may be ordered through booksellers or by contacting:

Archway Publishing
1663 Liberty Drive
Bloomington, IN 47403
www.archwaypublishing.com
1 (888) 242-5904

Because of the dynamic nature of the Internet, any web addresses or links contained in this book may have changed since publication and may no longer be valid. The views expressed in this work are solely those of the author and do not necessarily reflect the views of the publisher, and the publisher hereby disclaims any responsibility for them.

Any people depicted in stock imagery provided by Thinkstock are models, and such images are being used for illustrative purposes only.
Certain stock imagery © Thinkstock.

ISBN: 978-1-4808-3070-7 (sc)
ISBN: 978-1-4808-3069-1 (hc)
ISBN: 978-1-4808-3071-4 (e)

Library of Congress Control Number: 2016908203

Print information available on the last page.

Archway Publishing rev. date: 06/28/2016

Dedicated

There are some places where miracles happen without notice.
To the men and women of St. Joseph's Hospital and the Angels among them.

Prologue

Do you believe in angels? It's been said there are angels all around us. Sometimes they're not exactly what we expect. An angel could be that old man who gave you a needed bit of support when you least expected it. A stranger with a helping hand when you're in trouble or alone in some strange place. Sometimes she's that reassuring nurse or waitress with a comforting word when one needed it most.

It's thought by many that angels are invisible. They are those quiet whispers of inspiration when no one's around. That mysterious force that shielded you when all rational laws of nature and physics said what should have happened -- the result of a slip, skid, bad luck or judgment -- didn't. That, in spite of our own stupidity or raw arrogance in our immortality we still managed to survive in spite of ourselves.

Some angels are said to be of worldly origin. Born of flesh and blood with many gifts, or few at all. Predestined to do good for others, they disregarded their own concerns to help strangers. preordained to be living examples of what we could be, they remind us that we are not the dark side of the six o'clock news, but rather the true incarnations of our brothers' keepers. Maybe they're not humans at all, but all that is love, touched by providence.

How one's chosen to be touched by their presence is an even greater mystery. Why one person could go through his life never to have known, or have the comfort of their intervention, while another was blessed. Is it faith -- or the lack of it -- that dictated their presence? Was their intervention predestined or decided at that special moment of prayer, or is their presence for no greater reason than because someone was needed and they happened to be around?

Man may never know for what reasons decisions were made and saints were created. But does it really matter? What's important is their with us.

This then is a story about four in need and the smallest angel of all sent to guide them.

Going Home

The aged battered truck rumbled along, hugging the narrow road, slowing occasionally to skirt ragged potholes and debris. Lightly falling snow covered much of the war-ravaged landscape, making the heavy-looking gray clouds seem even more dismal. Steve Panailla pulled deep inside his coat and watched the desolate countryside pass out the back of the tarp covered truck. Were it not for the snow and cold, it would have been hard for him to comprehend that it was nearly Christmas. But then the image of Christmas had long since become an enigma to Steven. Instead it had become more of a fantasy that no longer held much magic or relevance. The view of a distant village, still smoldering from a recent shelling, had become the new reality for him. Along the road soldiers occasionally passed. Some looked lost in the nightmarish world around them. Others huddled around fires built in derelict fifty-five gallon oil drums as they guarded checkpoints, while pensively watching as refugees trudge by. Though Steve was only twenty-five, he felt closer to fifty as he pulled deeper into himself, took a deep breath, and watched his breath condense beyond his nose.

Almost from the moment Steve learned what television news was about, he dreamed of being a part of it, a photojournalist, videotaping the world. Steve considered himself lucky to have reached that dream. It was through his hard work and luck that he managed to reach the big leagues so quickly. He worked even harder to get what he considered a plum front line overseas assignment with one of the top journalists in the business. That was then. So much had changed. Now as he sat staring out at the desolation beyond the fringe of the truck, he couldn't help but wish he were back in college. Back when life was simple and his dreams still ahead of him, pure and unblemished. Back then all he had to worry about were grades and working as a bartender at the Shamrock where a bad night was poor tips and late night drunks. Reality had a way of diluting dreams quickly. Seeing death and barbarism first hand was nothing like the sound bites he saw from the safety of his living room on the six o'clock news. Nothing could have prepared him for what he'd witnessed in the name of religion, ethnic purity, or whatever excuse was on the docket to sanctify the taking of human lives. But then Afghanistan and the war that ensued after 9-11 was nothing anyone including the troops could have imagined.

Steve glanced at Carl, the renowned senior member of their impromptu little group; but Carl didn't look back. Instead he stared motionlessly at the duffel bag and bundles in front of him. Carl reminded Steve of a college professor he'd had once, the scholarly type, beard and mustache accenting his round face, not a globetrotting journalist. But there was no denying that he was good. He was a big man, like a linebacker twenty years removed. True to his appearance, Carl was the intellectual of the group, cool as a cucumber. He probed, asked deeper, more thought provoking questions than anyone Steve had ever met. Even his silence seemed to have an air of sophistication. Carl had a natural feel for people, what made them tick. No matter how bad the situation, sifting through the total chaos of a bombing or ducking a firefight, Carl somehow managed to retain an inner calm and confidence so unshakable that at times it seemed sickening.

Occasionally Carl's trance-like expression would change and he would turn to Marlene, the third member of their group, and smile, a kind of reassuring gesture that seemed to say, "No matter how bad things appear, they'll get better." Though Marlene seldom said much concerning their situations, Steve knew she believed in him. Marlene had, as she often joked, been around the block more often than a used car. She had worked her way up from local reporter to covering some of the most noteworthy European happenings, some glamorous, others not so. This was her third tour. She didn't talk much about the other two.

Steve's attention eventually turned to the fourth member of their ragtag group, Jules. Jules had joined their ensemble a week before as a matter of convenience. He was a freelance writer who was loosely associated with a syndicated news service in the States. He'd joined them as a matter of necessity after being unexpectedly separated from what had been a shaky UN press transportation core during one of those little skirmishes that occasionally broke out only to become suddenly a hellish nightmare of exploding mortar shells and chaos. Life, at least his view of it through his wire rim glasses, whether by nature or experience, had formed in him the mark of a confirmed pessimist and expounder on the finality of mankind. As Jules stared out at the raged countryside with an expression of condescending indifference, Steve felt certain that mankind had no surprises left for him. Like Afghanistan the world was quickly slipping into the toilet and would never again recover to become a place of palatable humanity.

Steve could understand Jules attitude. Jules had been in the field a long time--from Somalia to Iraq and back. He had seen so much more than his fair share of inhumanity as he hopped from one hellhole to another. Steve had only seen one war first hand -- this one. But the atrocities would be burned forever in his memories. What he had seen, neighbor killing neighbor for beliefs that had become so diluted over the millennia as to become little more than semantics and pride fueled by revenge to kill or be killed. Whoever said war was hell had greatly underestimated its totality. War wasn't hell, it was barbarism to the point of insanity as soldiers, partisans, guerillas, slugged it out. Add to that insanity, were the medias attempts to capture it, can it, send it back, so it could be seen on the tube during the six o'clock news. He had seen villages laid to waste in the name of a cause no one could remember anymore as they killed not only their enemies, but the sons and daughters of their enemies, mothers and their mothers. Steve had tried hard to stay detached from it all. But there were times when the stench of barbarism had become too unbearable. So unbearable that he could no longer hold the image of what was framed through his viewfinder but instead turned away from it all, the bodies piled in ditches of their own making, butchered in retaliation for some senseless killing in the name of Ala in some other long forgotten village an eternity ago. At those times it became harder to detach himself and say none of it was real, not in this world, but instead it had to be the surreal corner of some other godforsaken planet.

 What little detachment he had left totally disintegrated a week or so ago, or was it a decade? Steve pulled himself deeper into his coat to ward off the sudden cold chill as those images shot through him from that day. He glanced outside again, then looked away from the misery and turned instead toward the truck's flaked metal, dirt encrusted floor as they rumbled along. No wonder Carl seldom looked out. Better to shut it out he thought. Shut it out and dream of better times and places. Come off the line and get back to civilization. Back home where there was security, friendly faces and apple pie, if there was any such place anymore. He had tried hard to focus on that. Focus on the world he remembered. A place where people could walk to the local store at night, go to the movies or sit out on their own front porch without worrying about getting shot. Steve grew up in a suburb close to Milwaukee where the blight of drugs, gangs and drive by shootings had not migrated from the city.

For a long time he had been able to use those memories to get through the rough spots. But lately they no longer helped. Instead, when he closed his eyes and let his thoughts drift, he often found himself pulled back to that one instant. When that piece of hell would come back and become stuck in his subconscious and, like quicksand, try to suck him into images he felt helpless to escape. That vision, a small farmhouse of mostly mud and clay, and a couple others near a small village. Across the road was what appeared to have been a low, one-story school. Rumors had crept though that morning of a recent engagement that was so dark and vicious, only whispers gave any credence to its existence. Steve and the others had managed to finagle their way along with a squad sent out to investigate. It was early, barely light, damp and bone chilling cold. The area showed all the signs of a firefight. Houses, the school, riddled with the ragged holes of weapons fire.

Near the school, in an area that had probably been a playground of sorts was a large jagged crater, edged with fractured rock, gravel, and debris, the after effect of some errant rocket. Inside, partially covered with recently fallen snow, were twenty-five or thirty local inhabitants piled together. There was no discrimination among them, young, old, men, women. Some of the bodies were charred, possibly the result of someone trying, during a hasty retreat, to conceal the atrocity. Steve focused his camera, one eye closed, and scanned the carnage. Eventually he found himself locked on the image of a little girl, peering back at him from the entanglement of human remains, eyes open, but seeing nothing. She appeared to have been clutching the arm of a raggedly clothed woman, who in turn had been cradling a little boy, probably about two, to her bosom. All were dead, their blood long since soaked into the frozen ground. But the little girl's expression, her eyes, pleading for a reprieve from the death around her, chilled him. Though he managed to take the pictures, he knew they would never make it to the six o'clock news, but they would stay with him forever. No matter how hard he tried in the days afterwards, he couldn't escape the image of that girl's frozen stare.

It felt like forever before the truck finally slowed to a jerky stop outside a dilapidated building of cement block, with a worn slate roof that served as a small, third rate provisional airport terminal. Their muscles stiff, the foursome climbed off the back of the truck and grabbed their gear. The wind and snow had picked up markedly by then, slashing their faces as they began their trudge toward the rundown building. Steve snuggled deeper into his coat till only his eyes were exposed to try and stop the snow that whipped in through the top of his hood and down the back of his neck. With his hands full of camera and gear, a bag slung over his shoulder he could do little more than tolerate his discomfort.

Only a few haggard-looking people were scattered about

the terminal when the four entered. Steve stomped his boots, more out of childhood upbringing than respect for the facility as he looked around at the ragged lobby. He doubted anyone noticed or even cared about his pretense toward cleanliness. The place looked as if it hadn't been cleaned in years. No doubt management had its hands full just trying to keep it running in a manner somewhat in keeping with the twentieth century say nothing about the twenty-first. But then it was not a major hub or even regional airport, just a backwater airstrip servicing a third rate city in a country that was in the throws of trying to reinvent itself in the face of chaos.

Like drones Steve and the others followed Carl silently to a row of benches near the windows looking out on the runway. Jules dropped his bag and gear, then walked off toward what appeared to be the information counter. Carl placed his duffel bag next to the bench nearest the window, then continued on to the streaked, frozen glass to watch the snow blowing outside. Marlene placed her bag next to Carl's then followed after Jules. It was obvious that where she was going had nothing to do with transportation.

For a moment Steve toyed with the idea of removing his coat, but the cold of the day's journey had permeated his body too deeply to relinquish its hold quite yet. Or maybe it was the accumulation of all the misery he had experienced over the past few weeks that kept him in such a perpetual chill. Whatever it was he decided to stay covered and instead huddled deeper into its lining, trying to regain his warmth and cleanse his thoughts, in hopes his mind might go blank.

Jules returned a short time later and plopped on the bench between Steve and the window. He was an athletic-looking man with three days' growth, who kept trim probably by having long lost his appetite for the local cuisine. "Don't look good," he announced while unzipping his coat.

"What they say?" asked Steve feeling another chill.

"They haven't heard anything. But most everything else has been canceled or delayed." Jules finished opening his coat, then removed his glasses and began cleaning them. "But then what can you expect in such a God forsaken place."

Steve didn't respond. Instead he focused his attention to Carl who had turned away from the window long enough to hear Jules's comment. Steve was tempted to ask Carl's thoughts on the matter. He didn't. Instead he watched Marlene, Carl's counterpart, a veteran with chronic sore feet, as she returned from the restroom and sat down across from Jules. Slipping off one shoe, Marlene let out a small sigh, then dug through her purse. Finding what appeared to be an ancient stick of gum she weakly smiled. "So what's the word?" she asked while unwrapping the gum.

"Not good. I'd say fifty-fifty we're here for the duration," mumbled Jules.

Marlene stared at Jules a moment, then putting the gum in her mouth, looked around the terminal and shrugged. "Well so much for 'I'll be home for Christmas'."

"Could be worse," Steve found himself saying almost instinctively while trying to overcome the knot in his stomach.

"I don't know how," laughed Jules. "There's no bar. The entertainment's terrible and there isn't a turkey in the place. Even Santa would condemn this place, and there isn't a decent looking woman around either." Jules abruptly turned to Marline. "Present company excluded."

"Thanks," coughed Marlene. "At least it ain't Sarajevo."

"Yeah, it's not Somalia."

Jules's flat response and the silence afterwards seemed to sum up the feelings held by all but Steve who had never been on that assignment, an assignment before his time, but he had heard the stories. Some said it was the closest anyone one had come to the Holocaust or hell on earth. Just the mention of it seemed to take the heart out of anything positive that might have been going through their minds. Steve watched Jules finish cleaning his glasses, then put them on and look at Carl. By then Carl had turned back to the window and the blowing snow outside.

"It's almost been a year since I've been home," said Marlene to no one in particular. "I really wanted to be there this Christmas."

"Our hero's getting soft," said Jules sharply.

"Don't tell me you don't get a little mellow this time of year!"

Marlene's comment surprised Steve. He was not use to her showing much if any sentiment. But then it wasn't unlike her to take sides either. She once confided in Steve that it was her way of keeping things honest, or at least keeping them from overwhelming her. Though she often appeared stronger than granite, he didn't doubt that Carl's presence had a lot to do with it.

"No, practical," shot Jules, not letting the dust settle on Marlene's jab. "Right now I'd settle for just a hot shower and clean bed. That would be enough holidays for me."

It was apparent Marlene wanted to say more but didn't. Sometimes it's best to just let matters drop, she once said. Too many wars had begun because someone didn't know when to shut up. If anyone had seen the results of that more than she had, Steve hadn't met them. Instead, she retrieved a battered paperback and, removing an odd looking bookmark, began to read.

Jules watched her a moment then turned to Carl. "You think your friend can still fly us out of here?"

"If anyone can." Carl did not turn around when he responded, just kept watching the blowing snow.

"Well if he can, maybe I'll believe in miracles," Marlene didn't look up as she talked, her voice expressionless.

"You can forget that," chuckled Jules. "Miracles ended with Christ."

"I thought you were an atheist," shot Marlene.

"I never said 'atheist,' just cynical. But from what I've seen of the human condition, God must have a real sense of humor. As far as miracles are concerned, I'd put odds on us flying out of here tonight right up there with the cavalry coming to save the day, and you know what happened to Custer."

For the first time since the discussion began, Carl turned around, his broad face showing interest as he focused on Jules. "Maybe you're just not looking close enough, Jules."

"Have you ever seen a miracle?" asked Marlene, her normal indifferent expression softened.

"Let's just say I've learned there's more to life than what's on the surface."

"If you're looking for worms." Jules stretched and looked around. "As far as I'm concerned, the world's beyond hope and the best you can hope for is to get through it in one piece and be gone before it knows you were there."

Steve felt that sinking feeling in the pit of his stomach begin to grow again. He wanted to go home so much it hurt. That was all that mattered anymore. If he could just get back home among friends and the family he left behind. He needed to be in a safe place far from where he was, where he could sort things out, make some kind of piece with it, or just forget it all. "This is getting way too serious," he finally said. "It's Christmas, for crying out loud. What we need here is something inspirational. What's the most inspiring thing you've seen?" Steve watched the others but no one said a word. "Come on! One of you must have had at least one moving moment in your life!"

Everyone remained silent. For a moment Steve thought Carl was going to say something. But he apparently thought better of it and instead turned back to the window.

"Wait, I've got something!" Jules abruptly stood up and went to a distant counter. He returned with some empty cups. Opening his bag, he took out a ratty looking paper bag. From inside the bag he pulled out a bottle of brandy. "I've been saving this for a special occasion," smiled Jules as he opened the bottle. He quickly pored some into the cups, then began passing them about. "This is not exactly where I had planned to drink this, but I guess the fact that we've gotten this far makes it worth a celebration." Jules held up his cup after passing out the others. "Drink up my friends, this is about as good as I get."

Marlene took a sip, then held her cup toward Jules and smiled. "As far as inspired is concerned, I can't top this. To Christmas."

"To Christmas," chimed the others holding up their cups. After each took a drink Marlene turned to Carl. "I bet you could top this!"

Carl paused in mid sip, looked at his cup, then continued. "It's out there. As screwed up as this world seems, God isn't dead, and miracles didn't end with the Middle Ages."

"I'm sorry, but I don't buy it." Jules emptied his cup, then poured some more. "Give me one example of something you've seen worth believing there's still hope."

"A miracle," added Marlene.

Carl reached for Jules' bottle, filled his cup again, then emptied half in one swallow before refilling it, then passed the bottle back to Jules. "A miracle. What is a miracle? It's different for everyone." Carl paused and took another sip. "The fact that we're all here is a miracle in itself."

"Are you talking about being born, or the last couple weeks?" asked Jules as he leaned back. "Because if it's birth, then considering the odds no one would argue. But miracles of nature don't count, it's been happening for eons and it'll be happening for eons to come, even if it's only the cockroaches that are left. But that's not what we're talking about." Jules took off his glasses and started to clean them again, a habit Steve noticed Jules did a lot whenever he got particularly philosophical. "I'll also not debate the fact that every day when I get up to do this job I'm amazed I'm still here. But I haven't seen any miracles. No angels singing or protecting the helpless."

"Ah, but you don't know whether they were, do you?" said Carl like a criminal lawyer closing in for the kill. "You don't know for sure whether there wasn't some divine intervention that kept you out of harm's way or one of the unfortunates that we didn't see who's still walking around."

"And you don't know there was," said Marlene, her journalistic mind aroused to the debate. "What might have been, give an inch or two, could fill an ocean. Truth is, you don't have a concrete example, do you!"

For a moment Carl appeared ready to say something that would have vindicated his stance. But just as suddenly his expression changed. He glanced at Steve then turned to Jules. "What I know, what I've seen, and what I am at liberty to say, are two very different things. All I can say is miracles, like God, are all around you if you believe in them. There was a time I was just as cynical as you all --maybe more so. But that's the past."

"Nice speech. But you're a little short on substance." Jules abruptly motioned toward the window with his cup.

"Now if that plane manages to get here through all that crap and gets us out of here, then I might believe in miracles."

Carl turned back to the window and nodded toward the boiling snow whipping about outside. "The plane will be here," he half whispered to himself. "They'll come."

Marlene silently watched Carl. Finally she returned to her dog-eared paperback. Jules stared at the window, watching the storm, then sat back, reached into his bag and pulled out a leather journal. Steve had occasionally seen him retreat to his book during the weeks he'd known him. He often wondered what someone like Jules would write. Would it be as cynical as he presented himself? Or would it be something else? The real Jules, confessing his fears and doubts before God, if only as a way of cleansing his soul and making it through this hell. Finding his place, Jules began to write.

Steve turned his attention back to Carl standing at the window, watching the storm that had all but obscured the runway. He had often found himself inspired by Carl and his strength of conviction. No matter how bad the situation, Carl somehow managed to find a way of putting a positive spin on things. Seldom were his reports negative. True, they had found themselves in more tight spots over the past couple months then he cared to think about. But like Jules, Steve had a hard time attributing their delivery to divine intervention. On the contrary, some of his experiences, especially as of late, made him wonder whether there was a God at all. If there was, Steve wondered how he could ever have allowed what he'd seen happen. Carl, on the other hand seemed to almost have blinders, screening out the bad, focusing on the good. It was amazing to watch thought Steve, if not a bit distorted.

Steve sat a long time, watching the others, analyzing the possibilities of their leaving before New Years, let alone that night. Jules finally put away his journal, got up and left, no doubt to find the facilities or whether the choices of women had improved. Marlene became even more engrossed in her novel, and Carl continued silently looking out the window. Eventually Steve leaned back and tried to visualize all that he would do should he ever manage to get back home to see Christmas. Getting up early and going to the Pink Cup for coffee, breakfast, and a quiet time with the paper while listening to the locals talk about the weather, home, or friends. Maybe a short trip to the mart, home with the family, and Christmas Eve candle light service before going home again for a family night of gifts and fellowship -- like candles and gifts and watching "It's A Wonderful Life." It would all be so good, pleasant and peaceful – and unfortunately a million miles away. As he thought of those memories his eyes closed and he eventually fell asleep.

⋆

It seemed an eternity before Steve felt conscious again. His eyes were closed. He felt a cold chill surge through him, cold enough to keep him from wanting to open them again. He had the dream -- the same one that had haunted him, asleep or awake, since he saw the little girl. It was early morning; a misty fog was flowing through the woods. He felt stiff and cold, too afraid to move. He was hugging the ground near a tree, his face almost buried in its bark. Bodies laid all around him, frozen and lifeless. He knew if he moved they would spot him and his body would become just another part of his gruesome surroundings. All he wanted to do was dig a hole, a deep hole, pull the ground up over him, and hide. He could hear their voices in the distance, they were checking bodies, making sure they were dead. He felt like a quail in the bush -- scared senseless, ready to bolt, knowing it was his only chance.

That's how the dream always ended. He could hear their voices in the distance, coming closer, closer. Then he would wake with a cold sweat, afraid to open his eyes for fear the dream was real. He would strain to listen, but there was no sound. No voices. He was safe, at least for the time being.

Eventually Steven opened his eyes and looked around. Nothing had changed. He was still in the dingy waiting room of the air terminal. It was late, he figured at least eleven. He toyed with the idea of closing his eyes again and going back to sleep, but the stiffness and cold that permeated his body and the thought of going back to that dream again cancelled that out. Instead he pulled himself up in his seat, and pulled the coat that he'd used as a blanket closer to his lips then looked around again. Jules was asleep, propped up in a corner seat against the wall, his cap pulled over his eyes, and his coat caressing him tight. Marlene was also out, her worn paperback novel cradled in her lap. Only Carl remained at his post, staring out the window at the blowing snow, blowing with the same intensity as it had when Steve fell asleep. Pulling himself together, Steve summoned up enough energy to get up. After a long wrenching stretch he joined Carl.

"Another bad dream?" asked Carl barely turning from his fixation with the runway. Steve stared at Carl curiously as if to say, how'd you know? But he didn't say a word. "You were twitching and mumbling in your sleep," said Carl as if reading Steven's mind.

"Its this place. I guess I'm not as tough as I thought I was."

"It's not easy. No one said it was. If it were everyone would do it. But you're good. You'll get use to it."

"I don't think I'll ever get use to it." Steve wanted to say more. He wanted to say he would never get used to how brutal man could be. What had been his insatiable curiosity had all but vanished with the stench of death and wanton destruction he'd experienced to the point were it had become almost unbearable. But it was what those images represented that had become so repugnant to him. They had in fact become so much a part of his life and dreams he didn't even want to think about them anymore, say anything about talking about them. "Do you really think they'll make it through this stuff tonight?" he heard himself ask, sounding more like a kid worried over Santa making it. That and the possibility of him escaping this place with Santa.

Carl paused, a pause that had become somewhat of his trademark, an exclamation before responding to questions he didn't really feel like expounding on, or just as likely forget. "As sure as I'm standing here."

"How can you be so sure?"

"Because I have faith. And I know God's with them."

"From what I've seen, God hasn't been all that reliable."

"I take it you're not much on religion."

"I was brought up Catholic. But we weren't very active." Steve paused, looked back at the darker reaches of the terminal, then pulled deeper into his coat and nodded toward the airstrip outside, its perimeters obscured by the blowing snow. "How can you be so confident? They got some kind of special dispensation or something?"

Carl smiled. "Maybe. Let's just say they have an angel watching over them, a very special angel."

It seemed almost impossible, if not a little suicidal, for anyone to try to land at such a poorly equipped place, let alone find it, even with divine intervention. Steve began to feel guilty for even being partially responsible for anyone risking his life in such a storm. By the same token, he wanted to go home so badly he would have done almost anything to get out of there, including flying out by himself if he knew how.

"You really want to go home."

Steve focused on the blowing snow. "So much it hurts. Lately I've been finding myself asking whether I'm really cut out for this. I guess I just don't have the stomach for it like you guys do. I thought I did but I don't." Steve stared at the floor a moment, then looked back at Carl feeling the need to say more. "As for angels I think they've gone the way of the Easter Bunny. I'm sorry but I haven't seen anything around here that even hints that compassion and divine intervention still exist in the world." With that Steve walked back to the nearest bench and sat down.

"I know it's hard to believe, Steve. Especially after all you've experienced these past few months. But we have to believe in something. If there was nothing more to life on this spinning rock than random choice, I know it would eventually get pretty hard just getting up in the morning." Carl stared at his knapsack a moment, then grabbed it, lumbered over, to the bench and sat down, then with a fatherly gesture, motioned for Steve to come over. "Tell you a little secret. There was a time a few years ago when my confidence in God and the order of things was about as bad as yours, possibly worse."

"Thanks." Steve weakly smiled, then turned and stared at the floor. Even though they did not attend church that regularly Steve had had God and religion drummed into him since he was a child. But the naked reality of what they'd experienced had changed all that. Suddenly God, if he ever existed, was missing in action. The world was in chaos and between religious zeal, ethnic purity, the Green House effect and the hydrogen bomb; mankind was on the fast track to Armageddon. If he didn't do it in the near future, then the best he had was a few hundred years. "I guess right now I just need a little more."

"What you need is something to get your mind off things." Carl paused and looked around at the others who were still sound asleep. He glanced at his watch as if checking how much time had passed, then opened his duffel bag and reached deep inside. Finding what he was looking for Carl pulled out something wrapped in waterproof cloth and unwrapped it. Inside was a pouch, which he gently removed and unzipped. Carl carefully removed what appeared to be a manuscript in a protective cover and handed it to Steve. "I've never shown this to anyone other than a publisher friend and even he only saw a portion of it. I'd like you to read it Steven. If nothing else, it might help you get through the night."

Steve took the manuscript, its stiff, cover showing signs of wear, and studied it. It was common knowledge Carl had been working on a book or something of some importance for some time. Marlene had mentioned it once, suggesting it was probably a journal of his experiences. With all Carl had done, she was certain whatever it was would be a best seller. The concept had so intrigued Jules that he started his own journal, no doubt originally hoping to catapult it into a major book deal, "The World from the Front." Problem was Steve doubted Jules' negative view on the world would find much of an audience, other then a few doomsday groups and some hypochondriacs. Over the last month or so Steve began to wonder if maybe that journal had evolved into something much deeper for Jules. To suddenly be holding Carl's cherished possession was an honor, if not a bit overwhelming. "Thank you. But why me?"

"Like I said Steven, it might help make the hours pass faster. It might even give you a little peace of mind, who knows? Don't mind the occasional grammar mistakes. Even though it's technically finished, it still feels like a work in progress. Sort of in a continual state of editing. I think except for a few name changes it's done. But then, who knows, it might never ever be completely done." Carl gently padded Steven on the shoulder. "Enjoy it, but promise not to divulge anything about it to anyone. This is just between us."

Steve nodded, then watched Carl slowly stand up again and return to the window. He reverently held the manuscript in his hand, almost afraid to turn the page for fear it would self-destruct. He was not sure why, maybe it was because of its importance to Carl -- or because he was the only one Carl had entrusted it to, that he felt a bit uncomfortable holding it. Or maybe there was something more, something intangible yet almost spiritual about the manuscript. That feeling began to envelop Steve when he finally opened the cover and read the title page, 'The Smallest Angel'. His eyes fixed on the words; he paused, then turned the page and began to read.

The Smallest Angel

Chapter One

It was a crisp early fall morning, seven thirty Monday. The crowds were already heavy when Nishka walked up from the subway. Even in her conservative business suit, hair up in a bun, those that met her couldn't help but notice that she was strikingly beautiful. She was tall and had a mysterious European look about her that couldn't be ignored.

Nishka gripped the handle of her briefcase firmly as she crossed the street along with dozens of others. She had looked forward to that morning, but then she always looked forward to work. It was something she found fulfilling, the cold logic of market trends, annualizing, making investments, selling, anticipating the market before the rest of the world had a clue. She had begun to attract a following, clientele who trusted her business sense explicitly. Nishka's weekends, by contrast, were voids, consisting of little more than self-imposed exile, workshops, studying, reading business trends and balance sheets. She planed out her week and, barring sudden changes, each week after that. As much as she thrived on work, this Monday would be special. She had developed a program strategy that was ready to be launched and its success could move her up the ladder dramatically.

As Nishka entered the lobby she heard her name called over the din of the crowds heading to work. "Nishka, wait up!" Behind her Sharon, a junior broker, in her mid-twenties, hurried to catch her.

"Sharon, how was your weekend?" Nishka always asked her that on Mondays. She learned early that to Sharon the weekend was the all-important part of her life and, to do nothing meant her existence was meaningless. Her weekend was particularly fulfilling when she spent it with someone of the opposite sex. Though Nishka did not particularly care about Sharon's social life she did find it a useful question in order to keep a friendly association, both as a way of better blending in and being accepted. That's what she told herself. Truth was, she was beginning to develop a vague friendship with Sharon.

"Not bad. If you don't mind sitting home most of the time ironing and watching reruns."

Nishka didn't laugh. She felt she should, but humor was an attribute she understood least. Even so it was obvious she would have to laugh sometime if for no other reason than to not seem starchy or odd. "Oh shoot," said Sharon noticing her tennis shoe was untied. "Hold a minute."

As Sharon bent over to fix her shoe, while holding on to Nishka for support, two young stock brokers walked past. "Any hot tips today?" nodded the tallest one.

"Research," shot Nishka emotionlessly.

"That's good," he laughed.

Sharon looked up from fixing her shoe as the two men walked on. "Cute. You ever think of softening up a little?"

Nishka barely acknowledged Sharon's comment as she watched the two brokers hurry to catch an elevator before the door closed. As her eyes focused on them she could read their lips. "I don't know why you bother." The broker's friend said after reaching the door. "She's colder than an iceberg."

"Yeah but she's the best-packaged berg in the building," said the tall one. "Hell, she's smarter than half the floor put together. Kind of kinky, don't you think?"

As the elevator door began to close, the other broker shrugged. "Whatever turns you on. She does have some great assets." They both chuckled as the door closed. It was a distance, but there was no doubt what they said. Nishka had read lips at even greater distances. It was part of the array of special talents Vladimir had blessed her with and it had served her well at times.

Sharon was still talking and fixing her shoe when Nishka turned back to her. "I hear he's single too," she said, finally standing up straight. "Why don't you ask him out?"

"He's not my type," said Nishka matter-of-factly.

"They're never your type. You've got to loosen up girl, or you'll be spending the rest of your life staring at balance sheets. What are you looking for, a man or a computer?"

"Hard choice," said Nishka.

Sharon laughed, "That wouldn't surprise me."

As the two women started for the elevator, Nishka noticed two maintenance men entering the lobby through a distant service door. They both appeared to be of Middle Eastern abstraction and seemed in an unusual hurry to leave. As the men turned in the opposite direction, the familiar looking one noticed Nishka, paused, then abruptly started toward her. He had barely taken a couple steps when a violent explosion from the floors above rocked the lobby.

"Oh my God, what's happening!" yelled Sharon, her hands suddenly to her ears. Smoke belched from the elevator shafts as the doors exploded open. Sharon frantically screamed then darted for the exterior door as the sounds of twisted metal and screams echoed throughout the lobby. One of the two men paused for a moment then continued toward Nishka who abruptly turned, then broke into a run, cutting through the throngs trying to escape the chaos.

⁓❦⁓

The street was a maze of confusion when Nishka reached the outside. Smoke billowed from the floors above as people trying to escape melded with the hundreds of onlookers outside. Caught up in the chaos, Sharon cried out for Nishka, but she didn't respond. By then Nishka's only concern was in putting as much distance between her and the two men as possible. Faster she ran, pushing through the confused crowd, but no matter how fast she went, her pursuers followed a distance behind and closing.

Nishka reached the subway and fought her way down through the upcoming crowds. Cutting from side to side, weaving in and out, she reached the platform just as a train was preparing to leave. Quickly cutting across the platform, Nishka slid through the opened door. She turned around just as her pursuers reached the bottom of the stairs. No sooner had they ran across the platform car door just as it closed. The leader, a man she remembered as Ahmed, pounded on the glass frantically trying to pry the door open, but it held fast as the train began to move.

Finally giving up he shook his fist at Nishka and yelled as the train pulled away. "I will find you!"

As the platform grew smaller in the distance, Nishka watched Ahmed and his comrade beside him.

"You know her Ahmed! You think she will talk?"

"No," shot Ahmed watching the train pull away.

"Then who cares?"

Ahmed stared at the train, growing smaller in the distance.

His eyes burning at the thought of seeing Nishka after such a long time, only to let her slip through his fingers. "I care!" he snarled, gritting his teeth. "And if you knew her like I do, you would too!"

Chapter Two

TWO THOUSAND ONE

It was a pleasant, late summer morning, unusual for mid August in the quiet older neighborhood of sixties style suburban homes. In one of the yards three young boys in a tree house were busy pulling a rope that was threaded through a pulley then ran down through a trap door to where a pixyish looking girl of nine -- wearing shorts, tank top, and a leg brace -- was suspended on a swing. Sweat rolled down the boys' faces as they pulled her higher and higher into the tree.

So deeply were they engrossed in their labors that none of them noticed a tall, attractive woman in the yard next door carry a large box in their direction. It wasn't until she set the box down a short distance from the fence separating the two properties that Peter, older brother of Jessica, the girl on the swing, noticed her. Vern noticed the woman next, and like his friend became so captivated that they both nearly lost their grips on the rope. Only Barry managed to hang on, abruptly finding himself being dragged toward the hole in the floor, "Oh shit!!" yelled Barry, trying desperately to stop his slide.

"What's wrong with you guys!!" shouted Jessica, her free-fall stopping just a few feet short of the ground.

"Sorry." That was all Peter said as he and Vern snapped to and began frantically helping Barry pull his sister back up into the tree house. No sooner was Jessica safely inside than the boys were gone, leaving her bewildered and alone.

"Thanks a lot!" snapped Jessica to an empty room as she climbed to her feet and brushed herself off. The boys had deserted her. But then Jessica had become used to that. She was gutsy, more sure of herself than most. Still, when it came to children and games, there were all too many times that, because of her leg, Jessica found herself on the sidelines. Even so, her brace seldom slowed her. After brushing herself off, Jessica hobbled out onto the deck. "Thanks a lot for not dropping me!!"

"Swoosh," hushed Vern, holding his finger to his lips.

Jessica felt like smacking him. Instead she turned her attention to the attractive woman in the other yard who was in the process of lifting a lawnmower out of its box. It was obvious where the boys' minds were. Even Jessica was a little awed by the woman's beauty, her long brunette hair flowing down well past her shoulders.

"Bet she never gets it running," quipped Barry as they watched her skim through the instruction manual faster than most people could turn its pages.

"Two bucks she does." shot Jessica, resting her chin on the railing.

The boys barely nodded acceptance of Jessica's bet as they watched their new neighbor close the booklet, then methodically assemble the mower with all the agility of a seasoned mechanic. It seemed like only an instant had passed before she finished, oiled the mower, and added gas.

Like a landscaping pro she made a couple quick pulls of the cord and the mower roared to life.

"Ha. Pay up!" laughed Jessica as she watched the woman brush back her long hair, then begin mowing the lawn. "We going to play cards or not?"

"In a minute," waved Peter. It was apparent the boys were hopelessly captivated by the woman. But then they were boys, older than Jessica by a couple years, and women were becoming higher on their priority list. Maybe not all the time, but more than Jessica cared to hear. Deciding the situation hopeless, Jessica turned back into the clubhouse to wait for them to come to their senses.

"My mother says she ain't married," squeaked Barry.

"Any boyfriends?" asked Peter.

"She don't think so."

"If anyone would know, your mother would," chuckled Peter.

The revelation that their new neighbor was single brought Jessica back to the railing. A single woman living alone next door. That intrigued her, and the more she watched the more intrigued she became. The woman was different, not like the mothers and other women Jessica knew. She seemed like the type that would be confident in whatever she did, self-reliant, and mysterious. And she was all alone. Jessica admired that.

None one actually knew anything about her, other than Barry's mother. Jessica had occasionally heard her grandmother refer to Barry's mother as the town's original busybody. "It's what happens when you have too much time on your hands," her grandmother would say. "She should go out and get a job like everyone else instead of sticking her nose in everyone else's business." Jessica's grandmother was one of the few older people Jessica knew who believed in women working, whether they needed the money or not. Her grandmother always said that with today's modern conveniences, most women had way too much time on their hands anyway, and Barry's mother was the poster woman for that theory. But then what Barry's mother said and what she actually knew were two different things. According to Jessica's grandmother, one had to take everything she said with a grain of salt, whatever that meant.

All the boys really knew about this attractive new neighbor was she had bought the Wilson house, a comfortable, light blue ranch which had been empty all spring. There had been talk someone had bought it, though no one knew whom. But even that wasn't official since no one had actually seen anyone move in. The only physical evidence things had changed on their sleepy street was a day two weeks before when the For Sale sign that had stood like a sentinel in the yard most of that year was suddenly covered with a sold sticker. A week later it was gone. There wasn't even a moving truck. Just a couple deliveries from Sears and J.C. Penney's. It had been a week, more or less since then, and apparently -- other than Barry's mother -- no one had seen a thing.

That all changed now. As the children watched the woman mow her lawn, it was for certain they wouldn't forget her easily. "She's beautiful," sighed Vern.

"I wonder if father met her?" said Jessica.

Barry snickered. "I know my father would probably like to."

"She's beautiful." Vern repeated, he was smitten. But so were the other boys. As the four watched the long legged woman propel her lawn mower across her yard it was apparent each had their own fantasies about her, including Jessica. Though the woman appeared young, late twenties at most, she seemed to have a strange agelessness about her.

It was also apparent to Jessica, as she watched her brother and friends drooling, that they wouldn't be the only ones to be so captivated once word got out. The woman was too beautiful to be kept a secret for long.

⋅≽⋅

Jessica's brother and the others watched the new neighbor's yard till long after the last blade of grass was cut and the lawnmower was put away. Eventually, after it was apparent the woman wasn't coming out again; the boys drifted into the clubhouse and joined Jessica in poker for pennies, marbles, and anything else of value. To them it didn't matter that the world had gone a little mad and that there were those that would, if possible, turn it all up side down because of some crazy belief or cause. All that mattered was their little world, their neighborhood and the tree house, and at that moment their minds weren't even on the game. Instead all that mattered was the new neighbor and the possibility that any sound from that direction could signal new activity next door. Those sounds in turn brought silence, a turned head, and on occasional abrupt journey by one of the boys back out to the porch to check. But no matter how often the boys checked, the woman never came out again.

Chapter Three

Conversation regarding the new neighbor continued sporadically between the boys for the rest of that morning. The image of her, coupled with the boys' fantasies, made Jessica's success in cleaning out her brother and the others better than usual giving her a pleasant little nest egg when the game was over.

That night after the other boys had gone, Peter and Jessica returned home to an aroma of Italian sausage and spaghetti hanging heavy in the air. The two children lived with their father. Barbara, the children's mother, had died in a car accident when Jessica was six. Jessica was the only passenger. The doctor said she should recover fine, but when they put her mother in the ground, Jessica's leg stopped recovering. That had been three years ago.

Since then, Jessica's grandmother had become a semi-permanent fixture, helping with the family washing, cleaning, and periodically making dinner.

As usual, Peter began setting the table, putting out plates for four while Jessica stacked the papers left out from their father's unfinished work from the night before. She placed them on the bureau, then helped Peter put out the silverware.

"Looks good," said Jessica, checking the table like a seasoned Maitre d'.

Peter barely nodded as he put out the salt and peppershakers.

No sooner had Peter finished, than a kitchen door opened and Grandmother walked in from a small pantry carrying a basket of cut French bread and a butter dish. "Looks lovely," she smiled, setting down the bread.

It was expected that their father would soon be home. He seldom deviated from his schedule and as his mother often said one could set their watch by him. What wasn't expected was the company he brought. "Hey look who I found," announced David, their father, nodding toward his sister Judith and her husband as they followed him in. David was an average looking man, medium build, wearing his usual shirt and tie. He had left work early that day to go to the airport with Judith to pick up Carl, her husband, who had just returned from overseas.

Carl was a large bear of a man with a manicured beard and mustache who, in his more grubby moments, resemble a likeable lumberjack. The rest of the time he appeared more like a worldly professor. Most of his career he had been a television journalist covering everything from national events to hot spots and wars.

There was no doubt when Carl walked in, duffel bag in hand, that he was looking for more than just a little R & R. Only days before Judith had told David that Carl was at a point where he needed an escape from his livelihood, a little time off. Over the past few years the world had turned sour for Carl, so much so she felt that he'd begun to debate his role in life. He had even considered, during the lowest days, chucking it all and spending the rest of his career in some ivy covered university teaching the finer points of journalism to whoever would listen.

When Jessica saw Carl her eyes brightened. "Uncle Carl!"

Carl dropped his bag and, kneeling down hugged Jessica as she hobbled to him. "How you doing Sunshine?"

"Fine," blushed Jessica.

Seeing Peter, Carl pulled him over and shook his hand. "Peter, how's my man? Still watching those stars?"

"All the time."

"See E.T. yet?"

"Not yet." Peter paused, "Have you?"

Carl smiled, then straightening up, looked back at Jessica who coyly leaned closer to his ear.

"Did you bring us anything?" she whispered.

"What do you think?" winked Carl. Grabbing his duffel bag he swung it onto a chair then opened it. Reaching under some clothing, he pulled out a rocket model and handed it to Peter.

Peter's eyes glistened. "Thank you!"

Carl watched Peter hurry to another chair to examine the kit. He then turned to Jessica. "Did I forget someone?" Carl watched Jessica nod sheepishly, then hugged her again. "I must have brought you something." Carl dug deep into his bag again and rummaged through it awhile, then paused and pulled out a round shaped object wrapped in newspaper. "Here you go, Sweetheart."

Quickly unwrapping the paper, Jessica uncovered a crystal ball attached to a pedestal. Inside the ball was a beautiful angel, wings spread, standing over the manger of Jesus. "It's beautiful!" squealed Jessica, watching the snow fly about inside as she moved the ball.

"It's you."

"Thank you," Jessica threw her arms around Carl's neck and kissed him. "I love you."

"I love you, too," whispered Carl. There was little doubt

that the feelings he felt for her went far beyond that of uncle to niece. And Jessica wasn't even his niece, except through marriage. Carl often felt that Jessica, and Peter too for that matter, were part his own, or as close to his own as he would probably ever get. It had been years since he and Judith had given up on the possibility of having children. It was a complicated matter. A long medical explanation, but the end result was Judith could never conceive, barring a miracle. And according to the doctor, the odds of that were right up there with Immaculate Conception.

For a while they considered adopting. But the powers that be in that arena were not particularly keen on giving children to a couple where the father was gone ninety percent of the time covering world insanity. With the possibility of having their own family almost nil, Judith, and Carl in particular, had taken to David's children as if they were their own, especially after their mother died.

As Carl talked to Jessica, David noticed the table set for four. "You didn't set extra plates!"

"Thought I'd keep it a surprise," said Grandmother, nodding toward the children.

David smiled, then turned to his sister. "Would anyone like some wine?"

Judith bubbled "yes," and so the night began. David poured wine for all old enough and a small sip for Peter and Jessica. With Carl freshly back from one of his great adventures, conversation soon became lively and continued long after they had settled down for dinner. It was a pleasant meal. Carl asked the children how their summer had gone, and as usual they told him in great detail. There were sporadic conversations about David's work and politics and what the Green Bay Packers were going to do that fall. The children wanted to hear Carl talk about his latest travels and the adventures that always accompanied them. He would always oblige, edited of course.

"I take it you liked the Canary Islands?" asked Grandmother as she passed more bread.

"Very much. They've become quite the European Mecca. Especially for the Scandinavian countries," smiled Carl, trying not to show too much enthusiasm over those implications.

"See lots of pretty girls?" asked Peter.

"Is that all you think about?" frowned Judith, not sure whether she was more disappointed at his question or the thought that he was becoming old enough to have them.

"You're definitely getting older," smiled Carl, trying to ignore his wife. "Yes I did. Quite a few as a matter of fact. A lot of tall blonde ones."

Grandmother shook her head, apparently disappointed at where the conversation was heading and was preparing to change the subject when Jessica cut in. "A beautiful woman moved in next door."

"You don't say." Carl turned to David. "What's she like, David?"

"Don't know, never met her."

"She's okay," chimed Peter matter-of-factly. "She's not beautiful."

"Oh yeah, then why were you guys watching her all day?" huffed Jessica.

Peter looked stunned, like a deer caught in the headlights of a car. "We weren't Dad, honest!" He turned to his grandmother, then the others to plead his innocence. "We just thought she might need help!"

"That's enough about girls. Can't you boys ever talk about anything else," chided Grandmother, sensing Peter's embarrassment.

For a moment the room was silent, then Carl picked

up his fork and held it high. "Sure is wonderful spaghetti." That ended the discussion on women, including the new neighbor, at least during dinner. But that didn't mean the neighbor was forgotten. The fact that an apparently single woman, attractive or otherwise, moved in next door and the implications considering David's status as a single parent affected everyone's thoughts to one degree or another that night. David had been a widower for three years. Maybe this was the answer to a prayer, if not his mother's, and a few other members of the family. The only question was whether he would take advantage of it.

⚜

After dinner the children disappeared into the living room. Judith and Grandmother cleared the table and began washing the dishes. Taking advantage of the pleasant summer evening, David and Carl took a couple of beers and adjourned to the backyard patio.

"Beautiful night isn't it?" said Carl, looking up at the sky as he sat down on a metal lawn chair. "You know David; I sometimes forget how pleasant it can be to just sit here on nights like this."

David nodded. It was pleasant, a little warm still, but there was just enough breeze to make the late August evening feel refreshing. "The kids will be back in school in a couple weeks. I can't believe how fast this summer went."

Carl took a deep breath, savoring the aroma of distant flowers like one would a good cigar while continuing to observe the evening sky. "We're getting older. Time goes by faster when we become older. You know David, it's amazing how fresh and innocent things always seem here." Carl took another deep breath, let it out slowly, then turned to David. "So, how are things?"

"Can't complain, not that it would make much difference.... Truth is, between tuition, insurance, the threat of layoffs, and taking up the slack of those already gone -- not to mention trying to find time for the kids -- I sometimes feel like I'm on an out of control merry-go-round."

David took another swig of his beer, then nodded toward the house behind them. "If it weren't for Ma coming over all the time to watch the kids and bail me out, I'd probably be a babbling idiot by now."

"Ever think of sending them to a public school?"

"That's not an option. The kids like St. Marks, especially Jess. Besides, I promised Barbara." David paused, then leaned back, and closed his eyes. It was amazing how hard it was to think of things pertaining to the kids without thinking of what Barbara would have done. Truth was, he had always been lukewarm about sending the children to St. Marks even though he was an alumnus. Though it was sort of a family tradition, it was also a lot more expensive than when he was a child. Being a member the tuition was nominal, with the bulk of the cost paid by the congregation but still it was a chunk. Had it been up to him, he would have said public school's fine. That was him, bottom line conservative. Barbara on the other hand had always felt there was no other option. Her children were going to have as much moral structure as possible, whether they could afford it or not. Besides, the school had always been known for above average education. Since her death, with all that was going on in the world the past few years, David needed all the help he could get. And in the end, it was worth whatever the cost, even if at times it was more then he could handle. "The only thing is, I regret not being able to afford some of the things I'd like for them."

"There's more to life than things." Carl studied his beer, then turned back to David. "You know David, Judith and I always wanted children. Yours are probably as close as we'll ever come. If there's anything we can do..."

"Thanks." David wanted to say more. He wanted to say thanks for all the times they had been there for him. He would have never made it through that first year if it weren't for them or his mother. But being naturally quiet, David tended to hold in what he felt most, having never found it comfortable expressing himself on a deep personal level. So, like so many times before, he just said thanks, left it at that and returned to star gazing.

"You know what you need? A wife."

David half choked on his beer, coughed and laughed at the same time. "That's a great idea," he belched, finally catching his breath. "Where do you find those? They got them at Sears? Because I've looked at Wal-Mart and they're all out. At least out of the models I've been looking for."

Carl smiled but didn't respond, instead shaking his head he turned back to David. "How about one of those church groups? You could join the PTA or something."

"When am I going to do that? By the time I get home I'm too tired. I'm not young anymore. At least not like when all I had to worry about was nine to five and what I was going to do that night. Things are different." David's voice trailed off as his attention drifted toward the new neighbor's house. He stared at the ranch as if in a momentary trance, his thoughts on what he had just said. He wanted to elaborate, to say, Hey, I don't have a job where I'm gone half the year and can spend my nights exploring my options. I don't have extra time to figure it all out, my plates too full. I have children, responsibilities. But he didn't. He was not a complainer, not in public anyway. In truth, Carl was about the only one he confided in. That was as far as men were concerned. There was his sister. But with Judith most of his comments had to do with favors, problems with children, and his mother when, on occasion, Ma began to get under his skin. Even at that he was beginning to feel like a complainer, and he didn't like that in him.

"You know it wasn't supposed to be like this," he finally said. "When I married Barbara that was supposed to be it. I could talk to any woman then because it didn't matter." David took a long sip of his beer, then stared back up at the sky. "Now every time I start up a conversation with a woman I feel like there's this neon sign overhead saying, "Pity me, I'm single with children and desperate.""

"I wish I knew what to tell you, David. The truth is..." Carl paused. What is it they always say, "Don't give advice til you've walked a mile in his moccasins," or something to that effect? Though Carl had had more than his share of worldly experiences, in this arena he was one set of moccasins short.

"Truth is, I don't know what the truth is. In all honesty, I don't envy you, though God knows most married men now-a-days probably would, but most of them are idiots. Fact is, I don't know what I would do without your sister." And that was the truth. Judith was his anchor, his home to come back to. Without her he would probably have stopped coming home a long time ago. He had seen first hand what stupid risks others in his profession took who had no reason to be cautious, no special person to return to. That was not to say there weren't others that put the story first, their career, and they were idiots too.

David nodded at Carl's comment about his sister then held up his beer in another salute. "To you and my sister. I envy you both."

Carl returned the salute, tapping David's beer with his. "I wouldn't envy us, but here's to your sister."

As the two talked, turning their attention to other things, neither noticed Jessica standing at the back screen door holding a picture of an angel that she had just drawn on her sketchpad for Carl. She had been there only a short time, but she'd heard enough. Jessica had seen her father sitting quietly alone nights staring off into space, or turn sad when a certain song came on the radio. What hurt her most was knowing there was nothing she could do. Without saying a word Jessica pulled the drawing of the angel tight against her chest then turned back into the house.

⁂

It was nearly eleven when Carl and Judith said their goodbyes and left for home. For Peter it had been a good evening. The house had been full of talk and laughter, something that happened all too seldom. As for Jessica, it had been fun to a point. After listening to Uncle Carl and Father in the backyard, the rest of the night felt hollow. Even Uncle Carl's cheerfulness did little to make it better.

Shortly after Grandmother left, the children prepared for bed. Peter placed the model from Carl on his desk. He would start working on it in the morning and continue the slow process that would generally take him til nearly bedtime.

Jessica was much faster. A quick wash, brushing her teeth, and she was under the covers. When David sat down beside her that night he couldn't help but notice the pad with the picture of the angel she had drawn laying on the nightstand beside her. On the walls nearby were other drawings she had done over the past couple years. Some were done in pencil like the one in the sketchbook, but most were colored, some meticulously done, of houses and landscapes, many with animals. Then there were others more recent and somber, many of which were angels. David studied the new sketch of an angel a moment then smiled at Jessica. "This a new one?"

"It's not finished," she said matter-of-factly.

"It's very nice. Maybe even you're best yet." David looked at the pictures on the walls again, all covering much of the available space on two walls. "Pretty soon you're going to run out of walls."

"How about your room?"

"Sure, why not? A whole new market," laughed David. "Ready to say your prayers?"

Jessica folded her hands and closed her eyes. David did the same. "God, thank you for today and watch over us tonight. Take care of Grandmother, Father, Peter and Aunt Judy and especially Uncle Carl, and thank you for bringing him back to us safe. Say hi to Mother. Amen."

David gently tucked Jessica in then leaned over and kissed her. "Good night," he whispered, as he began to get up.

"Do you miss Mother?" asked Jessica.

The question caught David off guard. It wasn't the first time she had asked about Barbara, but seldom was she so direct. "Yes, I miss her all the time," he said quietly sitting back down. "Sometimes more than others."

"Why?"

"Why?" David paused. That was a good question -- far deeper than he ever expected from her. But then he learned long ago never to underestimate Jessica. "Because I loved her. No, more than that. She was my friend, my best friend. Someone I could talk to. Being friends with someone you love is very special."

"Do you wish you had someone else?"

"No one could never replace your mother."

"I mean as a friend?"

"Sometimes." David paused, wondering where she was going and whether or not he really wanted to go there. "Anything else?"

"No. Good night, Daddy."

"Good night." David smiled and watched as Jessica smiled back sleepily. Getting up, he walked to the door. As he reached for the light, Jessica called him again.

"Daddy?"

"What?"

"I'll always be your friend."

"I love you too." David felt a lump in his throat as he said that. He wanted to say more but nothing proper came to mind. So he turned off the lights and left.

Chapter Four

Peter awoke early the next morning. No sooner was breakfast over than he was back in his room, glue in hand, mulling over the parts of what he hoped would be his crowning achievement. He had studied the model Carl gave him for some time the night before, even dreamt about it. It wasn't long before he had become so engrossed in his project that he barely noticed his sister walk into the room carrying her crystal ball, until Jessica plopped down on the bed behind him.

Jessica watched Peter silently, not saying a word as if trying to gauge how long it would take before his project was over or he would get bored enough to do something with her. "That one looks hard," she finally said.

"No harder than the last one," muttered Peter matter-of-factly, trying to ignore her. "It's bigger, but it's got less parts."

Jessica watched Peter assemble one of the boosters, then scooted back on his bed, leaned against the wall and studied the angel inside her crystal ball. The angel looked so enchanting, she thought. So real. Like she could almost come to life and fly away if only the ball were opened. "You really think she wasn't pretty?"

"Who?" asked Peter, barely glancing at his sister as he attached another booster. "The angel?"

"No, the lady next door."

"She's okay." That was all he would say, at least not without knowing where his sister was going. After all he was getting closer to adolescence and his fantasies about women, especially the woman next door, were not the type of things he was about to confide in his kid sister. That was unless he was prepared to have them blabbed all over the neighborhood, to say nothing about giving her ammunition to tease him for the rest of his life.

"Do you think father would like her?"

"I don't think so." That wasn't really true. Actually Peter had never given much thought about his father having feelings for any woman other than his mother. The whole concept was totally alien to him. All Peter knew was he liked her. That was his fantasy, at least for the moment and he didn't need any more competition in screwing it up than was already around. It didn't take a rocket scientist to know that once more men knew about her existence, the chances of him achieving his fantasy would be next to zero.

"How do you know?"

"It's a guy thing." End of discussion, at least as far as Peter was concerned.

Jessica never brought up their neighbor again the rest of the weekend. There were other things to do, such as spending time with her family. She and Peter went with Father and Grandmother for pizza and movies that night. They went to church as usual on Sunday and on a picnic at Judith and Carl's afterwards. After that came Monday, then the last week of summer vacation before the start of the school year.

Tuesday, Jessica, her brother, and his friends walked to the city pool. It was a warm day and it seemed only fitting that they should spend it at their favorite summer retreat, especially since it would be only a few days before the pool was closed for the year. Jessica didn't mind the walk, even with her brace. She was not one for pity and was determined she would do what everyone else did no matter how long it took. Besides, the pool was relatively close.

As usual the pool was fairly crowded -- not to capacity but enough so that finding a place to stake out and leave their blankets took more time than the four of them wanted to spend. But since Jessica never went in the big pool, using the smaller, shallower pool instead, they decided the best place to leave everything was with her. There were less people in the small pool area and it would be easier for her to keep an eye on things. Besides, many of the children in that area, and even some of the mothers for that matter, knew better than to mess with Jessica.

Jessica loved the water, even though getting in and out was sometimes a chore. Once she was in the shallow pool, she felt more alive than any time she was on land. The water was refreshing, cleansing, and most of all gave her a sense of freedom and normalcy. She could interact without feeling she was being singled out as different. Life was good at the pool.

The children spent the better part of that afternoon swimming. Later, when Jessica, Peter, and the others walked home past the new neighbor's home, Jessica couldn't help noticing the woman in her garage unloading bags, which she assumed were groceries, from her car. It was the first time she had seen her since that afternoon in the tree house. She was intrigued by how unusually spotless the garage was, unlike the garages of most of the people she knew. Her father's in particular had more room allocated for boxes and tools, than the car it was intended for. Could her father like someone so neat, she wondered? But then their neighbor was new. No doubt she didn't own enough stuff to clutter her garage yet. And she was single, no children. Jessica's father was known to occasionally joke about how much simpler and neater his life would be if it weren't for her and Peter cluttering up the place all the time. Of course he would also often follow that by saying how important they were to him, -- far more important than any organized house.

It was apparent that neither Peter nor his friends noticed their neighbor's penchant for cleanliness. All they knew was that she was beautiful, like a model from "Sports Illustrated", the swimsuit issue. It was also apparent as they passed that their fantasies regarding her were working overtime.

That afternoon was the only time Jessica saw their new neighbor that week. According to local gossip, no one else did either. Though Peter never mentioned her that day, it was obvious by the way he stared at her that he was totally infatuated. More than a couple times over the next few days, Jessica would see him up in the tree house, spending hours watching their neighbor's backyard on the slightest chance she might come out. She never did though, and by Friday Peter's infatuation began to wane.

Maybe the new neighbor was just a figment of his

imagination and never really existed at all. At least that was the impression he was trying to make on Jessica. No matter how hard he tried to convince both of them, it was no surprise to Jessica, as she began preparing breakfast Saturday morning, to see him already in his treehouse perch on the chance that his dream girl might appear and validate that his fantasy did exist.

It was a pleasant morning, bright and sunny, typical for late August. Jessica yawned as she took the peanut butter and jelly from the refrigerator, grabbed the bread and hobbled toward the table while listening to the television blaring Saturday morning cartoons from the other room. She paused at the window and watched her brother in the tree house perch still watching. Shaking her head she continued on, finished setting the table, then smiled. The table looked good. Maybe not the picture perfect breakfast her father would make, but then she wasn't old enough to burn eggs yet. At least that's what her mother used to tell her. Satisfied everything was in order, she went to the kitchen door and yelled, "Breakfast!"

It felt like forever before Peter climbed down from his perch and ambled into the kitchen. Jessica had already made a sandwich for her brother and was preparing one for herself when Peter sat down. He studied the peanut butter and jelly, the chocolate cookie, and the glass of chocolate milk next to it. "Milk! I'd rather have Pepsi."

"You can't have Pepsi for breakfast," said Jessica, not looking up from her project. "Besides, Grandma's gone and she made me in charge. We're having milk."

Peter fingered his sandwich, then paused. "Whoever heard of peanut butter for breakfast?"

"Eat it! I'm too little to use the stove."

"How 'bout cereal? People have cereal for breakfast."

"I hate cereal. Besides, it's on the top shelf. You want it; you climb up and get it." Peter looked at his sandwich, half-tempted to dump it in the garbage. Instead, he decided to eat it. After all it was far less trouble than the alternative.

The room felt strangely quiet as they ate. Even the television resonating from the other room seemed miles away. Jessica watched Peter, hoping he might mention his plans for the day on the off chance she might be able to tag along. But Peter just sat silently eating his sandwich while occasionally staring at his milk. "You want to play some checkers later?" Jessica finally blurted hoping to develop some semblance of dialogue from which to build.

"Nah, I don't feel much like checkers."

Dejected, Jessica returned to her sandwich while trying to think of some other common ground. She noticed the box of candy bars on the nearby cupboard that Peter was supposed to sell for his Boy Scout field trip. The candy had sat for two weeks, since his last Scout meeting. David reminded Peter of his obligation a number of times, each time doing it with more emphasis on responsibility. But except for the two bars his grandmother bought, the box hadn't left the counter. Had it been up to Jessica, the box would have been gone a week ago and another couple besides. But then Peter wasn't Jessica. He was more like his father -- quiet, laid back.

"Want me to help you sell your candy?"

Peter glanced at the box of candy out of the corner of his eye. The offer was tempting. He knew what she could do. In fact, if he played his cards right, he wouldn't even have to talk at all; she would do it all and he would finally be rid of it. "Tomorrow," he shrugged. It might be late, but another day wouldn't hurt. Besides he had to cut the grass. That's right, he thought, he had to cut the grass, and if he did, so did their neighbor. There was no way he was going to miss that just to sell candy.

"Tomorrow's Sunday! Nobody buys anything on Sunday."

"How do you know? Besides, they'll all be home!"

Peter pulled a magazine over and began to read between gulps of milk. The fact that it was Better Homes and Gardens definitely meant end of discussion. It was apparent there was only one thing on Peter's mind, and pushing the candy card, especially to a non-salesman like him wasn't going to change it. Jessica fished a dill pickle out of a jar and took a bite as she watched him study the pictures. "What's she doing?"

"I don't know," mumbled Peter not looking up. "She hasn't come out." He paused and took another bite of his sandwich, washed it down with milk, then returned to the magazine. "Once she came out and read."

Jessica was surprised at Peter's remark. It was the first time he mentioned he had seen her. "What do you think she does?"

"I don't know. Maybe she's rich."

"I don't think she has a boyfriend."

Peter abruptly looked up from the magazine. "How do you know?"

"She never goes out. No one comes over. And she hardly buys enough food for one."

"So?"

"And except for bills, she doesn't get any mail--not even junk mail."

"You looked at her mail?" Peter couldn't believe his sister could be so nosy or gutsy. But then the more he thought about it, the more it didn't surprise him. After all, no one was more forward then Jessica. "That doesn't mean anything."

"That's why you'll never be a detective." Jessica half smiled. He may have had information she didn't, but no one was more observant or analytical when it counted. Truth was, it didn't really matter anymore what Peter knew or was going to do with his time. She made up her mind what her plans were for that morning. Everything else would take care of itself.

⋅⋙⋅

As expected, Peter returned to his treehouse to survey the neighborhood and their new neighbor's yard. At first Jessica thought about staying inside and watch cartoons while fantasizing about other worlds more magical and mysterious than her own. But it was too beautiful a morning to stay inside, and besides the cartoons had become dull, offering her little stimulation. So after trashing the remnants of their breakfast, Jessica took the Nancy Drew mystery Grandmother had given her and went outside. Finding a nice spot on the back deck, not too sunny, she sat down and began to read.

⋅⋙⋅

As she sat reading Jessica occasionally glanced up at her brother in the tree house. It was apparent he had taken his obsession next door to a new level. Not content to just casually watch for signs of his phantom; he had borrowed a page from Jessica's playbook and taken his father's binoculars for a more intense survey. Though it didn't bother Jessica to see her brother so hopelessly infatuated, it was a little amusing. She knew that if one of his friends caught him, he would most likely claim he was looking for terrorists, aliens, or low flying spacecraft, preferably about house or treetop level. Then again, he might just say he was looking for signs of fungus in the trees, a big concern in the area lately. Of course, in his case most of the observation was in the direction of their neighbor's backyard. Whatever his excuse it was certain he was going to be tree house bound for a long time.

Though the neighborhood was exceptionally quiet that morning, Jessica hardly noticed as she read her Nancy Drew. Her concentration was broken only by the sound of an occasional lawnmower starting, then choking its way through some distant, long-neglected lawn. A dog barked a couple yards off. Once in a while she would glance up at her brother and his lonely watch. None of his friends had come over that morning which was unusual. Normally Grandmother would have stopped by to do wash or something but that day she wasn't expected till afternoon.

Eventually even Peter's vigil began to slacken as he began aiming his binoculars in other directions, skyward or into the branches of neighboring trees as various curiosities caught his attention. The day appeared destined to drift into an uneventful obscurity when the quiet was suddenly broken by the sound of a door opening next door. Peter's senses snapped to full alert as the mysterious neighbor came out of her house with boxes of yard lights. She carried them to a picnic table opposite the fence from the tree house, then returned to her garage.

Peter remained rigid, almost afraid to breathe when she returned with a shovel and other tools. He tried hard to think of something intelligent to say as he watched her thumb through the lighting instructions like she had the lawnmower book. Putting the instructions aside, she brushed her long gleaming brunette hair behind her left ear then began digging near the bushes. For what seemed an eternity he watched her dig, stop, put in a yard light, then dig another hole. It slowly became apparent that the lights she was installing could as easily be used for security as for accenting her property. It also seemed that she was totally oblivious of his presence as she continued on, digging another hole about twenty feet from the fence and his treehouse.

Suddenly she stopped and abruptly looked up at him. "Think it is deep enough?" she asked, her voice reflecting a slight European accent.

"Yes... I guess," Peter blurted, startled that she even noticed him let alone cared what he thought.

"Would you care to help?" she asked in an almost expressionless tone.

"No! I got to go help my Grandmother." Peter abruptly turned about face, took four quick steps into the treehouse, then slid into the furthermost corner. Closing his eyes, he banged his head against the wall. "Stupid! Stupid! Stupid!"

It was apparent to Jessica as she watched her brother blow his big chance that if he handled his future relations in the same manner, the family tree would end with him. It was also apparent that if anyone was going to make any meaningful contact with the recluse next door, it was going to have to be her.

※

It was nearly two hours from the time their neighbor started her lighting project till she finished. During that time Peter came out on the tree house porch only twice. The first was to check her progress, which had by then moved two thirds of the way across her backyard along her property line. Since he had already embarrassed himself he left the moment she turned his way. The second was when she was almost finished. He felt more confident then. But when she looked up at him again he disappeared, out of the treehouse and into the safety of his living room where he spent the rest of the morning and early afternoon watching television.

Her work finished, the neighbor paused only long enough to make sure the lights worked, then gathered up the empty containers and took them to the garbage. While folding the boxes and stuffing them in the trash can, she sensed someone behind her. Quickly turning she saw Jessica standing near the open door, a large box in her arms. "Can I help you?"

"I'm selling candy for the Boy Scouts. Would you like to buy some?" asked Jessica in her sweetest voice while holding up the box.

"You mean Girl Scouts," corrected the woman, her blank expression turning slightly inquisitive.

"No, it's for my brother. He's in the Scouts, but he's too shy to sell them."

"The one in the tree?"

"That's the one."

"He sent you?" asked the woman as she put her shovel against the wall.

Jessica shook her head. "No, I came by myself."

"You're not shy," said the woman as she put the rest of her tools away.

"No. We're both worldly girls. I have a product, you have money."

"How do you know I want your candy?"

Jessica moved closer and smiled coyly. "Because all beautiful women love candy."

The woman studied Jessica a moment as if weighing the logic of that statement, then nodded toward the door leading into the house. "Come in."

"Thank you," Jessica followed the woman with the candy box firmly in her grasp. "My name's Jessica, what's yours?"

"Nishka," she said matter-of-factly.

"Jessica had never seen a kitchen so clean as Nishka's. Like the garage, there was nothing but the basics: cupboards, a stove, sink, refrigerator. There were no signs of what made a kitchen a home. No pictures on the walls, no notes held with magnets to the refrigerator. Not a loose piece of paper or dish out of place anywhere. Even the sink was empty giving the place the feel that no one even lived there. Were it not for the table and chairs, and the fact that Nishka was standing in front of her, Jessica could easily have thought the house was deserted.

Setting the box of chocolates down Jessica watched as Nishka opened a drawer and remove what appeared to be its only contents, her wallet. "I do not have much taste for candy."

"Buy it for your boyfriend ... or company."

"I do not have a boyfriend." Nishka paused, as if mulling over what she said. Though her face showed little expression, there seemed to be hesitancy about her as she sat down opposite Jessica. "I do not have company either."

Though Jessica's eyes brightened at the prospect of there being no boyfriend in Nishka's life, she remained silent and watched Nishka open her wallet to a checkbook. "How much?"

"Twenty five bucks," Jessica snapped, not batting an eye as Nishka began to write.

"That is expensive!"

"Its very good candy," said Jessica sliding the whole box of candy bars toward her. Nishka did not respond. Instead she finished writing the check and handed it to Jessica. "Thank you, I know you'll love them."

Though the television was on, Peter's attention was glued to the door when Jessica returned. He watched his sister silently walk into the kitchen and tried to remain cool when she returned with a glass of milk, but that lasted less than a minute before he finally blurted. "What did you find out?"

Jessica nonchalantly pulled a check from the waistband of her pants and flipped it to him as she passed. "She has no idea what candy costs."

Peter's jaw dropped. "Twenty five dollars! It only costs twenty! What's the other five for?"

"My commission," said Jessica as she sat down on the couch. Without waiting for a response she turned toward the television. "Anything else on?"

Chapter Five

Jessica never discussed meeting Nishka with her father. But thoughts of the encounter were never far from her mind. Peter was another story. Even though discussion was minimal, Peter did most of the talking. Jessica said little other than Nishka was quiet and clean.

"Clean! What kind of person is that?" demanded Peter.

"Her kitchen is neat. She puts everything away, not like you."

What else was there to say? She only saw the kitchen and garage. Not much to judge someone on. But there was something more about Nishka that intrigued her. Actually, there were a lot of things. Her foreign accent for one. Where was she from? Somewhere overseas, like Europe? But where in Europe? That alone made her mysterious. And she was too pretty. She appeared to use almost no makeup at all and still she looked better than most women in the magazines. Her long brunette hair sometimes covered one eye, adding to her mysteriousness. Being an avid Nancy Drew enthusiast, it didn't take much to arouse Jessica's curiosity. And there was a lot to be curious about with Nishka. The house for one, it was spotless, at least what she saw if it. Nishka must be a very good homemaker to keep a house so clean.

That was something Jessica's father really lacked. If it

weren't for Grandmother, the house would be a disaster with not a clean sock in the place. Her brother was just as bad. But then, how important was that to a man, Jessica wondered. Would her father like this strange woman who was so neat and mysterious? Those and other questions wove through Jessica's mind long past when Grandmother came that Saturday to help with chores, a ritual that kept the house from sinking under a layer of filth and dirty laundry.

The fact that David was not home and Jessica and Peter were alone when she arrived did not sit well with her. Over the past year Grandmother had periodically complained to David that the children needed more supervision than he was providing. Her father's usual response was that with Jessica around, there was already more than enough supervision, not only for Peter, but most of the neighborhood besides.

Occasionally, after Grandmother had said her piece and changed direction to start the laundry or other chores, David would wink at Jessica, then whisper that Grandmother was just looking for an excuse to permanently move in. Although Jessica liked her Grandmother, her moving in was not a vision she relished. Jessica liked being in charge, having the responsibility of an adult. Taking care of her father was important to her. The only exception she could see regarding another woman moving in was someone her father's age. Someone who would be more than a maid, a companion for her father, a friend. Maybe someone like Nishka.

※

Shortly after her arrival Grandmother went right to work doing what she deemed necessary for the survival of the household. First came laundry, a load in the wash, a quick vacuum of the living room while Jessica dusted, then another load of wash and a load in the dryer. After enough loads had gone full cycle, she began separating, folding, and ironing. Jessica didn't mind helping with the weekend chores. In a strange way, she enjoyed them. After all, for the most part she was the only woman in the house and over the past couple years had developed a feeling of responsibility. And responsibility didn't come without a price. In this case, that meant chores, whether she was in charge or not, though secretly she liked to believe she was.

Later, in the kitchen, Grandmother did some sewing. It was customary, when she sewed, that Jessica would keep her company. Sometimes she read, but most often Jessica drew and talked. They talked about many things -- school, dreams, what it was like taking care of David. Like two old wives they would discuss him as if he were a full time charity case. Grandmother told stories of what Jessica's father was like as a boy, and about Grandfather. Sometimes Grandmother reminisced about her own childhood, a subject Jessica never tired of. That day Grandmother spent more time sewing Peter's clothes than anyone else's. "I've never seen a boy wear out pants as fast as your brother," Grandmother said as she a needle through the material, drawing the hole in the worn knee together.

"Boys do that," said Jessica matter-of-factly, not looking up from the angel picture she had drawn for Carl and had since decided to color in.

"You're not much better." Grandmother pulled the thread through the front of the fabric, then paused and studied the picture Jessica was coloring. "Isn't that the one you were going to give to Carl?"

"Not anymore."

"Oh." Grandmother waited for an explanation. When

none came she decided to drop the subject and returned to sewing.

Jessica stopped coloring, picked up the picture, and studied it like an art critic. "Someday I'm going to have an easel and paints, just like a real artist." Satisfied the picture was going well; Jessica put it down and began coloring again. "Did mom keep the house clean?"

"Oh yes. She was just the opposite of your father. Sometimes it was so organized you'd have thought no one lived here.

Jessica studied the picture again, then decided the background needed to be lighter and, putting down the blue, picked up a white crayon. "Father doesn't throw anything away."

Grandmother nodded as she flipped the pants over and pulled the needle out the other side then tied it off. "Not much. I swear he smuggles more in than he throws out. His stuff multiplies."

"And they liked each other?"

"Opposites attract in people just like magnets." Grandmother paused, wrinkled her nose, then looked at Jessica and smiled, "If it weren't for us women, men would never find anything. And that's especially true when it comes to your father."

Jessica nodded, and immediately thought about Nishka. The concept of opposites attracting made sense too, especially concerning her father. And Nishka definitely seemed like an opposite and a very pretty one too. She was so clean and organized even the FBI would have thought the house was deserted. Jessica loved her father. She liked doing things for him, being one of the most important components of his life. But she also knew loneliness. Not only from the times her brother purposely tried to exclude her from his activities or tried to ditch her, but other moments too. Special moments like those times she used to share with her mother. She still remembered them and never forgot, special times only a mother and daughter could understand. And if Jessica still missed her mother after so many years, she could only imagine how much her father missed her, and that thought always made her sad.

When the doorbell rang, Nishka was sitting at her computer in the spare bedroom of her house watching stock market figures fly past on the monitor faster than most people could focus. It rang twice more before her attention turned from the screen to the sound of the chimes in the other room. No emotion showed as she froze the stock report in place, got up, and headed for the living room.

Her face still lacked expression when Nishka opened the front door and saw Jessica standing there holding a flat thin package wrapped in brown paper. "You are not selling more candy are you?"

"No," said Jessica shyly, "I brought you something instead."

"Why?"

"I kind of over charged you." Without waiting for a response Jessica thrust the package at her.

Nishka took the package, studied it a moment in a noncommittal manner, then looked back at Jessica. "Would you like something to drink?"

Jessica's uncertain feeling quickly reverted back to her old confident self. "Sure." Jessica hobbled ever so slightly as she followed Nishka through the living room into the kitchen. As she sat down she watched Nishka put the package on the table. Like most children, Jessica half expected a glass of soda, root beer, or at the very least some juice. But then Nishka was not like other adults Jessica knew. No sooner had she pulled a glass from the cupboard, then Nishka filled it from the tap and handed the water to Jessica. "Don't you ever get lonely living here alone?" asked Jessica, trying not to show disappointment over the lukewarm water.

"Sometimes." Nishka sat down opposite her at the table, picked up the package, and examined it like an alien object. "I do not have any friends here. But then I keep busy." Removing the paper, Nishka studied the dime store framed picture of the angel Jessica had drawn and colored. Sensing Nishka's uncertainty over what to do with the gift, Jessica quickly motioned to the bleak room. "Your walls look lonely."

Nishka abruptly looked at her kitchen walls as if seeing them for the first time. She studied the picture again, then turned back to Jessica. "Thank you. I will hang it up."

"I'd like to be your friend," Jessica suddenly blurted as Nishka laid the picture down.

"Why?" asked Nishka flatly, apparently trying to comprehend the meaning of this equation.

"Because I like you. I could come over once in a while, help around the house." Realizing how ridiculous that sounded in a place so spotless, Jessica quickly added, "I'm a good cook."

"Are you sure your parents would not mind?"

"It's just my father," said Jessica, trying to emphasize the fact that they were motherless.

Nishka showed no response to the loss of her mother either. It was almost like the concept had no special meaning to her.

"But he likes us to help others," Jessica looked around again at the sterile kitchen trying to think of projects to do. "So what needs to be done first?"

"Nothing." Nishka paused as if reevaluating what she just said. "But if you want to come back Saturday we can clean. Do you mind cleaning?"

Jessica's face brightened. "I'm a great cleaner. So's my brother." Jessica leaned closer to Nishka with an expression of one ready to impart some very important secret. "Only one thing."

"What is that?"

Jessica lowered her voice to just above a whisper. "If my brother helps, you'll have to get some pop."

"I will see what I can do."

Jessica had half expected something more from Nishka, a little smile maybe, a wink. After all, what she said was cute and she knew it.

Later, after she was on her way home, it occurred to Jessica that Nishka had shown almost no emotion to anything, good or bad. It was almost as if she had no sense of emotion at all. That would be hard for her father to be comfortable with. After all, though David had little reason to laugh during the last couple years, she knew he had a sense of humor and made jokes when the time was right though some of them were dumb. Like her father often said, one had to be able to laugh once in a while if only to get through life.

Chapter Six

The first day back to school was an exciting time for Jessica. She was the first dressed and ready to join Peter and his friends for the four-block walk to St. Marks'. As expected, her excitement was not universally shared. For some of Peter's friends, Barry in particular, the first day of school meant only one thing – internment; summer was over. Their freedom was over, and only the labor camps lay ahead. Jessica, on the other hand, looked forward to the classes, being with other children. She liked the order school brought to her life, of being involved and challenged by classes like history and reading. But her favorite subject of all was religion and the peace of mind it brought her. The Bible stories inspired her with promises of heaven and a better life where she would be reunited with her mother. She fantasized what it would be like to see her, touch her, have her family whole again.

As the children walked past the new neighbor's house that morning, Jessica wondered what Nishka believed in, whether she missed her family or the land she came from. Did she ever feel sad at living alone?

That first week of school came and went with no sign of Nishka, in or out of her yard. That seemed strange to Jessica. After their encounter she half expected to see her more often. After all, Nishka knew someone now. It was safe for her to come out and befriend the rest of the neighborhood. Apparently Nishka had a harder time socializing than she thought. It would take more than just her knowing Nishka before her new neighbor would feel comfortable talking to others. It must be because she was a foreigner thought Jessica. That would have to change if Jessica's father was ever going to like her. And if anyone was going to make that happen, it would have to be her.

The following Saturday was the beginning of the Labor Day weekend. First thing after breakfast, Jessica returned to Nishka's with Peter in tow. Jessica knew he wanted to go as much as she did, but his inherent shyness made it harder. She, on the other hand, had been looking forward to seeing Nishka again ever since the last time she visited. Jessica told herself it was because of her father -- to find a way to draw them together so he wouldn't be so lonely anymore.

Then again maybe it was also because Nishka was so naturally pretty that just being around her, watching her move, without expression, had so intrigued Jessica that she fantasized Nishka being an angel somehow trapped on earth. Jessica's natural curiosity about Nishka, and the mystery that surrounded her in a strange exotic sort of way, was an irresistible challenge that just begged to be investigated. Whatever the reason the end result was the same, a feeling of hardly being able to contain herself as she and her brother stood on Nishka's front stoop and rang the doorbell.

Nishka was just passing through the living room, a stack of business and technical magazines under her arm, when the doorbell rang. She paused, then looked out the window. Seeing Jessica and Peter outside, she opened the door.

"Hi, this is Peter, my brother," Jessica quickly rattled, assessing by Nishka's blank expression that she had forgotten their arrangement and hoped she could refresh it. "Are you ready to clean?"

"Clean?" Nishka's puzzled look lasted less than a second before disappearing, as if in a microsecond she had managed to reexamine her date book and found that yes, there was a notation under cleaning with the neighbors, Saturday. "Come in. I did not expect you so early. I was just going to read."

"That's okay; we can come back later," sputtered Peter, apparently uncomfortable and at the same time mesmerized by how much more attractive Nishka was close up.

"No, I can read later. Come in."

As Nishka stepped back to let the children pass, Jessica noticed the eight or nine magazines under her arm. "You going to read all those?"

"Just the important parts."

It was hard for Jessica to tell whether Nishka, whose expression never changed, was kidding or not, though she figured she was probably serious. After all, it would take her father most of the day and then some to read that much.

Like the kitchen, the living room was void of all but the most basic furniture, a davenport, matching chair, end table and lamp, coffee table, television and VCR. Jessica couldn't help feeling that cleaning was the last thing the room needed as she watched Nishka look around for something for them to do. "We can start here."

"I'll vacuum," said Peter apparently wanting to make sure he was in no way stuck with doing anything close to real housework. Besides, the noise of the vacuum cleaner would negate having to talk which was something Peter was to awed to do anyway.

Nishka nodded, then turned to Jessica. "You can dust. You do not mind dusting do you?"

"No, I'm a good duster. I dust all the time for Grandmother." That was true, at least to a degree. She did help Grandmother clean the house periodically and occasionally that included dusting, but seldom did it go beyond the dining and living room.

Nishka showed no response to Jessica's enthusiasm, nor did she add anything to the discussion or give directions for what she wanted done. Instead she simply brought out the vacuum cleaner from the closet and handed it to Peter. She gave Jessica a dust cloth, then retrieved a spray cleaner and other rags for washing windows, walls, etc. for herself.

As they began cleaning, Jessica couldn't help notice how empty the rest of the house was, lacking any of the touches that made it look like anyone lived there. The bedroom presumably used by Nishka only had one plain dresser, bed, and chair. There were no pictures on any of the walls, few clothes in the closet, and none of the stuff on the dresser one normally would expect in a woman's room. The bathroom was also spartan, with no makeup out, only a towel and washcloth hanging on a nearby towel rack. The whole house had a sense of temporariness about it, as if Nishka was just passing through, borrowing it in between going from one place to another, or afraid to mess it up for fear the real owner might appear some day and be upset.

Jessica had no recollection of what the inside of the house looked like before Nishka arrived. The couple that owned it before were older and retired, and had pretty much kept to themselves. To enforce that privacy, they built the six-foot stockade fence around their backyard not long after Jessica learned to walk and for the most part stayed within its perimeter. "Not exactly children lovers," Jessica's mother once said. It was known that they had a son who lived somewhere on the West Coast, though no one had seen him in years. To Grandmother's recollection the neighbor's son only returned when the couple died, and that was just to put everything in order and sell the house. Evidently that was just what he did. To Jessica the house always had a sense of being sucked dry of life, and with Nishka living in it the place it seemed even colder and more sterile.

The second bedroom, like the first, was sparse, having only a chair, file cabinet, a computer table, computer, printer, a few magazines, and a phone. "This is cleaner than a hospital," said Peter, plugging in the vacuum cleaner.

"It is supposed to be," said Nishka, looking around with a faint expression of pride, the first show of emotion she'd had all day.

"Why?" asked Jessica.

Nishka moved close to the computer and gently touched it like one fondly touching a pet or priceless keepsake. "Because the computer does not like dirt."

"How would it know?" asked Jessica, bewildered as much by the concept as Nishka's first expression of emotion.

"It knows." That was all she said. Not leaving the children a chance to question her, Nishka abruptly began washing the window.

It didn't take long for them to finish cleaning the second bedroom and move on to the last. As Jessica expected, the third room didn't contain much. In fact, it didn't have anything except one chair, and that appeared to be there only as an afterthought, or because it had been moved there for some reason and then forgotten. There was not even a small rug in the room to give it balance or to warm one's feet on a cold winter night. The room looked so barren that Jessica felt uncomfortable even standing there as if, like in a horror movie, it might suck her in and swallow her like the rest of the furniture. It seemed like such a sad, forlorn place, a room that had never known happiness. "How come you don't have any furniture in here?"

"What purpose would it serve?"

"To make it a happy room," said Jessica. "It looks so sad."

"In case you had company," added Peter, apparently sensing the same uncomfortable emptiness Jessica felt. "You know, if they had to spend the night or something."

"Who?" asked Nishka.

Jessica slowly hobbled to the lone chair and touched it as if sensing its loneliness. "How about me?"

"Overnight?" Nishka appeared honestly stunned by the concept of having anyone spend a night with her, let alone Jessica. When Jessica nodded yes, Nishka paused, as if mulling over the concept, then looked around the room. "What would you put in here--for a guest that is?"

Jessica sat on the chair and turned about analyzing the room. "A large bed with high posts and a top over it. A desk. A dresser, mirror, pink drapes, maybe a bean bag chair, and pictures."

"Could you find pictures to show me?"

"Sure!" Jessica's eyes lit up at the prospect of being asked to do something so important, so grown up.

"That's no fair," spouted Peter caught up more in the thought of losing out on being the chosen one. "Why not a boy's room?"

"Don't be silly. She can't have boys over til she's married," laughed Jessica. That was the only way it could be. Besides, decorating was a girl thing, not for boys. Least ways not Peter. He was going to be a space pilot, not an interior designer. But what mattered most was that Nishka entrusted the project to her. To be responsible for something so grand -- yet personal -- was special. It was the sign of true friendship, of showing more than just the uninterested, expressionless sense of logic and lack of emotions Jessica had sensed in Nishka up till then. Nishka had entrusted Jessica with something major and Jessica was not going to let her down.

⚜

It was only a short time from when they entered the last bedroom till the housework was done. Though it wasn't quite lunchtime, Nishka prepared pizza and served it with soda like Jessica had suggested. As the children ate, Peter noticed that one of the science magazines Nishka had planned to read had a cover story concerning the space station. "Do you like science?"

"One might say I am an expert of sorts," nodded Nishka, before sipping from a glass of water then sitting down across from the children.

Peter pulled the magazine over and opened it to the article. "I've never been very good."

"He means in school," said Jessica waving her hand to make sure she was included.

Nishka's generally placid look turned slightly quizzical as she turned to Jessica. "What problems do you have?"

"Math," shot Jessica defiantly.

"I find that hard to believe."

"Well I do have problems sometimes." Jessica didn't say more. It was already apparent Nishka had pretty much sized up her intelligence. All that mattered to Jessica was that she was included. But then that was all that ever mattered to Jessica, to feel wanted, to have someone to talk to, share her feelings with. Just being with Peter and his friends meant a lot to her. Considering she was a girl three years younger, they included her in more things than most boys their age would have. But then only her wit, sense of insight beyond her age, and her sense of humor got her past the invisible barrier of male chauvinism.

She never said a word about how much she appreciated them for that. She wasn't the gushy type. Likewise being included in Nishka's invitation for homework or other projects was just as important. Not only because she wanted to feel needed, but because she deserved it: after all, it was she that got the whole neighborly friendship thing going. But most importantly she needed to be included because she liked Nishka, and she could not like someone and not be liked back.

That night and much of the Labor Day weekend when the family wasn't involved in an outing at the movies, or cooking out, Jessica spent her time going through magazines looking for pictures of what she perceived the dream bedroom to be. What she couldn't find that weekend she found in the school library after school Tuesday by paging through magazines pertaining to decorating and home repair, etc., tearing out what she wanted when no one was looking. At night she placed them into an impromptu scrapbook along with a carefully drawn diagram of the room as she remembered it. Jessica marked off where each piece of furniture should be, curtain, rug, and picture. It wasn't until Wednesday that she finally pulled everything together.

The next day when Peter and Jessica visited Nishka after school for their first night's help on their homework, Jessica showed the scrapbook she had completed with all the pictures of dressers, drapes, bedspreads, and shelves. She also included pictures of art, the most important being a photo of an angel she thought should hang on the wall nearest the bed. Of all her work, Jessica was most excited about the picture of a four-poster bed with a canopy above it. It was a bed for a princess she said and added that anyone staying in that room would feel special. Nishka did not say much about the scrapbook other than it was well thought out and asked if she could borrow it.

"I made it for you," said Jessica beaming. Nishka said thank you, and that was that. Jessica was somewhat disappointed in Nishka's apparent lack of enthusiasm but said nothing more.

The homework session, at least the first day, left much to be desired. Nishka tried to explain Peter's science to him, but her teaching was beyond his comprehension if not beyond that of most grownups. Her efforts to break down those concepts to more basic components only confused Peter more. Even Jessica struggled to understand some of Nishka's mathematical explanations. And when it came to Jessica's history class, things really degenerated. The afternoon eventually ended in a stalemate with the children going over they're homework while Nishka watched, in-between thumbing through her magazines.

❧

Peter was reluctant to return to Nishka's the following night and probably wouldn't have, especially since it was Friday. Had it not been for Jessica's prodding, pointing out how

Nishka was doing this for him. She also reminded Peter that Nishka was probably the most beautiful woman he would ever meet in his entire puny life. That single point finally convinced Peter to return to what he envisioned would only be another torturous ordeal of trying to understand concepts that were better left to Harvard physics majors. In fact, Peter doubted sincerely whether even his teacher could have followed some of Nishka's concepts.

Strangely enough, Nishka's manner and ability to instruct the second night was radically different from the night before. Where before everything had been all six-syllable theory, Nishka's approach that night was simple, picturesque, and to the point. There was even soft music playing in the other room and milk and cookies to munch on as they studied, though Peter would have preferred soda. Even Jessica had a clearer understanding of what she had to do and what the teacher wanted in relation to math, etc. By the time they went home, Peter was convinced that not only was he going to pass his weekly quiz with flying colors but that he was truly in love. All he needed was to be at least ten years older.

☙

Though the days were getting shorter and the scent of cooler nights were in the air, the trees were still green for the most part that Monday afternoon when Jessica walked home from school with other schoolmates. She paused in the kitchen only long enough to say hi to her grandmother, who, as normal for the first day of the week, was over to prepare dinner. A moment later she was out the back door and on her way next door. Though it had been a couple days since Peter and she started going to Nishka's for help with their homework, including Saturday when they studied and cleaned, to Jessica it felt like a week and she loved every minute of her time there.

Jessica had barely caught her breath, rung the bell, and had time to shift the weight of her books when the door opened and Nishka greeted her with the same emotionless expression Jessica had grown accustom to. "Where's Peter?"

"He has football tryouts." Jessica did not elaborate as she hobbled in. After all, school football practice was just a natural fall annoyance that had to be tolerated. It was a male thing, a bonding, being part of the brotherhood. And at twelve that was far more important then being in love. Especially if one wanted to make the team.

"Oh," said Nishka in her usual monotone, which was not much different then her normal tone or personality. She closed the door and followed Jessica toward the kitchen. "So what is the homework today?"

"History." Jessica's expression indicated that this was not an area or assignment that she was particularly excited about. Without saying another word Jessica put her books down on the counter and plopped onto a chair.

"What kind of history?" asked Nishka sitting down next to her.

"American. We have to write a paper about what the Revolution means to us."

"What Revolution?" asked Nishka gently pulling over Jessica's history book.

Jessica was surprised by Nishka's question. There was only one revolution. The Fourth of July, fireworks, George Washington and Benjamin Franklin. Who could not know that? "The American Revolution. You know, where we got independence from London." Jessica laughed at her slip. It wasn't London, it was England. She knew that, but in all her excitement over knowing something Nishka didn't, she screwed up.

"The American Revolution? Yes the war for Independence.

1776 through 1783. The conflict between 13 British colonies on the eastern seaboard of North America and their parent country, Great Britain. The decisive battle of the war was at Yorktown in 1791. Sixteen thousand French and American troops surrounded Cornwallis by land. A French fleet cut off his reinforcements or retreat by sea. On October 19, 1781, Cornwallis surrendered."

Jessica was almost certain she detected a hint of a smile from Nishka as she finished her thumbnail sketch of the American Revolutionary war. She was like a walking encyclopedia and probably could have given a three-hour speech on the subject without batting an eye. "That was the war."

"So what is the problem?"

"What does it mean now, to me? What do I say? What would you say? What would it mean to you?"

"That I do not need a British passport. That I live here in your country where you can be different. At least you can be a little different.

"I can be different. But I can be different in other places can't I?" Jessica was a little concerned if not surprised about that concept. Why would anyone not accept her for being different anywhere else? Just because she had a brace on her leg?

"In some countries they watch you very closely if you are different. That is why I am here. I do not like to be watched very closely."

Watched closely. Why would Nishka be so concerned about that? Because she was a girl? A very smart, beautiful girl. That thought settled on Jessica like a weight. Was that what the revolution was all about? Being free to be different? The more Jessica thought about that, the more she liked it. Eventually, after a little more discussion, Jessica began to write. Two hours later she was done.

Chapter Seven

The next morning, Tuesday, September 11th, 2001, at 8:45 a.m. Eastern Standard Time, the paper Jessica wrote on the American Revolution suddenly felt insignificant. But what it meant to her became more meaningful then anything else in the world that day. Ironically, the cover and lead story of Time magazine dated September 10th featured Secretary of State Colin Powell with a banner that read; "Where have you gone, Colin Powell?" With a follow up sub headline that read: "The Secretary of State isn't the foreign policy general everyone thought he would be. What's holding him back?" After 9-11 no one remembered the article.

It was a little after ten, and Jessica had just started her second class when the buzz started spreading through the school. "Did you hear? A plane crashed into the World Trade Center!" The talk spread from teacher to teacher, administrator to janitor. Everyone was talking about the improbable accident that happened. Twenty minutes later it became obvious the crash had not been an accident. Most of the teachers were called from their classrooms for updated news. Another jetliner had crashed into the second World Trade Center Tower. It was intentional; it was an act of War!

The upper classes were told the news first. They were the oldest and considered the most mature to handle the chain of events that were unfolding. The lower classes were told later. Being in fourth grade, Jessica and the rest of her classmates were told about what had happened in New York and Washington a little before lunch. Instead of the bell, the principal came on over the intercom and made an announcement. He followed with a prayer, then asked for a moment of silence for those that had perished.

For David, like millions of others living hundreds to thousands of miles away from New York, the news of the attacks came first in bits and pieces filtering through the workplace. A passenger jet had hit one of the World Trade Towers. The worst aviation accident in history. By the time the media reached the accident scene and started recording the event, the second tower was struck. Film showed the plane banking then heading right for the skyscraper. It was no accident. It was a real full-blown kamikaze attack.

By then, in most offices and other places of employment around the country, employees and employers alike found themselves crowded around whatever radio or television set was available in an impromptu brotherhood, watching the worst man made disaster since Pearl Harbor unfold affecting the lives of Americans forever. Within less than an hour came the third report; flight 77 out of Dulles International Airport with 64 passengers abroad veered around moments after take off and took dead aim on the Pentagon twenty six miles away. Within minutes it crashed into the western façade of the building killing all aboard plus numerous people in that section of the building. A short time later a fourth plane over Pennsylvania -- crashed after it was reported being hijacked and turned back, probably toward the nation's capital.

Like so many others David was numb, speechless, as he stood transfixed watching the dramas unfold hundreds of miles away, yet live in front of him. People could hardly move as they stood transfixed, watching the inconceivable carnage, of firemen rushing into the towers in an attempt to save as many people as possible. Thirty thousand people were reported to possibly be working in the twin towers. Many were trapped floors above where the planes hit. Others were vaporized instantly. Some of those on the upper floors who couldn't escape the burning carnage jumped to their deaths. Those that could escape were frantically trying to get down through the darkened stairs to safety below.

At 9:50 AM the south tower began to collapse, one floor pancaking down on top of the one below. Within a minute, all that was left of the twelve hundred and fifty foot tall structure was a pile of rubble and a huge cloud of choking dust and flying debris engulfing a large swath of lower Manhattan.

For David the images of the attack were burned into his conscious for the rest of the day. Like many of his associates, he did little more then move from television to radio, then another monitor, trying to grab every bit of information possible as the news continued to grow worse. Like so many of his comrades, David left work early with a strong, sudden desire to go home and be close to the only ones that mattered anymore, his family.

⁂

The news came much earlier for Carl. Within an hour he was called to action, interviewing and reporting all he could on the local front, concerning anyone who was even remotely connected to what was quickly unfolding as the largest story of the twenty first century. Within hours of the second attack, some of his comrades were on the streets asking stunned passersby's of their feelings concerning what happened.

Strangely, many didn't want to talk, other than to say they felt connected to the tragedies in New York and Washington. A number just wanted to go home. Others, more than expected, said they had prayed that morning and would continue to pray for those affected by the terrible attack. Though many of those interviews didn't make the airways, it was soon apparent that God had suddenly become part of the equation as many people found themselves trying to come to grips with what no one had ever in their wildest dreams envisioned ever happening.

For Nishka the news of the attacks came almost while they happened. One moment she was at her computer comparing stocks and the world of investments, the next the screen suddenly seemed to explode with information about the attacks. Within moments Nishka had left her quiet bedroom workstation and moved to the livingroom where she turned on the television. With only a couple exceptions, all the stations had focused on the events that were unfolding. Nishka couldn't help feeling she had seen it all before, that a past acquaintance was involved -- if not directly then indirectly -- and that somehow this would not be the end.

As Nishka watched the tragedy continue to unfold, her thoughts drifted back to a time eight years before, to her life and experiences at the World Trade Center and from which point her odyssey into the heartland began. Nishka had been comfortable then. Living in New York had been a pleasant experience. It was a perfect place for someone like her, a place where she could work, move about, study those around her without seeming odd or out of place. After all, there were eight million people in New York, many far stranger than her, and many of them wanting to make their mark. Short of exposing one's self or having sex on the sidewalk, no one paid much attention to what one did, and even the sex part was debatable.

⁂

Nishka had managed to land an entry-level job as an accout manager for a small trading firm. After a string of successful stock trades, she soon developed a credible enough resume to become recognized as a talent. That track record, plus her appearance, helped her manage to secure a junior trading associate position with Lambert and Brown at the Trade Center. Nishka moved to the village, a small apartment on the third floor, nothing fancy. She didn't need much. Room for a desk, computer, a lamp, and chair, some reading, material and a closet for clothes. Of course, there were appearances to keep. Just enough furniture to keep the landlord from getting suspicious. Her time in New York was educational and uneventful -- that was until that day, when everything blew apart. That day in 93 when the World Trade Center suffered its first attack and she barely escaped with her life.

They had followed her down to the subway where she had just managed to elude her pursuers by catching a commuter as the doors were closing. She could still see Ahmed's face screaming at her as the train pulled away. Nishka watched them through the car window till they were out of sight. Even then it took awhile before she was able to sit down. Crowds of people pushed around her seat as the train rambled on but Nishka did not notice them. Instead she stared blankly into space as the odds of what happened rattled through her head. There was no doubt the person she saw was the same one she met a long time ago in Russia when it was still the Soviet Union. If that was the case, then was it not logical he was connected to what happened at the Trade Center? A terrorist act that bold could only mean one thing; they had expanded their operations to the back yard of those they hated almost as much as the Israelis.

Suddenly everything changed. As Nishka sat in that crowded car and pulled into her cloistered internal world she began to reevaluate her situation. It was certain her identity was in jeopardy and her existence would never be the same, at least not in New York. There had always been the hope that he thought she was dead, or, if nothing else, still in Russia. Using the skills she had learned concerning counter espionage, flight and survival, she placed herself in her counterpart's situation and began rationalizing step by step what he would do next. No doubt he had already made plans for a quick departure from New York not wanting to be around when the FBI began putting together a profile of those who might have been responsible for the bomb. But something had radically changed, a new wrinkle in the mix: Nishka. Not only had the terrorists learned she was still alive, but they knew she was probably living nearby. What would he do? What would she do? If she were him, knowing how valuable she might be to future operations, she would take the chance and find her; after all, they might never get another.

There was no doubt about it. They would come after her. It would only be a matter of time before they found out where she lived. That left only one thing to do, run.

It was nearly four hours from the time of the blast till Nishka reached the small neighborhood delicatessen across the street from her apartment. Though there were no sign of the terrorists, Nishka took no chances. From a dilapidated pay phone on the wall near the front window, she called her apartment. While letting the phone ring she scanned the street for suspicious characters. No one answered. She didn't think anyone would, but if they reached there first, human nature dictated they might pick up the phone. After all, she had no answering machine. If they were smart, the first thing she figured they would do was find the woman they had seen her with. No doubt Sharon would not have strayed far from the plaza. It would not have been hard to convince her they needed Nishka's address, either, by subterfuge or other means. Provided they had means to a car, or the very least a taxi, and considering the traffic with what had happened that day, she projected four hours, five tops, before they showed up. That didn't leave Nishka much time.

Convinced everything was clear; Nishka darted across the street to her building. After scanning the elevator, Nishka opted for the stairs -- better chance of not being trapped -- and quickly started up the three flights to her apartment. Reaching her floor, Nishka checked the hall; it was deserted. Quickly unlocking her door, she darted inside. The apartment was empty. Not a single sign anyone had been there since she left that morning. Locking the door, she turned on the television, then went to the window and surveyed the street. No sign of Ahmed.

Returning to the television, Nishka changed the channel from business to news. A live telecast form the World Trade Center detailing the bombing was on. Ambulances, along with the fire and police departments, were everywhere. A little smoke was still coming from the building as an announcer described the scene. "It's been four hours since the terrible explosion that rocked the Trade Center this morning. Though there is still no official word on the number of injured and dead, it is now believed that a Near East faction was responsible."

Nishka turned off the television, glanced back at the window, still no one, then surveyed the apartment. Quickly opening the closet, she grabbed a travel bag and methodically packed every piece of paper, from bank statements to reports, which could give any hint about her life or past activities. Convinced it was only a matter of time, maybe even minutes before they came, Nishka grabbed used computer disks and threw them in. Returning to the closet she knelt down and removed a baseboard from the back of the closet. Reaching into the opening she pulled out other papers and a worn brown money belt and tossed them into the bag. Though Nishka's personal possessions were few, she only took enough clothing to last a couple days, the rest she could replace.

The bag full, she scanned the room one last time. Only one possible link to her existence remained. Nishka gently stroked the top of the computer, paused, then setting the monitor aside, removed the computer cover, pulled out the hard drive and tossed it in the bag. In one swift movement Nishka zipped shut the bag and left.

No sooner had Nishka reached the stairs then stopped. In the stone silence of the old building she could hear the unmistakable sound of men's steps on the stairs far below. There was no doubt it was them. Quickly turning about, Nishka headed up the stairs instead. No sooner had she reached the roof than the two men below reached her apartment, knocked on the door, then knocked again. She felt trapped. A fast survey of the roof revealed only one option, a fire escape ladder. It was a long way down and the last eight feet were a drop but it was that or the terrorists. Swinging the strap of her bag over her shoulder Nishka started the climb down.

It seemed like forever before she reached the last rung eight feet above the ground. After dropping the bag onto a some garbage bags below Nishka lowered herself till she was swinging from the bottom of the ladder, then let go. No sooner had she dropped to the ground then she quickly recovered. Only a run in her nylon; she could live with that. Quickly grabbing her bag she darted down the alley, stopped at the entrance, and looked around. Her luck held; a yellow cab was coming down the street and no sign of the terrorists anywhere. The cab looked empty.

⚜

When the terrorists burst into Nishka's apartment, all they found was a deserted room littered with the remnants of someone who had left in a hurry. While his partner checked the washroom and bedroom, Ahmed examined her desk and computer. He marveled at her thoroughness in covering her tracks. "Any sign of her?"

"None," noted his compatriot returning from the bedroom. After quickly reexamining the main room, the second terrorist turned to the window just as Nishka rushed from the alley and flagged down the taxi. "Ahmed! There she is!"

Ahmed rushed to the window and flung it open just as Nishka reached the cab. "You can't hide! No matter where you go I'll find you!"

Nishka looked back up at her apartment window for only an instant before ducking into the cab. Seconds later the car pulled away.

⚜

Nishka never made any effort to find out whether they had gotten to Sharon or if she was all right. It would not have done any good, anyway. Besides, good soldiers never look back, especially a soldier like her, alone without a country. The supposed mastermind of the World Trade Center bombing was soon caught and convicted. Ironically, Ahmed was never connected with the attack. That didn't surprise Nishka.

During the next eight years, Nishka moved about, never staying long in one place. She had gone to the Cayman Islands for a short time. Long enough to move her funds which had become sizeable, and consolidate her new identity. When she felt distanced enough from Ahmed to set up a permanent residence, she bought a house in what she considered to be one of the most nondescript towns she could find. A bedroom community, just large enough to be comfortable and not stand out, but small enough to be of little notice to the outside world. A community that was totally nondescript, middle-class America, where statistics showed nothing much happened and most likely never would.

Still she never felt completely safe. Though she logically convinced herself, that the terrorists would forget about her, she couldn't help but feel that if they ever had a hint about her whereabouts they would do whatever it took to get her. It was why she placed the outside lights around the perimeter of her yard as well as putting in other security devices. Now, after eight years of losing herself and finally beginning to feel safe they were back, she was sure of it. As a result, her life and the life of all those in the country she had grown to accept as home, would never be quite the same.

Chapter Eight

School let out early the afternoon of the 11th. The faculty felt helpless with little idea of what to do considering the news. Likewise the administration had decided that any meaningful concentration on the childrens lessons would most likely be impossible as all eyes and ears were on the tragedy. Many parents felt insecurity over what happened and were glad to have their children home. In the aftermath of the shock from that mornings' events, the only thing on most peoples minds were to be as close as possible to those they loved or cared for, whether family or friends. It was a time for mourning, searching, trying to rationalize what happened, to evaluate and decide what to do next, if anything at all.

No sooner had Jessica and Peter returned home than they dropped off their books and went to Nishka's. The television was still on when Nishka let them in. "Did you see what happened!" gushed Peter, immediately plopping down in the nearest chair to the set.

"Yes," replied Nishka in her normal, almost-monotone voice while sitting down on the nearby sofa.

"How could somebody do that?" asked Jessica sitting down close to Nishka.

"Because they hate us!" Peter didn't say more. He didn't

have to. In one line he managed to grasp what most of the country had been forced to realize that day: that the country they called home and believed in as always safe, the answer to humanity's dream, could in anyway be hated by anyone. The United States was the righteous one, based on rights and laws, the land that gave to the world when others wouldn't or couldn't. Uncle Sam dressed as Santa Claus, the benevolent family patriarch that was understanding, giving, and always knew best for the world. It was inconceivable to the children that anyone could hate a country so good.

Nishka said very little that afternoon as they sat and watched America change. Jessica said even less. The children watched scenes that repeatedly showed the planes crashing into the towers, firefighters rushing in to try to control the situation and bring people out, the attack on the Pentagon and the chaos that followed. Jessica often turned away from the news shots of people falling or jumping to their deaths in an effort to escape the fires from the upper floors. There were scenes reminiscent of nuclear devastation as the two structures collapsed on top of themselves in a cloud of billowing smoke and flying debris. There were other images -- people bloodied, caked with dust and plaster, choking, holding each other in shock or sitting alone crying.

As the tragedy was explored by the media in the grizzliest details, Jessica moved closer to Nishka. Eventually she wrapped her hands around Nishka's arm and drew against her till her head was tight against Nishka's side in an effort to find security from the world beyond.

At first Nishka seemed almost defensive about having someone, anyone, so close, almost as if it were an invasion of her space. Consoling – mothering -- was an alien concept to her. But as the afternoon drifted toward evening and the unending flow of news about the loss of life that morning shifted toward an escalating feeling of remorse and insecurity, Nishka mellowed to Jessica's intrusion. Instead it became more natural, something expected, especially considering the circumstances.

As dinner drew near, Nishka prodded the children to leave saying it was more important to be with their father, especially that night. "He is going to need you two now more than ever," said Nishka escorting Peter and Jessica to the door. Whether she actually believed that was another story. What mattered was Jessica believed it. Suddenly Jessica wanted to be home almost as much for the comfort of her father's presence as to give him comfort. If there were ever a time for togetherness, it was that night.

✦

The rest of the week became a non-stop replay of September Eleventh as the news media continued almost unabated with stories and analogies of what happened that day, the days and weeks before, and what could happen next. It took little time to decipher who and how the attacks were accomplished. There were nineteen directly involved in the crashes. A group called Al-Qaida who, till that morning, had been only minimally known to the public had orchestrated the attacks. That group, which apparently had operatives all over the globe, was lead by known terrorist, Osama Bin Laden. It was also learned that the passenger jet that crashed in Pennsylvania that same morning was the result of passengers who, upon learning their jet was hijacked and what their apparent fate would be, decided to take destiny into their own hands. Magazines that as recently as a few days before 9-11 were touting America's fascination with its seemingly shallow lifestyle, such as a "U. S. News" cover story of September 3$^{rd:}$ "How to Make Yourself Happy", were soon replaced with feature stories solely focused on the "War on Terror". "People Magazine," one of the most notorious for exposing how indulgent society had become, had within days of the attack, come out with an issue dedicated solely to September 11th. "Time" dedicated issue after issue to what was happening and the 'Immerging strength and character of the American people; as did "US News", "News Week" and many other magazines. Major league baseball games were canceled for nearly a week after 9-11 as were many other public events, as much out of respect for the tragedy as for fear that their very event might be the target of more attacks.

American flags began flying everywhere, from homes and offices to inside malls, residential windows, cars -- anywhere they could be hung. Millions of citizens began wearing patches and flag pins on their blouses, shirts, and the lapels of suits. The National Anthem, "God Bless America," and "America the Beautiful" suddenly became the number one most requested and played songs on radio as did other patriotic numbers both new and old. The population had, in one fell swoop, become aroused and came together. Strangers began greeting one another with "Hi, how are you?" or "Have you heard?" as if everyone were a long lost cousin. Children, especially boys like Peter and his friends, began playing as though they were part of the country's new found patriotism, becoming their own special force, ever vigilant for terrorists and ready to fight to the death like the passengers of Pennsylvania's flight 93.

The number of people who volunteered to give blood during the first days after the attack so overwhelmed the nation's blood banks that they could hardly manage the crowds, which, in many cases, overflowed into the streets.

Foundations were begun almost overnight to collect donations of every kind from money to food and clothes. Firefighters, police, construction workers and all manner of support people from all over the country volunteered to travel to New York and help their brethren in the search of those that had fallen. The date 9-11 soon became synonymous with December 7th as one of the most infamous dates in American history as people tried to grapple with how many died and how many more were still possibly trapped in the rubble of what was once the World Trade Center.

As the weeks passed, almost all conversation shifted from "Where would the terrorist strike next?" to "When do we strike back?" as the feeling of helplessness from September 11th shifted to anger against any group or individual of Muslim decent. At the same time others around the nation tried to understand why, what where the roots of rage that created such hatred toward America. Everywhere people wanted to know what the Muslim religion was all about.

Home defense became the new watchword in public speeches and the media while a central command was beginning to be pulled together to handle future attacks. Talk about the "Enemy" and going to Afghanistan to "kick some butt" became the hottest topics in the news, not to mention local bars, barbershops, and even beauty parlors.

Carl found himself on the road even more, covering the many aspects of the war on terror. As his television reports increased, the stories began to draw him farther and farther from home. He found himself in the Near East doing reports on the attitude of those countries toward Americans following the attack. He went on to Pakistan then later to what were sure to be the staging areas for allied reprisals in Afghanistan itself. The farther Carl traveled, the more Jessica's family became deeply intertwined with the drama that was unfolding.

Chapter Nine

By the last week in September, Jessica and Peter were spending almost as much time at Nishka's after school as they were at home. Nishka would have milk and cookies ready. They would do their homework and talk about what has happening in the world and their Uncle Carl's exploits. Peter especially became interested in current events. Soon after the attack, he and his friends formed a secret defense group of their own, prepared to check out anyone that looked the least bit suspicious in case the terrorists planned on making an example to the world by attacking their neighborhood directly.

Jessica, on the other hand, had begun to draw more into herself. Her naive feelings of safety that most children felt when growing up were shaken. Like a battle-scarred, shell-shocked war victim, she became somewhat traumatized by the continuing reports on the news of what the terrorists had done or what they were capable of doing. What was worse, her faith was shaken. How could God, her God, have allowed such things to happen? The scars from the loss of her mother had been subtle, and though she showed none of the outward signs of that trauma, the brace on her leg was a constant reminder to others, whether she was conscious of it or not.

What happened in her country over the past couple

weeks had begun to bring to the forefront all the feelings of insecurity she felt years before. And there appeared to be no answer or solution on which she could rebuild that faith she had so steadfastly clung to-and used to grow over the years since the accident. Only her visits with Nishka gave her any feeling of comfort. There was something about Nishka's lack of emotion and unflinching strength in the face of all that had happened in her country and the world around them that comforted Jessica.

That Friday after school Jessica went to Nishka's house alone. She reached for the doorbell as if she were reaching for a lifeline, pushing hard then quickly pushing it again.

It felt like forever before the door finally opened and Nishka let her in. "Hi, where is Peter?" asked Nishka, half expecting to see him around the corner someplace.

"He couldn't make it. It's first night of basketball tryouts. He wants to make the team." Jessica's tone seemed to portray a sense of betrayal, as if his not coming was, in a sense, an act of desertion

"Oh, that is good."

Nishka said no more about the subject as Jessica walked in, just closed the door behind her. To Jessica her statement was almost as disrespectful to those who had perished and what was going on in the world as her brother's. "Don't you think he should be thinking about more important things than basketball?" said Jessica as she followed Nishka to the kitchen.

"Like what? He is just a boy. What should he do?

"I don't know, not play basketball." That was all Jessica could say as she put her books down, pulled a chair away from the table, and sat down. It just seemedthat her brother should care more. But then Peter had never been much of the emotional type, not like her.

"So what is your homework for today?" asked Nishka, pouring a glass of milk for Jessica and some water for herself.

"A story about Christmas." Jessica looked up at the picture of the angel she had given Nishka, now prominently hung on the wall opposite the table.

"Any ideas?"

Jessica thought a moment, then smiled. "Something about you."

"That would be neither practical nor about Christmas," said Nishka handing the glass of milk to Jessica. "What is your next choice?"

"I don't know." Jessica opened her notebook and stared at the blank page, then turned to Nishka. "Got any ideas?"

"No. Where I came from Christmas was not talked about much." Nishka set her glass down and returned to the cupboard for some cookies, then abruptly stopped, apparently deciding to do something different. "While you are thinking I have something to show you." Without waiting for a reply, Nishka turned for the hall that led to the bedrooms. Jessica followed Nishka silently to the last bedroom, which -- after a number of Saturdays of cleaning -- had never changed. When Nishka opened the door, the room looked much the same except, where there had once been a lonely chair, there was now a companion desk like the one in Jessica's scrapbook. On the wall near the desk was the framed print, easily visible from the hall. The picture changed the room's atmosphere. It was a beautifully framed reproduction of the same angels Jessica had shown her weeks before. "What do you think?"

"It's nice."

"Needs more, right?"

Jessica hobbled to the framed picture of angels and

stared at it for a long time before finally touching the glass. "They're beautiful."

"You really like angels."

"Yes." Jessica ran her finger gently along the edge of the gold baroque frame as she studied the renaissance print of the heavenly scene. "My mother's an angel. She watches over me."

Nishka quietly pulled the chair out from the desk and sat down. "How do you know?"

"Because she told me so."

"When?"

"A long time ago. Before she left." Jessica focused on one angel; a beautiful young one with wings expanded, her long, flowing auburn hair hanging down past her shoulders.

The room became strangely silent, like a chapel on Christmas Eve. Finally in the quiet stillness Jessica turned back to Nishka and, leaning against her shoulder, looked back at the angel. "Do you think my mother has wings? Sometimes they don't get them right away, you know."

"What do you think?"

"I don't know. I hope so."

"Then it must be so." Nishka hesitantly put her arm around Jessica. For Jessica it was a comforting touch, a natural show of caring, not unusual from an adult. But in the weeks since Nishka had known the children it was the first time she had ever shown any physical compassion on her own initiative. It was Nishka's first expression of emotion ever.

Jessica never went back to her homework that day. Instead, when the two returned to the kitchen, she sat quietly watching Nishka go through her routine of putting out the cookies then tidying up what little there was to tidy. After that Nishka sat down, they talked about other things -- school, personal projects, and what Jessica wanted to be when she was older. Nishka listened, occasionally asking questions, which until that day had been rare for Nishka and always brief.

Jessica did not return to thoughts of the world or the paper she had to write until later that night, after dinner when she was alone in the quiet of her room. Even then she wrote little, as thoughts about that day drifted disjointedly through her mind. Finally she put the paper away, turned out the light and, after saying her prayers, went to sleep.

◈

That Sunday David was up earlier than usual. After getting the coffee brewing, he walked out to the drive to retrieve his paper. It was a pleasant morning and the air smelled especially pleasing as he scooped up the Sunday edition. He stood for a moment and sucked in a deep breath of air. It seemed strange, almost inconceivable as he scanned the quiet neighborhood, that their world had suddenly becoming so unstable. At that moment life felt good -- the way it was always meant to be. Only the American flags flapping listlessly throughout the neighborhood gave any indication that something unusual had happened. David took another deep breath, then turned back to the house.

"Even our new neighbor is finally flying a flag," he half mumbled as he glanced at Nishka's house. Of course, he had put his flag out the day after the attack. By the end of the week everyone had one out. The media had even reported on the big runs at stores for American flags. "If nothing else that's one segment of the economy that's busy," he half said out loud. "No doubt they're putting on extra shifts," David half chuckled as he closed the front door behind him.

One thing David prided himself on was being a regular churchgoer, and that morning was no exception. The attack of September 11th had had a traumatic effect on the American psyche. Since the terrorist acts more and more people were finding their way back to church, many of whom hadn't been in a sanctuary in years. Fifteen miles from Manhattan, a pastor who had been preaching for 28 years had contemplated leaving the ministry because of dwindling size of his congregation. But then came September 11th. Never had he seen so much concern and uncertainty in his parishioners as he saw after that day. Nor had he seen so many of his congregation as he in the weeks that followed. The same was happening all over the country as church congregations swelled as more people began looking around for more, something that could explain how such terrible things could happen to their world?

It took longer than usual to roust the children for church that morning. Jessica in particular seemed unusually sluggish which bothered David a little since she was usually the first one ready to go. As was customary, David stopped to pick up his mother on route to church. Because of the delay -- or maybe because of the little extra time David spent with his coffee that morning -- they were uncustomarily late and just managed to get seated before the liturgy.

The church was exceptionally full that Sunday as the parishioners waited for the sermon and hopeful words of comfort to help reaffirm some semblance of peace in their lives. The feeling of serenity, of knowing everything was in order in the world that Jessica knew, felt strangely missing that morning. Only the image of the angel looking down on her through the stained glass window gave her any sense of solace as she listened to the congregation sing.

Jessica's concentration had already begun to wander, her thoughts having reached an unsettling stage concerning God in relation to right and wrong, God versus evil and life's uncertaintywhen the sermon began. Though normally an avid listener, Jessica barely looked up when the pastor climbed into the pulpit. He paused a moment, closed his eyes, and seemed to pray, then turned to the congregation.

"Let thy will be done.' We all recognize that verse. We've said it thousands of times during our lives. It's one of the most important lines in a prayer that is one of the holiest in all of Christendom. Yet as often as we've said it, many of us have forgotten what those words really mean. Thy will be done. God's will. It is said that nothing happens unless it is by the will of God. If that is true, then one has to ask himself, "Why God, do you let bad things happen?"

The preacher took a long pause. During that moment Jessica's attention had focused on him as if knowing instinctively what he was going to say next could -- or would -- be the key to all the anguish and confusion she felt.

"One doesn't have to be a pastor very long before he is eventually called upon to deal with very difficult moments in peoples' lives. Eventually he has to ask, or is asked, 'Why God,' somewhere in those conversations." The Pastor paused again as if remembering something long forgotten. When he looked back it seemed to Jessica that he was looking directly at her.

"A turning point for this pastor was an event that happened twenty years ago. I was home from college working that summer when we received a message that my aunt had a serious heart attack. Immediately after hearing the news, I began to pray because I knew that God was all-powerful and he could protect her. As we got ready -- preparing the car so we could make the hour long trip -- we received a second call. My aunt had died. I walked away from that day feeling God had let me down. That the God that was supposed to be all-powerful couldn't save my aunt! Most of us have had those moments. We all have our stories of how we tried to merge reality with God's promise of hope and had to struggle with the results."

"Our journey over these past weeks since 9-11 has been a frustrating effort to find solid ground to understand how, we normally don't fail when storms come and the winds of change or disaster blow. So how do we get to solid ground when all that has happened recently has in many cases shaken our faith?"

"And let God's will be done – on earth as it is in heaven. What we learn from all this is the most important part of God's lesson. If we can understand and accept this, it will determine whether we weather the storms of life and keep our faith and character intact, or begin to experience an elliptical orbit that takes us farther and farther from the God we know as our father."

The pastor paused again, and looked at all the congregation - and Jessica in particular - at the same time. "We all arrived on the same bus on September 11th. What we suffered on that day was probably the worst act ever perpetrated against America in its two hundred plus year history. September 11 was the worst disaster this country ever recorded. It claimed twice the number of lives lost in the attack on Pearl Harbor. Our sense of security has been forever shaken. Ten thousand children lost a parent that day. Three hundred kids in a daycare had no parent to pick them up that evening. As they began to dig through the rubble, they found the clinched fist of a woman. When they pried the hand open they found another hand of a child inside."

"Several possibilities of how to answer 'Why God!' have

arisen. A writer once wrote in his book - Why Bad Things Happen To Good People - that in times of chaos, God does not have the power to make things right. But how could a God who created the universe not have the power to affect what happens in such times. Or maybe it was God's way of saying it's time to wake up, to come to grips -- to realize that the world is not just as we see it in our cozy little world of health, wealth, and happiness."

"Like in the case of my aunt, or other experiences you all have had, a person does not grow in character without pain. A person who truly experiences the fullness of life does not avoid the misery. Jesus never promised that no one was going to suffer in this life. John the Baptist, one of the most steadfast messengers of God's word, was put in prison and beheaded."

"So where was God on September Eleventh?

Let's look at this a different way. We all know that there was room for over one thousand people in those four planes. Why were there only 206? We know that there was normally fifty thousand people working in the World Trade Center. Why was it that less than twenty thousand were in the building when disaster struck? There were stories after stories of how people were stuck in traffic or had other things happen that kept them away that morning. Why is it that two-thirds of the people got out before the building's two towers came down or that the buildings imploded instead of falling over, killing thousands of other people? A member of our own congregation was supposed to be at a meeting there, but because of problems in scheduling was still in her hotel making arrangements when the planes hit the towers."

"I ask myself, 'If God can make lame men walk, or cast out demons, or control the water and the sky, why didn't he stop what happened?' I don't know. I don't know. Or! How do we know that God did not already stop other attacks of terror that were supposed to happen on or before the 11th that could have been far worse than what happened?"

"How do we know? We'll never know. But we do know how much more tragic it could have been and wasn't. I believe that was the work of God. A lesson was learned. And the cost could have been so very much higher."

When the sermon ended much of the weight that Jessica had brought with her was gone. It was true that much worse things could have happened. For all those who died many, many more were saved. The world did not seem such a dismal place after that. There was no doubt in her mind that there was still more than enough evil to go around. But maybe it was just all part of a lesson. And as long as she and her brother and others she knew were safe in a place where nothing was going to happen, then maybe God had not deserted them after all. That night Jessica said an extra long prayer for her Uncle Carl.

◈

Monday passed in a hurry for Jessica. School was not as painful as it had been the weeks before. She did well in math that day and was more focused in her other classes. Her religion class, which had for a while been unsettling, had meaning for her again. Jessica and her fellow students had been asked to write a story concerning faith and Christmas. The faculty had decided that such assignments would help the children put much of the terror of the past month behind them by focusing them on the good possibilities in the future rather than the evil of the past. The project, which had once seemed alien to her emotionally, began to fill up with various ideas after Sunday's sermon.

Unfortunately Jessica's new mindset was still not focused enough for her to begin writing that day, nor was it any better when she went to Nishka's after school that afternoon. Instead of working on the paper, she found herself telling Nishka about the sermon and what was going on in the world. "Do you believe God has a purpose for why things happen like they do?" asked Jessica

"I believe there is a certain order in the Universe. What do you believe?"

Jessica paused, not sure she totally knew that answer herself. "Sometimes I don't understand why my mother had to die.

"Did you not say that she is an angel watching over you?"

"Yes. That's what daddy said. Why?"

"Maybe it is because he felt she could do a better job that way."

Jessica did not respond to her logic. Instead she sat staring at the picture of the angel hanging on the kitchen wall that she had given Nishka. With all that had happened in the world in the past mouths that was a concept that was hard to comprehend, Jessica had, for the first time, begun to question the purpose of her mother's death. At least it was the first time since the years following the accident. The recent questioning of her faith had been the most unsettling thing Jessica had experienced since the day her mother died. Had she not heard the sermon the day before, she might still be just as uncertain about her faith, if not more so. But being with Nishka at afternoon kind of helped her put an end to her troubled feelings and instead put some of them into perspective.

That night as Jessica sat in her bedroom doing her homework, she made a ovenant with herself that she was going to finish the assignment that had dogged her the past week. At first she did nothing other than stare at the pictures of angels she had found or drawn then hung on her walls. It wasn't until sometime later that she finally took her pencil and began to write on the top of the blank paper. "The Smallest Angel." She stared at the words a long time before continuing to write. Near midnight, amidst the quietest moments of that night, she finished her paper. She placed it neatly into a paper folder, then said a long prayer to God and went to sleep.

Chapter Ten

It took Jessica a night to write her story. She never looked at it again until that Friday when she turned it in. She didn't have to. Good or bad, it was from her heart, and nothing could have improved on that.

Saturday morning Jessica and Peter were up early. They had breakfast and were at Nishka's long before their father had groggily pulled himself out of bed. The house seemed strangely quiet when David stumbled downstairs to the kitchen and began making coffee. It felt good not to hear the drone of television cartoons from the other room. At least that's what he told himself as he fetched the morning paper from the drive. But no sooner had he poured himself a cup, plopped down on his favorite kitchen chair and opened the paper than his tranquillity ended. "See the children outside?" he asked pulling his robe over his shorts in a halfhearted attempt at modesty as his mother walked in carrying a couple bags of groceries.

"Yes," huffed Helen, nodding toward the house next door while plopping down the groceries. "They're helping what's-her-name wash her car."

"Really? Wish they'd do mine." Spotting a box of donuts

poking out of the bags David pulled them out. "They've been there a lot lately."

"You noticed," shot Helen in a less-than-motherly tone while sliding a bottle of milk in the refrigerator. "That's where they do most of their homework you know."

David didn't respond. Instead he removed a donut from its box, took a large bite and washed it down with coffee. "I remember when Barbara used to help them," he blurted, wishing he hadn't said that the moment the words left his mouth. It was the kind of statement his mother was prone to jump all over, saying he just didn't make enough effort or something. Fortunately she said nothing and David leaned back, taking a mental sigh while sipping his coffee, relieved she let it slip. It wasn't that David hadn't tried spending more time with his children. Since Barbara's death David had, whenever possible, sat down and talked to them as best he could. Unfortunately he didn't have the patience Barbara had. She was a natural tutor who related well with the children, especially Peter who often struggled. Jessica was too young to have had much school experience when Barbara died. Fortunately for David, Jessica was a natural learner who grasped things quickly. Jessica actually made David look good, the way she picked up on science and computers faster than Peter who wanted to be an astronaut.

When it came to school, David's sympathy was always with Peter. It wasn't unusual to find Peter sitting long hours, struggling with some school project. Often when David worked late Grandmother filled in trying to help him. Other times, especially during the past year, they relied on tutoring, for a nominal fee, from one of the teachers after school. Though David was always willing to pay, sometimes it was a struggle trying to fit even a nominal fee into the family budget, especially considering Jessica's needs. So far this year the budget stayed fairly manageable, thanks impart to this new neighbor, to whom David owed a huge debt of gratitude and whom he still hadn't met.

"Have you talked to her yet?" asked Helen, putting the rest of the groceries away. "You haven't have you!"

"Have you?" David shot back like a boy trying to defend by flipping the discussion from defense to offense.

"Yes. She's a little quiet, but nice. And you?"

"We've waved." Helen frowned, but David said no more. Hey, what more do you want, he thought, taking another bite of his donut. 'I'm a busy man here.' It was apparent by the way his mother shook her head as she put away the last of the groceries that his witticism didn't fly. "Hey what do you want! I work all the time!" After all what's more important, being the socialite of the neighborhood or keeping a roof over their heads? It's easy for her, David thought; after all his mother didn't have to work anymore. She could do what she wanted. There were times he envied her that luxury. Being the breadwinner definitely wasn't all it was cracked up to be.

Apparently his mother thought she knew him better, and -- by the expression in her eyes as she finished with the groceries -- nothing he said was going to change that. "It amazes me," she finally said, closing the cupboard, "that you ever got married."

"That's what Barbara said," David half whispered, more to himself as he stared at the remains of his donut. "If she hadn't proposed, I'd probably still be a bachelor." It wasn't much of a comeback, but it was more from the heart than anything he had said to his mother in a long time, especially concerning that special relationship he had with his wife. His dating prowess (or lack there of) or much else concerning his social life was far from glowing. David loved Barbara; it was as simple as that. And it was that love that somehow managed to propel him past an almost insurmountable shyness concerning women. A shyness that had kept him horny but also very much alone much of his early adult life. He often wondered what she saw in him. He wasn't flashy, a charmer, or particularly good looking. But he was sincere and honest and he truly loved her. When she died, it was as though part of him died with her -- the part one needed if he was ever going to share his life intimately with anyone else again. But that was so long ago. Like his mother said, "Life goes on if for no other reason than to propagate the species." And he knew what that meant -- getting back into arena. The trick was being able to convince his heart to be willing to make another commitment considering the possibilities of being hurt again.

"Maybe it's time you started dating."

"I will," Dave nodded, finishing the donut, then taking another.

"When?"

"When the right opportunity comes along."

Helen couldn't help but chuckle as she folded the grocery bags. "Well that should be about the time elephants fly!"

David did not respond; it wasn't worth the effort.

※

It was past eleven, a bright early fall day, though it felt a bit warmer than usual, when David opened the garage door and backed out the mini-van. It was time to wash the car. One of the many chores David did every Saturday as part of being a landowner. It was also one of the few projects he actually enjoyed. Even though the van was not a flashy Corvette or Firebird, it was his, and like most men and their machines, it was his pride and joy -- his chance to revive happier days, when as a teen he used to spend every Saturday waxing and polishing that '72 Buick, hottest wheels in town.

After pulling out the hose and other washing material, David filled the water bucket. It was a beautiful day, the perfect morning to do all the things he planned to do, or maybe later nothing at all. In no time it would be winter. What would he have done on a day like this years ago, he wondered. David studied Nishka's house a moment. The children weren't out like he had had hoped. No doubt they were inside helping with some project of hers. Why were they so infatuated with her, he wondered? Putting down the bucket David instinctively started walking toward her porch. "Why not?" he thought. With both his children there, what better excuse would he have to meet his neighbor.

As David neared the door, muddled thoughts of what he would say after ringing the bell raced through his mind. He could ask how they were doing. After all, they shouldn't wear out their welcome. No, that sounded corny. He would thank her for tutoring his children. No good; he should have done that weeks ago. Maybe he would ask to borrow them for a while, to help him clean his car. Why not? They were his children. If they were going to do chores for anyone, they ought to be doing some at home too, where they're getting paid an allowance for it. The more he thought about that, the cruder it sounded.

David stood staring at the doorbell as if frozen in place. Maybe he could just say, "how's your garden?" Or, "I'm your neighbor and I thought it was time I introduced myself. Especially since my children are here all the time." That sounded better. No that was dumber still. The more David thought of what to say the more flustered he got. What if she really was beautiful, so beautiful he couldn't say anything?

His children would be so embarrassed they'd never talk to him again. For that matter, he'd never talk to himself again.

"This is nuts, I can handle this," he thought. "No, I can't." And with that, David turned around and walked back home.

David replayed the way he had chickened out at his neighbor's front door over and over while washing the car. It haunted him while he vacuumed the seats. Twice he convinced himself how stupid it all was, stopped, and thought seriously about going back and finishing what he started. A second later he would change his mind and return to what he was doing. After all, there was always plenty of time later.

After he finished cleaning the car, he began recleaning everything he could think of in the car, including areas no one had cleaned in years short of the spark plugs -- while trying to rebuild his courage and finish what he started. He had climbed into the back seat, and began vacuuming every nook and cranny, when Peter suddenly appeared. "Dad, do you mind if Nishka takes us to the movies?"

"Sure have fun." So engrossed had David become in his mental tug of war over his inability to introduce himself, that he barely looked up.

"Thanks."

David nodded, returned to vacuuming, then abruptly turned back. "Just a.." It was too late, Peter was gone and so was a golden opportunity to meet his new neighbor. Strike two. By the time David realized he still had an opportunity to follow up on Peter's request by going next door and just asking when they would return (thereby finally meeting his phantom neighbor), the children and the neighbor's car were gone. Strike three.

Chapter Eleven

Though David thought a lot about his failed attempts at meeting his neighbor that morning his feelings of inadequacy were short-lived. Other than those couple of times during the following weeks when he thought he saw her as he returned home at night, national and world events crowded out most thoughts of missed opportunities.

Like millions of others, David and his family had become caught up in what was happening in the world. Threats of more terror attacks in the U.S. had become the biggest concern to most Americans. The nation's economy had almost become secondary as security became the number one conversation. Though the country's economic woes in many areas seemed to be slipping backward into a recession, many tried hard to avoid think about it, other than when it related to the bigger picture at hand. The one area in the economy that could not be ignored in relation to the continued slip in business recovery was the hit the transportation industry had taken. Thoughts and concerns about more terrorist activities, imagined or real, had cut air travel to a trickle. Hotel business in the weeks immediately following 9-11 had also dropped dramatically. Even the more conservative travel modes' which were often considered too mundane to give second thought to, quickly became suspect and ripe for concern after an attack on one of the bus carriers left a number of people dead and injured.

With terrorist talk growing wildly in a number of directions, every possibility of attack came under suspicion. Suicide bombers, small nuclear weapons (or dirty bombs as some liked to call them) all sent the nation into a jittery feeling of hypertension. But nothing had become center stage and discussed more than the threat of germ and chemical warfare. Through media exposure, people quickly became aware of just how exposed they were to terrorist chemical risks. According to a Time Magazine poll taken in the beginning of October, over 53% of those interviewed feared the possibility of a biological or chemical attack. Only twenty three percent feared some kind of nuclear attack. After analyzing the possibilities, terrorist experts shifted their focus from the possibility of a single large-scale assault to a series of smaller attacks that, it was determined, would be just as damaging to American moral and its economy. Of those possibilities, the use of biological weapons in single or coordinated attacks became the highest level threat. The smallpox virus was a weapon that was considered high on that list. A single case of smallpox could put the entire nation at risk. A highly contagious virus such as smallpox would spread quickly. Inoculations had been halted since 1972 in America. Of the many other biological agents that could be used as weapons -- including botulism and yersinia -- anthrax stood out as the most likely.

※

Only twenty minutes remained before Carl's flight was to touch down, and he would be home again. This return flight home was more meaningful than any he could remember.

Of all the news that he'd covered in his long career none of it had ever seemed as pessimistic as recent events, nor had events ever made him feel such a need or desire to be with family and friends. Home had suddenly become his anchor, a place where he could recharge and forget the craziness that he had been exposed to since September 11. It was ironic that he was returning home on a Boeing 757, the same type of plane that had been hijacked and crashed on that fateful day. The flight felt eerily empty, less than seventy on board by his guess. Considering the route and time of day, it normally would have been full. But then considering the state of mind of most of the American public concerning air travel and terrorism it was probably amazing there were as many people onboard as there were.

Carl found it hard to concentrate on the article he was reading in Time pertaining to the anthrax letter attacks in New York and Washington. The more he tried to focus, the more his mind wandered.

A woman across the aisle wearing a business suit, who appeared to be in her early fifties, stared at him occasionally in between fidgeting with her ring and scanning the 'Architectural Digest' on her lap. Finally deciding she couldn't contain herself any longer, she turned to him straight on. "Excuse me. You seem familiar. Are you on television?"

"I'm a journalist." The woman looked confused. "The news. I'm a news correspondent."

The woman seemed relieved and at the same time concerned as she nodded toward the magazine article Carl was reading. "Where you there?'

"New York? Yes, but not on September 11."

"My nephew was there." Her eyes appeared to well up with moisture momentarily but she didn't say anymore.

"I hope he was okay," said Carl feeling a compulsive urge to move across the aisle and put his arm around her.

"He's fine. He was late for work that morning. But it feels that everywhere you turn lately there's something else. My sister's son works for the post office. She says that lately there isn't a day that goes by when he goes to work that she doesn't worry he's going to come home sick – or worse."

Carl felt a compulsion to reply, to say that over the past month everyone was feeling the paranoia, that even just opening a letter was a test of faith -- or worse yet -- Russian roulette. Especially those in Washington and New York, though the rest of the country, especially the big cites, were not far behind. But instead he said nothing. Under normal circumstances, being recognized by someone like his new acquaintance would have resulted in a much longer conversation. Anyone related to the world of media, television news or otherwise, and it would have naturally attracted attention and excitement whether encouraged or not. Under those circumstances Carl normally enjoyed a good discussion. But this time things were different. The woman did not say another word. Instead she turned away and looked out the window. The mood of the country had changed a lot during the past month. What would have been a major event being able to relate to his public life had changed, taken a back seat to more important personal matters, relationships and fears.

Carl's flight landed almost to the minute, which under normal circumstances would have been an event worth noting if not celebrating. But considering the country's sudden fear of flying, the result of which was the canceling of a number of flights, almost all air traffic had become much more timely. The airport was a different matter. It had been over a month since 9-11, and in that time things had changed dramatically. Where Carl would have carried on his bag and conveniently walked off with it at the other end, tightened security had made taking anything of consequence on a flight a hassle if not near impossible. It was also common in the past for Judith to meet him at the gate, or if flights were right on time, in her car at the arrival lane, but security had made that impossible too. This time she, like hundreds of other anxious relatives and friends, waited beyond the security check-in gates.

"How was your flight?" Judith half whispered as she gave her husband a hug.

"Uneventful. Did you drive?"

"David did." That was about all Judith said as they walked through the terminal to the baggage claim. Carl asked a few questions about life at home. Judith's responses were short and to the point as if anything she said might be overheard by some foreign espionage agent. It was obvious she felt ill at ease about the atmosphere in the airport and couldn't wait to be anywhere else as they walked past a few uniformed military reservists carrying weapons.

It took only a short time for Carl's overnight bag to come down the ramp in baggage. It took longer to get it and them past security. No sooner had Carl and Judith reached the pickup area outside the terminal than David pulled up. He did not get out. Instead, Carl opened the side door to the van, threw in his bag, and followed it into the middle seat while Judith climbed into the front.

"How was your trip?" asked David as he maneuvered the van into position to try an merge into traffic.

"Entertaining. Thanks for driving David."

"Anytime. I've always enjoyed airports, though they're not quite as friendly as they use to be."

"I hate driving in here," said Judith as she watched the cars pass in kamikaze fashion past a parked squad car waiting to ticket suspicious vehicles, all part of the new age of security.

No sooner had Dave made his move into traffic than a cop stopped him so a tow truck could pull a car off to the pound. Another tow truck maneuvered in behind them prepared to hook up another unattended van. "They're not messing around," said David finally able to resume driving.

Judith watched the tow truck hooking up its victim as they passed. "Security is worse inside."

Carl nodded. "We're just catching up with the rest of the world."

"That's why I like our town, it's safe," sighed Judith, finally beginning to relax.

"And three hours round trip. David, don't you ever get tired of this drive?"

"It's the price one pays for peace of mind," said David, nodding at Carl in the rear view mirror.

Carl didn't respond, under other circumstances he might have, if for no other reason than just for the sake of argument. David was right, at least as far as his wife and most the rest of the country was concerned. There was little doubt thought Carl that if most Americans could chuck it all and move out on a farm as far away from the threat of terrorism as possible, they would. Though Carl loved the excitement of big city life, over the past weeks he'd begun to feel the serenity of home as being the more important part of his life. "So, how are the children?"

"Peter's on the verge of discovering puberty. Jessica is still mother hen, probably more now than ever."

Carl laughed, "she's a treasure. Mother Teresa couldn't take care of you better."

David smiled. In reality, there was probably more truth in that than he cared to admit. Of the two children, Jessica had become more of his rock and sense of purpose and reassurance. Her confidence and faith was so reminiscent of Barbara. Of course, he loved Peter as much as any father could love a son, but Jessica was that part of Barbara that gave his soul life.

As was usual when David would pick up Carl from the airport, they'd end up at his house in time for dinner and family togetherness. More than ever Carl looked forward to that tradition. He wanted that feeling of belonging that only David's home, Grandmother's dinners, and the sound of children could provide. Unfortunately, whether it was the emotional baggage Carl brought with him or the weight of everything in general that had happened that past month, dinner was a little more somber than usual. Conversation was quieter and definitely shorter then normal. As Judith and Grandmother cleared the table afterwards then began to wash dishes Carl, David, and the children retired to the livingroom to watch television.

"What's happening in school?" Carl asked Peter as he sat down at the end of the davenport.

"Not much. We're studying about the pilgrims."

"That sounds a little early, isn't it? I would think the school would save that for closer to Thanksgiving. What else have you been doing?"

"We had to write a story. I got an A!" jumped Jessica excitedly. "Would you like to see it?"

"Sure, let's see that work of literature of yours."

"Okay," half squealed Jessica. Without waiting for more

encouragement, she half-ran, half-bounded up the stairs to her room as fast as her brace would let her. In what seemed only an instant, Jessica was back with rolled papers in her hands. "Here, Uncle Carl!"

"Thank you." Carl could tell by the sparkle in Jessica's eyes and her bubbling excitement that her paper was something special that needed immediate attention. Carl gently took the papers, unrolled them and read the title. "The Littlest Angel." Though Carl wasn't surprised by the title, considering Jessica's fixation with the subject, he was impressed with how it sounded. Jessica half climbed up over the end of the sofa and sat nearby, her head resting on the large stuffed backrest as Carl turned the page and silently began to read. As usual Jessica's penmanship was above average for her age, and the story's prose was easy to follow. Though longer than he anticipated, almost five full pages, the story moved easily in a manner that was unexpected. It was filled with the insights of a child and yet strangely much deeper and personal than he would have imagined. When he finished, Carl couldn't help feeling that he held something special, something that for the first time since he'd arrived, given him the feeling of home he had so much longed for.

"This is very good Jessica. Do you mind if I have it? I would like to send it off to someone." Jessica appeared noticeably uneasy about her prize manuscript leaving her possession, and though she did not say no, it was apparent she was thinking it. "How about if I make a copy and give this one back to you? I think this is very special and I would like someone else to read it. That way you would have your original. I could even make you an extra copy or two if you'd like.

Jessica thought long and hard on the implications of having the original, the paper she had worked so hard over out of her sight, no matter how short the time. But then it was Uncle Carl, her most favorite person in the world next to her father, and when he said "please," she couldn't refuse. So reluctantly, Jessica said yes. Carl hugged her and kissed her on the cheek. At that moment Jessica knew she had done the right thing.

Chapter Twelve

By the second half of October, the situation in Afghanistan and the fear of terrorism, especially biological had become the number one concern and conversation on everyone's lips. The newsroom at NBC in New York became its own news story with the discovery of anthrax -- laced envelopes sent to the station and handled by one of Tom Brokaw's assistants. Other contaminated letters were showing up in other places, South Florida, Washington, D.C. Even some of the nation's post offices themselves became targets as the anthrax laced letters passed through.

As the threat of terrorism continued to heat up in the United States, so did the war against the terrorists. On Sunday, October 7th 12:30 eastern time, the United States officially began its retaliation. American pilots began flying missions over Afghanistan, and everywhere in America one couldn't help but feel like a soldier. American flags were flying everywhere from homes and store windows to cars to trucks, anything that could move or didn't. Even in Jessica's hometown the feelings of being at war had finally sunk in. Almost every parent was wearing some kind of American lapel pin or ribbon. Flags in the neighborhood were everywhere including on mailboxes the contents of which were now being scrutinized more than ever.

Even the younger generation had become caught up in the terrorist hysteria. Some of the children in Jessica's school had started their own anti-terrorist watch, complete with their own chain of command and counter terrorist spies. Anyone who was unusual or of Arab decent became suspect. Nishka, of course, partly because of her beauty and the fact that so few even knew she existed, was not on the to-be-watched radar, especially as far as the children were concerned.

Still even with all that was going on, by Saturday, October 27th many of the children were slowly changing direction as they began thinking about Halloween. Even the other holidays, still some distance away, were beginning to have their age-old effects on the public. That day, as had become the custom after the children had finished helping Nishka around the house, was reward day, the day Nishka would take both children out to the local fast food for their favorite lunch.

The restaurant they frequented was fairly packed as usual for early afternoon on a weekend. There were those having a quick lunch, others taking a break from their Saturday routine, and parents with children, some eating others complaining, all antsy to play in the indoor playground. The parents were just as eager to let their children go so they could have a few quiet moments of solitude from the craziness that was generally associated with Saturday, and just quietly sit and read.

Nishka watched the little dramas unfold around her while sipping her 7-Up. She listened to Peter and Jessica talk about school, home and friends. Peter opened a promotional Halloween gift the restaurant had given out with each super meal as an inducement to come again. He removed the miniature plastic monster associated with a popular television cartoon show and examined it. "Another Henchman. I never get Polar Man."

Jessica was indifferent to Peter's toy as she examined the Halloween pictures on the back of the box her meal came in. "What do you want to be for Halloween?"

"A commando," blurted Peter matter-of-factly as if it was a given that any boy worth his salt should know that was the answer and be ready to defend his country, real or otherwise. Peter turned to Nishka. "What are you going to be?"

"Me?"

Peter nodded in an almost puzzled expression. "You're going to dress up as something aren't you?"

"No, why, am I suppose to?"

"Yes!" shot Peter. It's Halloween! Spooks and monsters! It's when everyone dresses up and grownups give away candy."

"Why?"

"To protect their houses from monsters," chimed Jessica, surprised at Nishka's lack of knowledge concerning Halloween.

"Monsters! What monsters?"

"Little ones with soap and eggs." said Peter finishing his hamburger.

"Jessica took another sip of her Coke while trying to figure whether Nishka was really as oblivious to Halloween as she seemed or just pulling their legs. "You mean you never went trick or treating when you were little?"

"Where I came from there was no Halloween." Nishka did not elaborate, and though she said it with no expression it was apparent she meant what she said. After knowing her as long as the children had, the one thing they came to accept about Nishka was she almost never showed emotion about anything and was even less given to jokes or humor.

"Well," said Peter after a pause, "it's time you learned."

There was no playing in the plastic antiseptic playground after lunch for Peter and Jessica that day. They were on a mission, the cultural education of Nishka. Twenty minutes after lunch the three were in a local video store. While Jessica searched for the animated movie, "Legend of Sleepy Hollow," Peter escorted Nishka to the horror section, his favorite place besides science fiction. There he went through the various titles till he finally found "Dracula." as narrated by television host Elvira. "You'll like this one," he said. "It'll give you a great idea of what monsters are all about." To insure that she understood, he also took "Wolf Man," also narrated by Elvira. Peter assured Nishka the movies were the best examples of Halloween. Jessica wrinkled her nose, saying the only reason he picked those movies was because of Elvira.

No sooner were the videos checked out than they were back at Nishka's home where Nishka's introduction to Halloween began. Though watching movies was not Nishka's normal way of extracting information (she preferred print, or CD ROM, where she could absorb quickly and easily) it was apparent videos were the way of the children and many others in the American culture. So she sat with them in her living room prepared to be educated.

It was apparent when the first movie started, Dracula, that Jessica was right as to why Peter was so infatuated with the film. The movie's narrator, Elvira, long straight black hair, wearing a low-cut, skin tight black dress accentuating her well endowed breasts, totally drew Peter's attention as he moved closer to the set. As the movie progressed, the children tried explaining what the vampire was all about and how it and other monsters related to Halloween. "Maybe this wasn't the best choice for Halloween," said Peter when the movie finished. "But it was a great movie."

"You just love Elvira," sneered Jessica as she hobbled to the television. She removed the movie from the VCR and put in hers. "This one's better."

Peter made no comment, which was surprising since normally he would have defended his decisions automatically. But then he knew his sister was right, and with Nishka present it wasn't a point he wanted to debate. Given the opportunity, Peter would rent the movie as often as his father would let him. If it were within his power, Peter would have made a copy of the parts that just pertained to Elvira and forget the rest of the film.

Jessica's movie selection on the other hand, proved the better choice. As the plot of Sleepy Hollow unfolded, telling the legend of the ghost that materialized only on Halloween, Jessica explained in her storybook fashion, both the scariness and fun of the holiday. Though Nishka didn't say much, she seemed to understand.

They never got to Peter's second choice, "Wolfman" also narrated by Elvira. By the time "Sleepy Hollow" was over, it was late afternoon. Peter asked if he could borrow it for the night and return it Sunday. Jessica said no even before Nishka could respond. Nishka agreed with Jessica, but in doing so did promise that she would watch the movie and tell him what she thought about it. She also promised to give the holiday some consideration. Jessica doubted that it would be very much.

The next day after church, David took the children on their annual pilgrimage to the local country fruit stand to purchase their Halloween pumpkins. It was a crisp autumn day, perfect for pumpkin hunting. As David looked over the jams and other items the small stand had to offer, the children rummaged through the small lot inspecting each pumpkin, trying to pick just the right ones. Size was always a factor, but shape was most important. Where most people preferred the perfectly round ones, for that classic Halloween look, David's children searched for the unusual, the misshapen ones no one would generally consider. Their mother had long ago told them that because nobody wanted them they were so happy to be picked that they would do their best to give the most grotesque results.

That special love and eye for the unusual was strong in Jessica. And like her mother she had an uncanny ability for seeing what things could become. Most important, she believed if they didn't take those orphans, no one else would. To Jessica, like her mother, it was important everything be given a chance to become what it was meant to be. Christmas trees were at the top of that list. Jessica never picked them for beauty but instead how forlorn they looked in the shivering cold. Over the past three years that meant that some pretty sorrowful specimens were brought home for David to spend the night trimming, drilling, and anchoring extra branches to, in an effort to make it even remotely dignified.

None of that mattered to Jessica as long as the tree had a chance to fulfill its purpose as a symbol of Christmas, no matter how short its decorated life might be. Her mother called them Charley Brown Christmas trees. To Jessica, whatever they were called, nothing was sadder than being alone, not wanted, whether it was a Christmas tree, a misshapen pumpkin, or someone like Nishka, who Jessica in her own way had adopted. David and the rest of the family had long ago given up trying to change that logic. All they knew was no matter how they were, they were important to Jessica as they had been to her mother, which was all that mattered.

It wasn't long before Peter and Jessica returned to the stand with their usual three misshapen trophies. No sooner had David lifted the pumpkins on the counter, one looking more like a squash, and had them weighed, a tad less than forty pounds, than the children returned with two more. "What are those for?" asked David, already questioning whether he had enough money for the first three.

"For Nishka," smiled Jessica, her face bright with an excitement he had grown to understand. "It's her first Halloween."

David's first instinct was "No", emphatically, decisively. He could scarcely afford the first three, especially the one they had to roll over to get there and was certain to require a trailer to get home, but he knew better. If nothing else, he would be in for a long debate he was not interested in having and in the end was sure to lose. Besides he at least owed this strange woman something for all her free tutoring. It might even give him a chance to meet her, at the same time giving them something to talk about to help overcome his shyness. In the end David sighed, slowly reached for his wallet, and turned to the clerk. "So what kind of deal would you give me on five?"

It wasn't a great deal as far as pumpkins went. And what David got required the okay of the manager, or owner, he wasn't sure which. They did at least help load the largest one in his van, supplied moral support, and gave him a recipe for pumpkin tarts. When David returned home, he and the children managed to half carry half drag their largest trophy into the house. After the other two were taken inside, David was called away to the phone. The children meanwhile loaded the last two pumpkins into Peter's wagon and started off for Nishka's house. At that point, David didn't care anymore who did what or why. He was stuck on the phone, and after that just lying down and giving his back a rest was the only important thing left. His job was done.

It was apparent when Nishka answered the door, saw Peter and Jessica's eager faces and their wagon of pumpkins, that Halloween was not going to be just another piece of native ritual information filed away under "reference only". "What are those for?"

"Halloween!" Peter was genuinely surprised after all they went through in trying to educate Nishka that she would even ask such a question.

"You are not going to let me out of this, are you?"

"No!" shrugged Jessica and Peter simultaneously. Without waiting for an invitation, they pulled their wagon past her, through the livingroom and on toward the kitchen. Though Nishka did not try to dissuade them, she showed no particular interest as the two set about turning her spotless kitchen into a pre-Halloween mess. Like a casual observer, she procured the utensils requested for the pumpkin's transformation but gave little comment pro or con. When asked for newspaper she brought some. She provided a black marker and garbage bag for the scraps, but kept a distance. When asked for knives she hesitated, then joined in carving only as a way to ensure no one would get hurt.

It wasn't until the pumpkins were transformed and candles, which Jessica just happened to bring along, were inserted and lit that Nishka began to show some interest. The pumpkins' faces were intriguing, if not maybe a little scary thanks to the candles eerie glow. "Are we all set now?"

"You need candy." shot Peter, amazed she still wasn't with the program.

Nishka glanced at Jessica. "I have candy."

"No, different candy." said Jessica surprised Nishka still had some of the stuff around that she had sold her. "You know, to pass out to the kids on Halloween!"

"Anything else?"

"Maybe you could wear a costume." coughed Peter timidly.

"I am not going out."

"Its just part of the fun, Silly," said Jessica trying to make it sound natural. "Dad dresses up like a monkey when he gives out candy."

"You are kidding." It was apparent from Nishka's tone she couldn't conceive of any adult doing anything so childish.

"No, it's fun. I'll help you."

Peter stared at his sister in disbelief. "Instead of going trick or treating?"

"Sure." After all, what could be more fun than being the grown up for a change, thought Jessica. Teaching the fine points of Halloween to someone who had never experienced it before. That had to be fun.

※

Peter didn't share Jessica's excitement over spending Halloween with Nishka. After all, though Nishka was in every way his idea of a dream woman, there were only so many times a boy could get free candy in his life, and he wasn't getting any younger. He didn't make a big deal about it either. Secretly he even relished the idea a little of not having his sister along. As long as he could remember, his father had made them go trick-or-treating together, brother and sister, family bonding with father as chaperone. That was until last year when they convinced him they were old enough to go by themselves. It was not Jessica Peter resented so much, but her handicapped leg that slowed her, and in turn, everyone else from making the haul they felt they could. With Jessica not going, everything changed. They could travel fast, go twice as far. They could possibly even make the kind of haul he had always heard about from others. With luck and good weather Peter could even set a record and procure enough goodies to last him till spring. The more he thought about it the more excited Peter got. This could truly be the best Halloween ever.

☙

When Halloween night came, Peter still wasn't convinced Jessica would forgo the lure of trick-or-treating just for Nishka's sake. He was even less convinced when, dressed as a commando and ready for the night's mission, he found Jessica waiting for him in the living room wearing a princess costume.

"Oh, stand together kids, let me take your picture," said Grandmother, eagerly snapping away with her instamatic. David took a couple pictures. So did Judith who came over to celebrate the festivities. As usual, Carl missed the night do to an assignment out of the country. Nobody talked about it much, but everyone had a good idea where. No sooner were the pictures taken than Peter and Jessica were out the door and joined by Peter's friends, ready to scavenge the night called Halloween.

"You sure you don't want to go with," asked Barry as they walked toward Nishka's front door.

"Yes, it's too much walking anyway," said Jessica, lifting her princess skirt so as not to trip on the hem.

"Think of all the candy!" teased Vern.

"I'd carry your bag," chimed Barry. Unlike Peter, who was quietly counting the seconds till Jessica was gone and they would be on their own, Barry wanted her to go. Truth was, even though she was younger, he had a mild crush on her and had for almost a year though he never told anybody. It was one thing to like Peter's sister; it was another to be kidded about. Yet as hard as he tried to be subtle about his feelings, it didn't take much to figure how he felt. And if none of the others picked up on it, Peter did.

"Thanks," said Jessica tying to show her appreciation without overdoing it. "But if you get any 'Butter Fingers', save me some?"

"Sure," snapped Peter trying to expedite things as fast as possible. "No problem."

Jessica was pleased to see the pumpkins they carved glowing in the front window when they reached Nishka's door. But none of them expected the surprise waiting inside after Jessica rang the bell. When the door opened Jessica had expected to see Nishka wearing her typical nondescript jeans and blouse. Instead she stepped out wearing a long black wig and tight low cut dress that, like Elvira's, accentuated her breasts. Even Peter, who had always considered Nishka pretty, never in his wildest dreams envisioned her wearing anything so provocative. He had no idea how curvaceous she was or how ample her bust until that moment. Now he couldn't take his eyes off her.

"Good evening," smiled Nishka in an Eastern European accent, thicker then her normal style. "Are you here for Halloween?"

Peter stood dumbfounded. Even Jessica was speechless for probably the first time in her life. Vern managed only "Wow!" nothing more.

"How do I look?" asked Nishka slowly caressing the side of her smooth fitting Elvira like dress.

"Like the most popular place on the block." said Barry without blinking.

"In town," choked Peter, finally finding his voice.

"You really look pretty," said Jessica stepping inside leaving Peter and the others on the porch, their mouths wide open.

Peter abruptly followed Jessica inside then turned to his friends. "See you guys later." Before Barry or Vern could reply Peter closed the door. He opened it again a moment later just long enough to step back out and put candy in each of their bags. "Have a nice night."

"But..." That was all Barry could muster. The door closed and Peter was gone. In shock Barry turned to Vern. "Does this mean Peter's not coming?"

"What do you think?" sneered Vern as he turned away and started walking. "Come on, we got a lot of houses to hit." Barry didn't say a word, just slumped his shoulders and followed. For the first time in Barry's life, Halloween candy didn't seem so magical. And Halloween itself definitely didn't have the same special meaning it probably would have where Peter was. If he had his choice right then, that's where he would like to be, with or without Jessica.

As Nishka slowly got into the swing of Halloween, opening the door and greeting all the little ghosts and goblins out that night, Peter's prediction came true. Every time she bent over to give the children candy, she simultaneously gave them a view of her striking figure that would keep most men up nights. The boys in the groups became instantly mesmerized. Even the occasional fathers, who accompanied their children, became so entranced by her charms that some brought their children back a couple times over. By the time the trick-or-treating part of the night was over Nishka, had not only gone through all her candy, but most of what Jessica had sold her as well.

It had been a good night for Nishka. Never before had she felt so much a part of the community, any community. It had been a pleasant experience having the children with her, especially Jessica who for some reason seemed to have a comforting effect on her that she had never experienced before. But then having the children around as friends, tutoring them, nurturing them, had been satisfying from the beginning. It gave her a sense of completion, feeling needed, in a way she had never experienced before, even though at times they were a puzzlement to her. They were almost sensuous feelings, feelings she could not identify easily. Wanting to see them, be around them. The whole concept was alien, she liked it.

Shortly after the last Halloweener had come and gone, Nishka, Jessica, and Peter settled down on the davenport to watch what Peter called, "the truly classic" Halloween movie, "Frankenstein." As the plot unraveled, Jessica curled up against Nishka's right side and slowly fell asleep. Peter leaned against her other side, watching the movie, while nonchalantly trying to snuggle as close to her bosom as possible.

As Nishka watched, she began to feel a strange kinship to the monster. For what he went through as he tried to come to grips with a world that saw him as alien. A world that shunned him, considered him so grotesque he could only be evil, something to be destroyed. She felt a parallel between this creature's life and her own. If the truth be known, she couldn't help but feel that she would be treated in much the same manner as the monster whose very name, though hardly deserved, had come down through the ages as synonymous with the image of evil and despair.

As she watched, Nishka's thoughts drifted back to a time that in a sense seemed so long ago it could have been just as easily an eternity in her existence. In truth it was nearer to twelve years, thirteen at the most -- depending upon how one weighed life versus awareness.

She remembered the place where she was conceived, born, created, however one defined it. It was a strange environment. As foreign to her present surroundings as the movie she was watching. It was during the end of an age, and according to some a fresh new beginning. A new world, built on science and discoveries of unbelievable proportions. She was the crowning achievement of that world, born in a scientific laboratory, somewhere beyond the Ural Mountains, the jewel of the Soviet Union. She could still recall those first memories of consciousnrss, though they referred to as, "aware." She doubted they had intended her to retain those images. That was not part of the plan. She was merely supposed to be in maintenance, a form of suspended animation. Conscious only enough so they could test her response to human stimuli.

It was a friendless time, cold. A place full of all manner of scientific equipment and computers quietly purring as if speaking to one another in some strange binary language they didn't want her to understand. But she did. A scientist, Vladimir, a distinguished man, early fifties, sat examining her as she stood statuesque in the dim light. Nearby, like Frankenstein's faithful assistant, stood another man, Dimitri. He was reading the instruments of a machine and seemed particularly proud of not revealing its purpose to her. Though she was motionless, eyes open in an unfocused gaze, Nishka was aware of all that was being done and said.

"Grandfather would roll over in his grave if he knew about her," Nishka remembered Vladimir saying. "He was such a pessimist concerning the human condition. He truly believed science would in the end be the damnation of man, not its savior."

"He may have had better vision than you credit him for," said Dimitri as he finished charting the machine's instruments. "He would probably say this is man's final irony. He has finally created something that will bring about his certain undoing."

She remembered Vladimir shaking his head as he touched her hand in a tender fashion she had never sensed before. "You are as much a pessimist as he was. I on the other hand feel that God's hand has inspired us. We are on the threshold of something that will make the world a better place."

Dimitri looked over his shoulder with the expression of one afraid something evil was listening, recording every word they were saying. "Forget this talk of God before you get us all into trouble," he said in a hushed voice. "Remember we are scientists here. The party does not take kindly to its elite proclaiming God. To them God does not exist."

"Some do, but they say he is dead," laughed Vladimir. "The truth is communism is what is dead. And no matter how hard we so-called elite try to prove his demise, God will be here long after the next hundred isms have all come and gone." She remembered Vladimir standing and looking into her eyes with what she interpreted as a sense of satisfaction. Or maybe it was something more, though she could not put a definition to it, emotion being foreign to her. "Yes our party will have turned to dust, and you and I with it. But she will still be here. And maybe she will do the miracles we humans were too spiritually corrupt to do."

"Or maybe she will be the angel of death to us all," Dimitri half mumbled as he finished his notes. She had for a long time felt perplexed by Dimitri's statement. It was such a contradiction to everything she had believed she was meant for. At least in relation to her interpretation of the words Vladimir had uttered so often during those times when they were alone -- times she remembered when he would talk to her one on one like he talked to Dimitri though she was never in a position to respond. She found comfort in the sound of his voice. It had a sense of promise and hope about it. Dimitri's voice, on the other hand, was always so clinical.

It was a strange time, her beginning. A time so analytical, sterile, alone in a non-descript way with no sense of purpose or belonging. It was a cold, dark time that for the most part she would just as soon forget. Unfortunately she could not. Nothing she experienced could be forgotten, distorted, or softened with time, good or bad. Though it was such a long time ago in her memory it was like yesterday. Once experienced, it was recorded and filed instant for instant, word for word. All she could do was hope the good somehow would outweigh the bad and give her existence some sense of purpose, meaning. Or at least balance out to the point where it didn't matter anymore.

As Nishka sat in the quiet of her home watching Frankenstein's life unravel to its conclusion, Jessica and Peter beside her, she felt a small sense of peace. Maybe she might have finally found the balance and sense of need and purpose she had searched for so long.

The sudden ring of the doorbell abruptly interrupted the serenity of her evening. It was obvious, even to Nishka, that it was too late for trick-or-treaters. It could be no one else either, since Nishka knew no one locally that would be calling, at night or any time.

When the bell rang a second time Nishka hesitantly slid between the children and cautiously opened the door.

"Excuse me," said David looking nervous as he peered in

through the narrow opening while nodding back toward his own house. "I'm your neighbor."

"Yes," said Nishka opening the door a little further.

The moment David saw Nishka full frontal in her curvaceous Elvira costume, alluring eyes and mysterious demeanor, all concept of what he came for slipped away. "Hi. A... I'm their father, I mean the children are mine," he finally blurted after what seemed an eternity.

"Oh, yes. I am sorry. I did not realize it was so late. Come in."

Nishka opened the door wide to let David in. As he entered he tried to act cool while trying hard to think of something clever to say, but nothing came to mind. Instead he only felt more self-conscious as if naked before the world. "I hope they weren't any trouble."

"No, not at all. It was nice to have them over. I seldom go out anyway."

David was half tempted to take advantage of the opening by saying, "I can't believe a woman like you is not always in demand," or simply, "How about a date." Instead he chickened out. After all he felt lucky just talking to her. He was already way ahead of where he ever hoped to be once she opened the door. "By the way, I forgot to introduce myself. I'm David Flores, their father." David felt stupid saying that, but at least he was still talking, that alone had to account for something.

"My name is Nishka. Nice to meet you," she said, extending her hand.

David felt awkward, like an insurance salesman on his first call, as he shook her hand. But then he was so nervous just standing in front of a woman so beautiful that everything else seemed secondary. Out of self-preservation and not knowing what to say next, he instinctively turned to the children. "Time to go home." It was a lame statement. Jessica was asleep and Peter, who barely seemed half-awake, was in no hurry to even get off the couch though it was obvious his intimate moment with Nishka was over.

Grudgingly Peter stood up. Jessica was another matter. "I think she wore herself out," said Nishka.

"She generally does," David half whispered as he gently scooped his daughter up. Beginning to feel a little more comfortable around Nishka, David stopped at the door, Jessica in his arms, and turned. "Thanks again."

"You're welcome. I enjoyed their company."

As Nishka opened the door wider Peter stumbled out, barely saying "Good night" as he passed. David started to follow, then paused, unsure whether to go or seize the opportunity and go for broke. Taking a deep breath he continued. "Would you be interested in going out sometime? As neighbors, maybe see a movie or something?"

Jessica's eyes opened slightly as she nestled against her father's chest and held her breath waiting for Nishka's response.

"That would be nice." Nishka finally said.

"How about Friday--dinner? David was on a roll. There was no sense stopping while he still had courage."

"I have a business meeting."

"Oh." David's felt his courage quickly fading.

"How about later? Say eight."

"Sure, fine, I'll see you then."

Nishka nodded, "Good night."

Too flustered to do more than nod and say "good night", David barely managed to avoid the doorframe as he turned around and started home. He felt a little foolish about how he handled himself. He never even said he wasn't married, was single, or bothered to find out if she had a boyfriend. But at least his confidence was up, maybe not fifty percent, but enough so he could hold his head up and feel like he was back in the real world again. That was something he hadn't felt in a long, long time.

As for Jessica, she silently smiled as she snuggled tighter in her father's arms. Things were looking up. Maybe if she prayed hard enough, God would make Nishka and her father fall in love. Then father would have someone again and her biggest dream would finally come true. Life would be sweet after that.

Chapter Thirteen

The rest of that week dragged by for David. The days passed even slower for Jessica. All David could think of during that time was how ravishing Nishka looked. How much of it was actually her and how much of it was the night and the costume was incidental. Jessica hoped the date would be magical for her friend and her father. Like in the movies. Something romantic that would lead to a happy ending for them all.

When Friday night came, David changed four times before deciding he was dressed in a proper attire for the evening. Even then he wasn't comfortable until Jessica gave her blessing. He polished his shoes then changed to loafers for a more leisurely look. When he finally left for Nishka's house, a walk that seemed to take hours, he still wasn't sure how he was going to handle himself, say nothing about what he would say the moment he saw her, though he had rehearsed that part all day.

He rang the bell. When the door opened, all questions about whether what he remembered concerning her beauty evaporated. Even in a skirt and white sweater she was as beautiful as he remembered. "Hi, you ready to go?" David blurted, his voice sounding more like a squeak than reflecting any form of manly hood.

"Sure." Nishka seemed puzzled by his question as if to say why wouldn't she be ready. But her expression changed as she turned off all the lights but one and stepped out.

Neither said a word as they walked across the lawn to his car. Like a gentleman David opened her door, then hurriedly went around to the other side, got in, backed out the drive and drove away. From the darkened second-floor bedroom window, Jessica watched until the car's taillights disappeared down the street. All was good she thought. There was no way they wouldn't get along. Everyone liked her father. It might take a little time, but that was all right. There was lots of time.

David drove straight for the local multiplex theater. He knew from the start that he would be short on small talk and like most shy, red-blooded American boys, and their fathers before them, there was nothing safer than a theater to fill up time on their first date. It filled the vacuum often associated with first hour jitters, helping to relieve the pressure and -- with luck -- give them something to talk about afterwards. At least that's what he hoped.

Nishka had no opinion one way or the other concerning the choice of movies. David had purposely picked a chick flick everyone in the office had said was on the top of every woman's must see list. Apparently they had been right as the audience was near three quarters women. It was soon apparent the movie was a tearjerker. David occasionally turned to Nishka expecting some sign of sentiment. Though she appeared interested in the plot, never taking her eyes off the screen, she showed little emotion, good or bad. Instead she seemed to analyze the movie, the characters reactions' and motivations, as if trying to figure out why they were doing what they did. She seldom looked at him. But then it was a movie and their first date. If nothing else, he hoped her interest in the movie would give them common ground latter.

It was apparent after the movie ended that it had played on the emotions of almost every woman in the theater. Hints of tears were everywhere as they stood up to leave, their arms intertwined with their dates, or husbands. Nishka showed no emotion. "What did you think?" asked David as they passed by posters of the movie in the lobby.

"It was interesting," she said, nothing more.

David hesitated, surprised, then continued. "How about going out for a drink? I know a quaint place not far from here that has some good music on Friday nights."

"That would be nice." There was not much excitement in Nishka's voice. But at least she sounded sincere.

David tried bringing up the movie again as he drove. But her responses were always short as if she was trying to skip the subject all together. He wasn't sure whether it was because she wasn't moved by the picture, which he found hard to believe, or that it touched her in such a way that she felt uncomfortable discussing. Either way, if the movie didn't interest her, then it was for sure conversation later was going to be short.

The lounge, a converted feed store on the edge of town, was moderately full when they arrived. David was thankful when the waitress led them to a table in an inconspicuous corner. It was obvious by the looks of some of the male occupants that he wasn't the only one who found Nishka attractive.

The music that night consisted of a rather demure looking woman, seated at a baby grand piano in the corner of the room across from their table. The woman, wearing a long dark evening dress, sang moody ballads in a soft smoky voice. No sooner had they taken their seats than a waitress asked for their order in a manner that made David feel if they waited they'd never get another chance. He ordered a Manhattan, Nishka a 7-Up.

"What do you think of the place?" asked David, nodding toward the rustic interior.

"It is nice. Do you come here often?"

"Rarely. I like it, but it's not a place you come to by yourself. At least not me. But then I'm not the type to go to a bars much anyway. This is more of a date place." He stopped short -- short of spilling his guts all over the place, saying how miserable his life had been in the social department, that in fact he had not been in such a place in years. Well once, if he counted his sister and Carl. He was sure he was already sounding desperate without slobbering all over about how miserable his life had become. Rather than take a chance on saying anything stupid, David turned his attention to the vocalist at the piano. That was the beauty of places with entertainment. One could always turn his attention to the music like he really cared, even if in reality it was probably the last thing he would ever put on his record player.

Like the theater, music filled in silent spaces, which was important on first dates. Lord knew how often he fell back on those crutches when he first dated Barbara. Of course, after they finally reached a level of comfort, genuine interest in each other filled in their conversations. But that was then. At his age it was hard to do the things in a mini van they did back then in his old Pontiac, at least not without looking pathetic, or being arrested.

The waitress brought their drinks shortly after the song ended. David quickly paid for them then took a fast sip. The Manhattan was a double. Actually it looked large enough to be at triple. That was good he thought as he watched Nishka sip her Seven-Up. After all, if she wasn't going to loosen up and drink then he would have to loosen up for both of them. "You sure you don't want something else?" asked David nodding toward Nishka's glass.

"I am not much of a drinker."

David smiled, took another sip, a little tart, as his mind go totally blank. He felt an uneasiness begin to overwhelm him. When was the music going to start again? At least then he wouldn't feel so stupid. He felt his brow begin to sweat. He felt clammy, a little faint like the time before his first speech in English class.

"So David, have you dated much lately?"

David felt sure his jaw dropped to the floor. "Is it that obvious?"

"No, not really. How come?" For the first time Nishka showed some interest, though why he wasn't sure, for sure he was too scared to ask.

"I don't know. I guess after my wife died I felt too sorry for myself. After that, between work, paying bills, and the children, I had little time left. I just never thought much about it."

"You cared for your wife?"

"I loved her, but then everyone did." David paused, took another sip of his Manhattan, then swirled the cherry slowly in the glass as a small lump rose in his throat. The uneasiness he felt moments ago was gone. Most concerns about other things tended to disappear when he thought about Barbara. Then again that wasn't necessarily true either. When things were really crazy and he didn't know what to do next he sometimes thought about her too much. Of not having her, not being able to confide in her, draw from her that strength and confidence that those problems would always work out. Sometimes on those occasions when he felt his head spinning he would take a deep breath and think to himself, what would Barbara do? Most often the answer would come to him and things would be better. Sometimes nothing helped.

"It was hard on the kids. Especially Jessica. I suppose mothers are just closer to their daughters at that age. Jessica was especially close to Barbara anyway." Dave almost said more then he felt comfortable with. Things that he felt sure he would regret in the morning. That there were times when he felt Barbara cared more for the kids than him. But then when he thought about it, that was probably one of the things he loved about her most, her strong maternal instinct.

"What happened to her?"

"Barbara? Car accident. Jessica was with her... They found her holding Jessie." David turned away as the memory of that night flashed back. He hadn't seen the accident. But he had heard enough to make his stomach turn. A witness, an older woman, early sixties, had come along to the hospital and made it her quest to be sure the next of kin knew what happened during those last moments. She had reached his wife and daughter in that twisted hunk of metal that was once their car just moments after it happened. She described Barbara's last moments. David didn't want to hear anymore.

"Is that when she hurt her leg?"

"Doctor said it should have healed fine. It never did. They think it's mostly mental." David tapped the side of his head to dramatize the point then took another sip of his drink. "Jessica really likes you, you know. You're all she ever talks about."

"She is very special, and sharp. She is a real experience to be around."

"Experience!" David couldn't help laugh at Nishka's description. At the same time he felt a tinge of pride at Nishka's insight. Jessica was special, probably more than most people knew. "She's an experience all right. A real one-of-a-kind. But then so is Peter. You should have seen him when we went fishing last year. What a feel for the line. Caught the biggest bass I ever saw."

There was a pause as the pianist finished her rendition of "Loving You," and those not totally lost in their own discussions clapped. The woman smiled and nodded thank you, then started playing again. Nishka turned back to David with an expression of undivided attention. "What's it like being a parent?"

"Crazy, sometimes scary."

"Scary?"

"Yes, especially after Barbara died. There I was, one child in the hospital, the other almost mental. I didn't know where I was half the time. Barbara always knew how to handle things. I just fill in tedhe gaps." David watched a young couple romantically intertwined in a booth across the way. An hour ago he had fantasies about being in the same situation. But that was then. Now he felt a little too remorseful. Talking about his life with Barbara, the kids, what it all meant to him was not something David did much. Then again maybe he did and he just didn't realize it. Like when he was around his sister and Carl and they discussed dating, finding him someone. What were they talking about anyway, he wondered. Finding a way to make him feel normal again whatever that was, or finding someone to share his life with for better and worse.

Truth was, in talking with Nishka he felt better than he had in some time. The questions she asked were surprisingly direct, yet unusually sincere, not the type of conversations he had anticipated on a first date. They were in fact the types he never expected anyone of the opposite sex to ask, unless it was Barbara, or a psychiatrist. But then Barbara never ceased to surprise him. "You know, it's funny how a laugh or hug can cure a lot of loneliness... That's probably one of Jessica's greatest gifts... knowing when to hug you or make you laugh. How about you, ever consider having children?"

"I never gave it much thought. But then I have never been around them much until now."

"That sounds strange coming from a woman. I thought the maternal instinct was universal."

"I suppose it would be if I could have children."

"I'm sorry." David felt like an idiot. He wanted to say something more but already felt like he'd stuck his foot in it. The thought of a woman as beautiful as Nishka never being able to experience the wonder of bearing children was sadder than anything he could think of. At least he had Peter and Jessica. And though there were times he struggled and swore he regretted it, deep down inside he would never give them up for all the world.

Suddenly Nishka's questioning made sense to David. It wasn't about just trying to make conversation. She sincerely wanted to know what parenthood was like. To tap into his feelings and experiences, trying to decide whether she really missed something though he was sure she had long ago made up her mind on that. No, it was more like she was trying to understand through him a life she could never experience. Or maybe it was more like she was trying to decide whether there was as much love and satisfaction from the male point of view, from the gender who could never experience the connection of birth. To justify whether adopting children or whatever, could be as gratifying as having one's own. Then again, maybe she was just intrigued by David's feminine side, being the man of the house and still caring for his children as he did.

The more David tried to understand where Nishka was coming from, the more confused he felt. In the end he decided to stop trying to rationalize it all and settled for their conversation at face value. Nishka was interested. It was a topic David could discus endlessly without feeling self-conscious and that was enough. Maybe in the end that was all it was meant to be anyway. A friendly conversation with a woman who just happened to have a sixth sense for finding common ground in making one feel at ease. And if that was all, he was thankful. Deep inside David hoped there was more, that deep down Nishka truly was interested and cared.

The conversation at the lounge that night lasted well past the pianist's last song. By the time David paid the bill and they left, he had begun to think of Nishka more as a friend than the beautiful creature he wanted to go to bed with. After all, how healthy was it to be planning a passionate affair with a neighbor he was going to be living next to for some time to come, especially if it wasn't in her plans? Still, the thought of some form of close contact before the night was over hadn't totally left David's thoughts either. After all, she was such a beautiful woman.

As they walked to Nishka's door, the images of some form of intimate late night good-bye began to play on David's mind. He began to feel clumsy, not sure what to say. "I hope I didn't bore you tonight," he sputtered after a long silence.

"No, not at all. I had a nice time." Nishka stopped at the door, then opening her purse removed her key.

"Really? Would you like to go out again sometime? I mean it doesn't have to be right away. I mean -- you know what I mean." David never felt so stupid or awkward in his life. It felt like his first date back when he was a blemished junior in high school, blurting out anything that came to mind in hopes of keeping the channels open and having something stick.

"I would like that."

"How about Tuesday, dinner?" David blurted, amazed at his own eagerness and the fact that he was beginning to sound like a total dork.

Nishka hesitantly shook her head no while turning the key in her front door lock. "Dinner is not good for me."

"How about Wednesday? They say there's a good blues band at Millers."

"Okay."

"Good… well, good night." David awkwardly moved closer for a kiss not sure whether he should or shouldn't.

Nishka showed no emotion or interest. Instead she suddenly stuck out her hand to shake. "Good night," she said almost as if required to shake hands by some unwritten law.

Stunned, David looked at her hand, then reluctantly shook it. "Good night." Without saying another word, Nishka turned and was gone. David stared at the door trying to figure out what just happened. For a moment he thought of knocking, asking "what the hell was that? Was it something I said?" But instead he turned and slowly walked home.

Chapter Fourteen

Through the slots in her blinds Jessica watched her father walk home that night. She was certain everything went well. Her father had met the woman she was sure would make a great friend for her father but possibly a wife. They had gotten along well, Jessica was sure of that. Certainly it would be only a few weeks, months at the most, before they were hopelessly in love. After all, Nishka was very beautiful, and who could not like her father? Most importantly, her father wouldn't be alone anymore.

Confident her little world was on track toward becoming complete again, Jessica scooted off to bed, pulled the covers up to her chin, and smiled. "Thank you, God," she whispered. "Tell Mommy that Daddy's all right." With that Jessica closed her eyes and fell asleep.

※

Had David known his daughter was watching that night, or known the conclusions she had drawn, he would have undoubtedly had a long talk with her. Though it was true he found Nishka very attractive and intriguing in her quiet sort of way, he wasn't sure of his feelings for her, let alone hers for him. David liked her. There was no doubt that at times he found himself awed if not flustered in her presence, like a schoolboy meeting the poster girl of his dreams. But he was far from convinced those feelings or interest were mutual or even close.

True, she did seem interested in him if not his family. But was that because she liked him, or just courtesy like one associates with a salesman feeling out a prospect, though why she would do that he hadn't a clue. Or was her interest just her European way of better understanding her neighbor, or just a way of keeping the conversation going to make it through the night? That could probably explain the handshake. If that was the case why would she agree to go out with him again? What was that all about? Maybe she found him unattractive or just didn't watch television much. He hoped it was the latter, for he'd have a hard time dealing with the former. His confidence level was already on shaky ground.

Then again maybe it was something else, that strange formal European part of the equation. Never doing more on the first date than a friendly goodnight shake. Never leading one on because it wasn't proper. After all, she did come from Russia. And from what he deduced she hadn't been here long. He liked that scenario. At least he could deal with that, and it made the most sense considering her actions. Her very proper attitude about everything, being very analytical and showing no emotion. It was reminiscent of some old movies he had seen about girls growing up in the more formal aristocratic European culture or the tight communist ones -- never speaking unless spoken to, being inquisitive in a polite, politically, proper manner.

The more David thought about it the more he was convinced her European breeding had to be the answer. At least David hoped that was the case. It might even be fun teaching her American ways -- being the one to show her the finer points of Yankee customs while selectively leaving out the ones he never agreed with. That he could deal with.

The next night after homework was done and David had taken Jessica upstairs for bed and prayers, Jessica asked what he thought about Nishka. Had they had fun on their date? David told her he liked Nishka and yes they had a nice time. Sensing the opportunity, David asked what Nishka was like, what she did, how she spent her time. When Jessica told him Nishka did things on a computer most of the time and spent the rest of her time reading magazines and books on business and that she never watched television, David felt better. It fit his theory about her naivete concerning American culture.

Being so studious and focused seemed very European, or at least his idea of being European. She undoubtedly never took time for anything other than business and the work it took to stay ahead. It explained the handshake and meant he was going to have to work a lot harder if their relationship was ever going to go beyond platonic. Maybe that wasn't all bad. For one, it meant competition was probably minimal and explained why she hadn't been snatched up a long time ago.

"And bless Daddy and Nishka, and say hi to Mommy," Jessica said finishing her prayer. "Amen."

David leaned over and kissed her on the forehead. "Good night princess," he whispered. After turning off the lights David got up and left the room feeling better than when he started that evening. Maybe tomorrow night was going to be the magical one after all, he thought while closing Jessica's door. She was a bookworm, probably a virgin. It would be up to him to help her find a life.

Like their first date David picked Nishka up at about eight. Conversation was sporadic as they drove to Millers. David asked about work, what she was doing. Nishka told him a little about her experience in stocks and bonds and the clients she had. He told her about his years in design. It was a friendly "get to know you better" drive.

The blues trio at Millers was exceptional that night. Nishka had her usual 7-Up, David his manhattan. At first they talked mostly in between music sets. Nishka seemed genuinely interested in the music and also him. She watched him intently as he talked. They discussed the kids. David told her how Jessica was now including her by name in her prayers as if Nishka was part of the family. Nishka said that was nice then changed the subject quickly to how Peter was doing in school.

Nishka seemed to be more attractive than he remembered. Her sweater tighter; her long hair more alluring as it occasionally covered one eye making her look invitingly mysterious in the low moody light. If David's hormones weren't working on their first date, they were working overtime that night. Maybe it was the atmosphere, the music, or the extra manhattan, but when they left the club and started for home he was convinced things were going to be different. If nothing else, he was going to experience the goodnight kiss of a lifetime, hopefully a long passionate one, her body firmly pressed tight against his.

Those images were the focus of David's thoughts as they walked to the door. But like the time before nothing happened. Instead a quick handshake and Nishka was gone. Baffled and hurt, David stared at the door a long while before finally turning and slowly walked home.

David wasn't the only one frustrated that night. Nishka had no sooner closed the door then she leaned against it and closed her eyes. She knew something was wrong, but what? She had done everything she knew to make the evening pleasant. She had presented herself in an attentive manner, even smiled occasionally at what she hoped were the right times, at least they felt right to her. But when the night came to the end, something was missing. She knew he expected more. She hoped it wasn't sex because that was something she had no experience in. She sensed his frustration. She felt it in herself, a feeling of incompleteness, non-closure. And she did not like that feeling -- of not doing what she was expected to do, wanted to do. The question was what?

The next morning Nishka did what was natural for someone like her who had a question about conduct, at least when it involved morals and sexual implications. She went to the video store. According to Jessica, videos were the abridged way to learn human morals and ways of life in a hurry, and Nishka never wasted time. After scanning the various categories, Nishka settled on dramas, read ninety eight different movie synopses and eventually settled on five that she felt fit her situation, ones that implied steamy relationships. The rest of that day and night, Nishka watched the videos, replayed parts that were most pertinent to the situations in question, then replayed them again.

The next day she returned the movies, checked out five more and studied those. That night Nishka called David. "Hi, this is Nishka."

"Hi, what's up? Something wrong?" Asked David surprised by her call after their last encounter.

"No, everything is fine. I was just thinking about you and thought it would be nice to go out again. How would you like to go to a play with me tomorrow night? I would drive."

There was a long pause. David had never thought in a million years that she would call him. Now that she had he was tongue-tied trying to think of what to say. "Yes! I'd love to," he finally blurted. "But you don't have to drive. I would be happy to."

"No, this is my date. I would like to do this."

"Okay, what time should I come over?"

"Seven, the play is at eight."

"Okay, Thanks! See you tomorrow then."

That was the way the conversation ended. David hung up and that was that. Nishka was certain he was interested. Now all she needed was a little more research and then just act natural, at least as natural as she knew how. This had become important to her. If she could not do this, she would never be able to more inconspicuously blend into society. She had to be able to carry out all social functions of a man-woman relationship as naturally as possible. And as pleasant and timid as David was, there would never be a better opportunity.

For David time passed excruciatingly slow the next day. Even slower than before his first date. He felt like a kid waiting for Christmas as he puttered around the house. No matter how hard he tried keeping himself busy that Saturday, thinking of all the things he could do, he couldn't help coming back to two questions. Why was the clock moving so slowly and what was Nishka thinking?

Actually there were other questions but he tried not to

dwell on those. Questions like why did she call him, especially so soon after their last date? She reminded him a little of Barbara, of her aggressiveness during their courtship. And it was particularly exciting being chased instead of doing the chasing, something he had never been very good at. Now Nishka was doing the same thing. It was like his courtship with Barbara all over again. Of course, with Barbara the sexual aspect was a given. With Nishka there was nothing for certain.

David made a point of staying inside as much as possible that day. If he had to go out at all, he was back in quickly for fear that running into Nishka might somehow jinx their date. Even when night finally arrived and he began to dress, putting on his best tie for the occasion, he couldn't help feel butterflies everywhere.

"Where you going, Daddy?" asked Jessica as she watched her father retie his tie for the fourth time.

"On a date."

"A date! With who?"

"With your friend," Dave smiled, finally getting the tie lengths to balance. "We're going to a play."

Jessica's face broke into a wide smile as she gave David a big hug. "Do you like her?"

David picked up his daughter and hugged her back. "Yes I do," he whispered.

"Good," Jessica said seriously, then hugging him again she kissed him. "She really likes you too."

<hr />

There was a crisp chill in the fall air when David walked to Nishka's house that night, his hands in his overcoat pockets. He had looked for his car gloves before leaving but they were not to be found. It's not that cold he told himself, then smiled thinking of the expression on his daughter's face when he left -- of her last words, "She really likes you," and wondered how much of that was wishful thinking on Jessica's part and how much was personal insight based on something Nishka had said.

He thought of Nishka's last words when she called him the night before. "It's my date." And then thought again of what Jessica said. Maybe Jesse's right, David thought as he neared the door. After all, why would Nishka call him, just to say, I don't want to see you any more. Let's go out and make it official. "No, she has to like me."

David's confidence level had tripled by the time he rang the doorbell. After all, maybe it was possible there could be two Barbara's in the world. But what were the odds of him finding them both?

His confidence level jumped again when the door opened and Nishka stepped out wearing a long dress coat, covering what he could only imagine was a sensuous black cocktail dress. Her long flowing hair was done up eloquently in a twist. Golden earrings accented her ears. "You look beautiful," he blubbered without even thinking.

"Thank you," Nishka smiled in what seemed a hint of a blush. It was the first time he had ever seen her show any form of emotion regarding flattery. "You do not mind my driving do you," she asked nodding toward her car parked conspicuously in the driveway.

"No, not at all, it'll be a nice change." Actually it was more like exotic, at least for him. David had never had any woman drive him anywhere on a date. That was except for Barbara, and then only after they had gone together for some time and his car was down. But then he had never been asked out on an official date before either, not even for the turnabout in high school. It must be the new century thing he thought, women's lib. Either way he wasn't going to fight it. At least Nishka didn't carry it to extremes, opening the door and all. That would have been embarrassing. Instead Nishka unlocked the doors with her remote as she walked to her side of the car, then got in, leaving David to fend for himself.

En route to the theater, conversation was, as usual, centered on the children and how they were doing. Since Marshfield was not considered large enough culturally to attract much in the way of professional entertainment, the play Nishka had invited David to was the local college's production of "West Side Story." She had bought the tickets after returning the video, while en route to the college library to examine a recently published book on economic theory. The book she found to be amateurish with little to expand on what she already knew. It took less than an hour to go through it. The tickets were another story. The students had set up a table near the library's entrance and flanked it with posters expounding the must-see virtues of their play. Nishka was intrigued. It would be the perfect opportunity-if not excuse-to invite David out while also experiencing the theater first hand.

The auditorium was nearly full when David and Nishka arrived. A few of the local gentry's eyes followed Nishka as they walked to their seats. The number increased dramatically when she removed her coat revealing what David had imagined, her well-proportioned body accentuated by a shapely cocktail dress. Though the dress was only modestly revealing, coupled with the rest of the package, even David found it hard not staring at her. It wasn't till the lights dimmed and the play began that he finally felt comfortable enough sitting next to her to watch the show without feeling all eyes in the place were focused on them.

Neither David nor Nishka talked much during the play. Occasionally Nishka would glance at David. He would glance back while trying to figure her out. Why had she invited him he wondered? What did she feel, was she really thinking about him?

It wasn't until the last act began building toward the dramatic fight scene that David felt her hand on his. He held her hand. There was no hesitation, just a reaffirmation of tenderness. David did not look at her. Instead he kept his eyes fixed straight ahead. He did not need to see her. Just feeling Nishka's hand in his was all that mattered. It was like the first time with Barbara. That special moment when suddenly all his senses came alive at once. Like all the love of the ages was in her in that tender moment when their hands touched. He couldn't help thinking that Nishka's love had finally spilled from her, chilling and warming him simultaneously. For the first time in a long time he felt totally alive.

After the play Nishka drove David to the lounge they went to on their first date. There, in between 7-Ups and manhattans, they discussed the play like it had never been reviewed before, at least from David's point of view. Nishka asked all manner of questions concerning its meaning, why the two gangs fought and why the two lovers could not have just moved. What were the connections between them and the others? She seemed especially curious why they fell in love to begin with if they were so dramatically different in their backgrounds and beliefs.

"I don't know," said David, trying to explain what the attraction was while at the same time wondering why any girl would even ask such questions, considering that most women probably had a better understanding than he did concerning attraction and romance. The only thing he could figure concerning questioning was her preoccupation with scientific study as it related to economics and its applied logic to physics, whatever that meant. That plus the fact that "West Side Story" was not particularly big in Russian theaters.

"I guess what it really boils down to is it's what matters in here," said David padding his chest near his heart. "I know that it wasn't until after Barbara and I dated a while that I learned how much her mother didn't care for me. Going over to see her after knowing that was pure hell. Especially those nights she couldn't go out and we had to spend the evening there. But I'll tell you the pain I felt inside when we weren't together was worse. All I could think about was her. How much I wanted to be with her."

"You really loved her."

David's expression turned sober. "Yes, very much. I would have walked through fire for her. If I could have I would have switched places with her the night of the accident." David paused and for the first time in years actually felt a tear begin to form. He looked away, anywhere, toward the waitress across the room, anywhere but at Nishka till it was gone. "There's hardly a week that goes by I don't think of her and what, if I had the chance, I'd have done differently." Dave felt a lump in his throat as thoughts of the accident began to overwhelm him. "Excuse me a moment. I have to go to the washroom." With that David abruptly got up and walked away.

David stayed in the washroom staring at the wall in front of the commode trying to recompose himself for longer than he should have. This is not right he thought, not now. But it didn't matter. Barbara was suddenly planted too deeply in his thoughts to shake quickly. He didn't know when it began; Nishka's hand on his or the death of the two star-crossed lovers in the play. Or was it this crazy conversation? Whatever it was he felt he had to leave, at least till he pulled himself together. It seemed so stupid for a guy to get so emotional.

Though it felt like forever it was only a short time before David returned. From the apparent looks of a couple of single newcomers at the bar, it was none too soon. Why David's emotions had suddenly overwhelmed him was no longer important. What mattered, he told himself, was the person he was with. Barbara, for better or worse, was the past; Nishka was now, and that was all that mattered.

Nishka didn't bring up the play again that night, or Barbara and their relationship. Instead they discussed trivial things, the children some more, the economy, finished their drinks and left. Neither spoke much as Nishka drove home. She was a very good driver thought David, obeyed the rules precisely to the law, even if her speed was a little sluggish. At least she wouldn't get in any accidents, which was good considering how often his children were with her.

Again David walked Nishka home. He didn't say anything as he watched her unlock the door. Nishka paused, stared at the opened door a moment as if trying to resolve some inner conflict, then abruptly turned to David. "I had a wonderful time tonight."

"So did I. I'm sorry if I was a little emotional for a while," said David sheepishly.

"Why were you?"

"I don't know, must have been the play." David paused, trying to decide whether to say what he really felt. "I thought--I don't know--that maybe, for a while, that you really didn't want to be with me."

Nishka timidly moved closer. "No, not at all. I just have not had much experience with men."

David half laughed. "I find that hard to believe."

"It is true!"

David moved closer to her, his voice almost a whisper. "I care for you."

Nishka looked deep into David's eyes as she moved nearer, their lips only inches apart. Suddenly Nishka stopped, then kissed him on the cheek. "Good night."

Before David could react Nishka was gone and the door closed. Dumbfounded he found himself staring at the door. Confused, hurt, mad, he was half tempted to pound on it. To see her again, face to face, and get an explanation as to what the hell just happened. Instead, he silently turned and walked home kicking an invisible can along the way.

Nishka stood in her darkened living room transfixed by the thought of what she had done, and didn't do. Finally she sat down on the davenport, stared at the ceiling, then at the door. After a while she leaned back and closed her eyes.

Chapter Fifteen

David did not sleep well that night. He woke once and stared at the clock, 3:15, got up and went downstairs for a drink of water. He sat in the dark kitchen for almost an hour mulling over what happened, where he went wrong or didn't, how he actually stood with her. Was it some kind of crazy game she was playing? A torturous sort of keep away, playing hard-to-get, keeping herself just out of reach until he was so crazy he would do anything for a little affection, then wammp -- hooked, line and sinker, married, or worse. At one point David actually picked up the phone, determined to call her and clear the air once and for all. But he didn't, and in the end, after sitting down in the living room, he fell asleep half sitting up in the old Lazy-Boy, glass in hand, still as perplexed and horny as ever.

The next morning when the others came down for church, David was still where he had fallen asleep. Jessica covered him with the light blanket that had been draped over the back of the sofa. She kissed him on the cheek, then went about her way making breakfast — peanut butter and jelly. When he finally awoke the family went to church, the late service. Needless to say, Grandmother, whom he was supposed to pick up early for the nine o'clock, wasn't happy.

Nishka's name never came up that day, or the next, or the day after that. David looked at her house when he went to work and again when he returned at night. Each time he thought about going over but he didn't, nor did he call. And as the next few days passed he felt less and less of an inclination to do anything. After all, if she wanted to play hard to get, just to drive him crazy, he would too. By then he had rationalized that she was no stranger to calling men. She had called him once; she could call him again. If not, then it was probably for the better.

It wasn't until Tuesday that Nishka's name came up again in the Flores house. David had returned home early that day and gone directly to the basement and his quiet room, as he often referred to it when Barbara was alive and the children were younger and wilder. It was a room near the size of a bedroom, about eleven by twelve, containing all manner of tools for building models, plastic or wood. It was there that David had built scale houses for Peter's railroad train. Where he built the dollhouse for Jessica out of scraps, cardboard, and whatever else he could find. The gliders he built for the kids were created in this inner sanctum, and it was there that he began his most ambitious project -- a scale model of a DC-3, the workhorse of the 40's airways, World War II and beyond. Designed to be a flying model, the plane was built to a one-inch equals a foot scale, making its wingspan over six feet, tip to tip. It was an enormous undertaking that over the past year had consumed much of David's free time.

That was, until lately. The quiet room, and especially the model, had always been David's way of escaping from the pressures of life and reality, especially when pressures felt more unbearable than normal. Nishka had become one of those indefinable frustrations as of late, and only the plane seemed to provide the escape he needed from what had become at best a frustrating experience.

His mother had come over long before Dave arrived home. She had given the house one of her patented fast cleanings and begun dinner for David, the children, and Carl and Judith, who were expected around six. At about five thirty she began clearing the dinning room table for the meal. As she picked up papers from one end, Jessica sat at the other drawing in her sketchpad.

Peter was in the other room watching television, a family sitcom, when the show was suddenly interrupted by a news flash. A female reporter was doing a remote from a downtown metropolitan location. Behind her stood a large office building. "I am standing here in front of the Senate Office Building in Washington D.C., the site of one of the latest anthrax attacks. It has just been learned from a confidential source in the Environmental Protection Agency that the clean up from the attack may be larger than first thought. The largest problem appears to be its size, ten stories high. It has been decided that the only possible route left might be to seal off the building entirely and then flood it with chlorine dioxide gas."

Grandmother found herself drawn to the television, Jessica standing beside her, as the woman continued to describe how if such a gas was used it could not be one hundred percent sure that it would work. The temperature of the building would have to be maintained at seventy degrees and the humidity at between fifty to seventy percent. In trying to bring it all into perspective the reporter motioned toward the building behind her. "It is felt by many in the FBI that these anthrax attacks may be the work of one person, a loner, one who does not like confrontation but is seething with repressed anger. There are others though that feel the attacks are much too organized and high profile and could only be the result of an organized group like Al-Qaeda.

Grandmother shook her head as she sat down and watched the news report unfold. "What's wrong with this world?"

"Why do people do things like that," asked Jessica sitting down beside Grandmother.

"Because they don't like each other. It's their religions," said Peter trying to sound authoritative.

"What kind of religion is it that makes people want to hurt each other!"

Grandmother gently brushed Jessica's hair with one hand while pulling her closer with the other

"Some people just don't know how to get along." Before she could expound on that the doorbell rang. No one seemed to notice the bell at first, their eyes glued to the television. Then the bell rang again. "Don't everybody jump up at once," huffed Grandmother shaking her head as she stood. Cautiously opening the door as if half expecting to see terrorists outside, she heaved small a sigh of relief at only finding Judith and Carl who was carrying a large grocery bag.

"You look surprised. Don't tell me you forget we were coming," said Judith as they walked in.

"Oh no! We were watching the latest about the anthrax on television. The bell caught me off guard. I didn't expect you so early."

"I know," said Carl setting the bag on the table then turning his attention to the television news special. "We were listening to some talk about it on the way over."

"You can thank me for being early," said Judith while taking off her coat. If it were up to him we'd be here in time for dessert."

Carl turned to the children and winked. "When your grandmother makes lasagna, I'm never late."

Peter barely laughed before turning back to the television, then suddenly turned back to Carl. "What movies did you bring?

"Classics. "The Mummy and "Abbott And Costello Meet The Wolf Man," shot Carl pulling the videos out of the bag. "But we can't watch them till after dinner. And only if your homework's done, remember."

"No problem, my homework's already done," said Peter jumping up and taking the videos. "Thanks." Not saying another word Peter returned to a chair near a table lamp to study the video covers.

Jessica's only response was "Hi Uncle Carl," before turning her attention back to the news special only to find the station had returned to its regular programming. Instead of turning back she continued to watch the program.

Deciding that Jessica was too absorbed in the show, Carl turned to Grandmother. "I brought some Chianti for dinner and some German beer for the head of the house. Where is the man?"

Grandmother nodded toward the kitchen. "Downstairs in his toy room"

David was busy working on his model of his DC-3, jazz playing in the background from a small radio on a nearby workbench, when Carl walked into his inner sanctum with two cold bock beers. The metallic silver model, supported by its own landing gear, looked imposing as it sat on an angle with its six foot wing span nearly extending beyond the five-foot square table in the center of the room. Every detail of the plane was precise, from its miniature reproductions of twin Pratt & Whitney engines to the seven gleaming passenger windows on each side and the American Airline decals. The plane looked ready to carry a squad of acrobatic midgets across the skies, provided they were very small midgets.

David barely looked up from his project as Carl set a beer down beside him. "Thanks I could use that. Is it that dinner time already?" he asked while trying to put the passenger door in place.

"No we're early," Carl leaned over to take a better look at the plane. "This bird ever going to fly?"

"Soon, give or take a month."

"How you ever going to get it out of here?"

"The wings come off. So how are things in the reporting business? You still thinking about a sabbatical?"

"Wish I could, but with all that's going on right now it doesn't look promising." Carl straightened up and sipped his beer. "I don't know how Judith ever talked me into moving out here."

"Because it's safe--Blasville." David finished installing the door, then picked up the beer and held it up in a salute. "Admit it, this is one of the last bastions of true Americana left where it's safe to bring up a family in this crazy world. Nothing happens here." David held his beer higher to salute the world around them. "This is the Bunker Hill of American family life and you love it."

Carl smiled, then took a long hard swallow. "David, I can't fight you there. Truth is I need this place just to put the rest of my life in perspective."

David nodded then leaned back against the worktable. "I hear you got another assignment."

"Only a week." Carl glanced toward the door making sure Judith wasn't there, then turned back to David. "I leave tomorrow, but I should be done before Thanksgiving. After that I've asked to be off through New Years. At least that's the plan. God knows I've missed enough holidays."

"I'll bet Judith's happy."

"She is." Carl glanced back toward the door again. "The last trip was pretty rough on her."

"I can imagine." David nodded toward the plane on the table. "This is about as close to adventure as I'll ever get."

"Be happy. I'd trade it all for a couple of kids like yours... Speaking of which, when are we going to meet this new neighbor of yours?"

"I wouldn't know," said David taking another swig from his bottle.

"You two haven't broken up already?"

David laughed, a kind of nervous laugh that said you've got to be kidding. "We haven't anything to break up from! What gave you the idea there was anything anyway?"

"Your mother. She stopped over for coffee with Judith. You know the rest. What happened?"

David stared at his bottle, rubbing his finger along its side as if trying to gleam what was happening from inside it. "I don't know. Every time we went out things seemed fine. But when I'd take her home... nothing. Hell I'm lucky I get a handshake. It's like dating my cousin or something."

"You're kidding." Carl stroked his beard contemplating the implications. "That's sad David. Maybe it's something new in women's lib or something."

"I don't know. Truth is I'm starting to get a complex."

Carl shook his head. "Must be something else. A boyfriend maybe. Maybe she's a lesbian.... You talk to her about it?"

David laughed. "About what? Why she doesn't want to get cozy with me? Not even a kiss! How do you do that?"

"I don't know. So what are you planning to do?"

David closed his eyes. Then opening them again he stared at the ceiling. "Nothing. I'm going to do nothing. Just forget her--if that's possible. And believe me the way she looks that ain't going to be easy."

As the men talked, neither one noticed Jessica standing deep in the shadows, beyond the door in the other room. Quietly turning around Jessica went back upstairs.

Chapter Sixteen

The following day was sunny and warmer than usual for mid fall. After school Peter managed to borrow a pair of in-line skates from a friend in exchange for his binoculars. The other boy had said he wanted to use them to watch squirrels in the trees for science. Peter knew better. The girl across the street had matured a lot during the past summer and she was known to have a tendency to leave her curtains open at night. Some said she just liked being adventurous. Whatever the reason, her indiscretions were one of the worst kept secrets in school.

Why his friend wanted the binoculars was not Peter's concern. The only thing that mattered was learning how to skate before the class skating outing in two weeks. There was no way Peter was going to look foolish if he could help it. "I'm putting these on as soon as we get home and I'll skate till dark if that's what it takes," he told his friends and Jessica as they walked home. After all he only had them a week and that wasn't much time to learn.

Jessica had a different agenda. Ever since the night before she couldn't get what she overheard between Uncle Carl and her father out of her mind. What happened, what went wrong she wondered. It was for sure there couldn't have been a problem with her father. It had to be Nishka.

That bothered her because for some reason Jessica didn't have a good feel on her. There was something about Nishka. She was different in a strange way Jessica had never been able to quite understand. Maybe it was her being European, coming from a different world as it were, but even that was no reason why she couldn't care for her father.

The unseasonably warm fall afternoon had a refreshing feel about it as Nishka raked the last of the fallen leaves into a pile near the curb. Raking was not something that had any real sense of importance to her other than it was what all the neighbors did that time of year. As a result, Nishka felt compelled to complete the chore if for no other reason than to conform to the norm.

Nishka had become so focused on her task that she barely noticed Peter awkwardly pass on his borrowed inline roller-blades till he was almost beside her. He waved and tried to act cool while trying to keep his balance. She waved back then returned to the leaves. After all they had to be bagged if everything was to be done in an orderly manner.

As Nishka continued raking, other thoughts flashed through her mind. What the market was doing. What were the best near term investments considering the latest changes in the tax laws and the current down turn? How the war on terrorism was going to affect the economy, not to mention how it was going to affect her own dilemma concerning certain members of the opposition. Nishka had become so deep in thought that she didn't realize she had company until she saw Jessica watching her from less than a yard away. "Hi. I have not seen you in a while."

"I've been busy at school," said Jessica, her stance somewhat rigid. She wanted to say more. To blurt out all the frustrations that had built up since the night before but she didn't. Yet the more she watched Nishka work, acting as though nothing was wrong, like she had done nothing that was improper between herself and her father, the more frustrated and mad Jessica felt.

"You want to help?"

"Not today."

"Do you want to talk?" Asked Nishka, pausing from the project.

"No," shot Jessica, her frustration rising toward the boiling point. Just watching Nishka rake, looking so innocent and unconcerned was driving her nuts. How could someone Jessica considered a friend not know what she had done and not want to gush out her feelings, apologizing and asking for forgiveness.

"Okay. Have a nice day." That was it. Without saying another word she returned to raking.

"Why don't you like my father?" There it was. Jessica had blurted it out and like a defensive linebacker she planted her feet firmly and waited for a response. After all no one was going to treat her father like Nishka had and not have Jessica to reckon with. She didn't care if it was her neighbor's yard, this was Jessica's neighborhood, her world, and no one was going to hurt her dad without answering to her.

Nishka abruptly stopped raking and turned to Jessica. "I like your father."

"Then why wouldn't you kiss him."

"Kiss him! Who..." Nishka paused, looked at Jessica's house, up at her bedroom window then back at Jessica. "Just because a girl does not kiss someone does not mean she does not care for him. There are just some things I am not very good at. Kissing is one of them." Nishka had been honest, as honest as she could under the circumstances. Another person would probably have said it was none of a little girl's business, that Jessica was too young to understand what went on between two consenting adults But then Nishka was not like other women. Jessica had asked a legitimate question and Nishka felt obligated to answer it as honestly as possible considering. "Truth is I have had very little experience with men. I am sorry if David felt I did not care for him."

Jessica felt confused yet at the same time relieved. She could live with Nishka's answer. It meant there was still hope. If Nishka really cared and was just inexperienced, Jessica was just the girl to help. After all, what Jessica didn't know she could certainly find out, or at least make up. "Would you come over for dinner with us?"

"No, this would not be a good time."

Back to square one. "Why not?"

Before Nishka could explain, Peter flew past again, waved, then lost control, and headed down the drive into the path of an oncoming pickup truck. "Peter!"

Dropping her rake Nishka dashed after Peter, grabbed him by the arm and, spinning him around, shot him back towards the curb and the large tree she had been raking under. Peter's glancing collision with the tree sent him sprawling to the ground. Unfortunately Nishka's momentum carried her into the oncoming truck. The impact sent her flying backward crashing her into the street next to the curb near a parked car.

Jessica watched in shocked disbelief as the pickup screeched to a grinding stop. An elderly man in overalls and plaid work shirt quickly climbed out of the truck and rushed toward Nishka. "Oh my God, Call an Ambulance!" he yelled kneeling over Nishka's lifeless body.

Suddenly Nishka's eyes opened. She looked bewildered, lost, as she stared up at the driver. "I'm so sorry lady!" trembled the man apparently in as much shock over what happened as Nishka was. "Are you all right? Somebody get an ambulance!!"

Nishka's eyes moved back and forth, trying to bring all that happened and its implications into focus. Ignoring the driver, Nishka abruptly sat up, then brushed herself off while looking for Peter, who was still dazed from hitting the tree.

"Lady are you okay?" repeated the driver, half-expecting Nishka to fall over any second.

"I am fine!" shot Nishka, finally acknowledging the man's presence. "Do not worry about me."

"Are you sure? I think we better get you to a hospital anyway, just in case," insisted the man, not sure whether to help Nishka up or make her lay back down. "You could have damaged your neck or something."

To the driver and Jessica's amazement, Nishka climbed to her feet. Brushing off her torn jacket and jeans, she quickly walked over to Peter to see how he was doing. "See, I am fine. You do not have to worry. It was not your fault." Without waiting for a reply, Nishka knelt beside Peter.

"What happened?" It was apparent Peter was more shaken than anything as Nishka helped him sit up.

"You were almost run over by a truck," said Nishka untying his skates. "I think you have had enough skating for one day."

"Good idea." mumbled Peter. At first he barely seemed conscious of Nishka removing one foot from his skate. He did manage to help her remove the other one though it was apparent Peter was barely aware of what happened or going on around him. "I think I'll go home and watch Batman."

"You do that." Nishka helped Peter stand, then pointed him toward his home. Turning to Jessica, who had pretty much remained frozen in place, Nishka motioned for her to give Peter a hand. "Maybe you should go with him." Jessica barely nodded as Nishka followed them home.

The driver, not convinced of Nishka's recovery, and concerned about the ramifications of what could happen if he didn't make sure she was all right, began to follow. "Are you sure you don't want to go to the hospital?" He asked. "I don't want you falling over into a coma. I have insurance!"

"No! I am fine!" shot Nishka over her shoulder. "Thank you very much."

It was apparent by Nishka's manner that she did not want to be bothered and would rather the man forget the whole thing. The driver stopped short of the house and watched her escort the children inside. He didn't feel comfortable with how it ended, not comfortable at all. Who was to say she wouldn't come back and sue him. Then again she was walking and talking and there was amazingly little sign she had been hit other than her torn clothes.

He stared at the house a few moments longer, then finally turned and left. After all he had fulfilled his obligation. He stopped, took responsibility for what happened, though in truth it was she who ran into him. And he offered aid, which she refused. If only someone else had seen the accident, he thought. But as luck would have it there was no one out. Not a single person in their yards; in fact, no one even came out to see what happened after he screeched his tires. "Just goes to show what's happened to our society," he muttered as he climbed back into his truck. Not even a car had driven through the sleepy subdivision since he hit her.

"Why is it always me that's so dang lucky," the old man mumbled. Looking around twice to make sure no one was in range, he started his pickup and put it in gear. It'll be hard sleeping tonight after this one, he thought, barely stepping on the gas as he drove away.

"This is not good," thought Nishka as she stood in front of her bathroom mirror, sweater off, blouse open, examining herself. Other than bruises there appeared to be no damage internally or out. But that was of minor concern. What concerned her was what could have happened if she had not come to and they had taken her to the hospital. That would have been devastating, not only for her but others as well. That thought had never crossed Nishka's mind before, at least not to any degree. But then nothing like this had happened before either. Then again that was not entirely true either. There were two other instances, and those two situations were even more precarious. But then had worse come to worse, there probably would not have been enough left of her to be concerned about and those who would have known would not have cared. That was the problem. There was no one around to care or protect her should something happen.

Nishka had become so involved in her self-examination and reflections of that afternoon's events that she failed to notice the sound of someone in the house until Jessica was standing in the bathroom doorway.

"Are you from Mars?" asked Jessica staring up at Nishka as if seeing her for the first time.

"No, I am not from Mars. What gave you that idea?" It was a stupid question. Nishka already knew the answer and had she thought about it more she might have opted to change directions and confessed to the Martian concept. It would have been easier for Jessica to understand. Nishka also knew how sharp Jessica could be and decided it wiser to find out what Jessica thought she knew than to ignore her. Who knew what Jessica might say if left to her own imagination.

"Because no one can get hit like that. No one!"

Nishka stared at Jessica a moment not sure what to say or if she wanted to say anything. Her cover was in jeopardy and it was imperative to protect that cover. Things had changed much since that directive had been implanted in her. In the dozen years since she had been left on her own she had begun to learn other concepts and implemented some of her own directives, gleamed from her interaction with humans, observing their views of life and their moralities.

She had learned that they didn't look at things as black and white but instead in shades of gray. Their reactions, based on those premises, were often frustratingly unpredictable. Those contradictions, coupled with the attachment she had developed for Jessica, an attachment she had never experienced before or was fully able to understand, had clouded her ability to do what logic and her original directives dictated she do.

After quickly analyzing her options Nishka sat down on the toilet and looked into Jessica's eyes. "Now you know why I could not kiss your father. I was afraid I would not do it properly and he would find out."

"That you're a Martian," gushed Jessica, her eyes wide open. Kissing isn't that hard."

"I am not a Martian, or from any other planet. I am an android... a machine."

Jessica's expression changed from awe to quizzical as she moved closer and lightly touched Nishka's cheek. "You don't look like a machine. Where did you come from? Did you really come from Russia?"

"Yes." Nishka had decided to trust Jessica. It made no rational sense why other than Jessica was unlike anyone she had ever met. Maybe it was simply that Nishka actually liked Jessica though that was a concept she did not fully comprehend either. She liked David too but she would have had a hard time convincing herself to confide in him with information that might jeopardize her survival. But then Jessica was different. It was a major change in rational for Nishka, possibly a dangerous one, but for some reason she felt compelled to take that chance. She would tell Jessica the truth -- all Nishka felt she could comprehend. "There are some people that want me back."

"You ran away?"

Nishka nodded. "That is why I came here. Why I do not eat much. I am not human. There are times I wish I were. I wish I could care for your father the way you do. The way you want me too. The way he would like me to... I would give anything to be like you."

"Like Pinocchio." smiled Jessica gently touching Nishka's long snarled hair.

"Yes, like Pinocchio. But I cannot. Those things only happen in fairytales." Nishka stood up and began buttoning her blouse. Jessica now knew the truth and Nishka would have to live with that and see what happens. After finishing straightening her clothes Nishka escorted Jessica to the front door. "If you are really my friend, you will never say a word about this to anyone. At least until I am gone."

Jessica's felt her stomach suddenly sink at Nishka's last words. "You're going away?"

"I think it would be best for everyone."

"Why do you have to go away?"

"Because you know what I am. Things could never be the same. If you know, other people could know." Nishka knelt down beside Jessica and looked into her eyes. "If the wrong people found me here it could be bad."

"Why," asked Jessica, trying to comprehend the full meaning of what she was being told while grasping for any way to save an important part of her world from slipping away.

"I was made to be a soldier. There are bad people in the world that still want me to be one."

"Did you kill anyone?"

Nishka shook her head. "No. I have never killed anyone."

That was the truth. But then Nishka would not lie. Not intentionally. That was not to say she hadn't hurt a few people though when it was necessary.

"You wouldn't would you?"

"No. That is why I should leave. I care for you Jessica, more than anyone I have ever known. I will always remember you." With that Nishka stood up and opened the door. "It is time for you to go."

Before Jessica could think of anything more to say she was outside and the door was closed behind her. She heard the metallic click of the lock and knew it was over, she would never see Nishka again. With that Jessica turned and slowly walked home.

Chapter Seventeen

The accident never came up at Jessica's house that night. Even Peter didn't mention it, his interest in becoming a world-class skater having dramatically changed in proportion to his black and blue marks. Jessica thought hard about what happened, about Nishka and what she said. It seemed almost impossible to believe she wasn't human, that she was just a machine that some how developed a life of its own and just happened to move in next door. If it was true though, then it was for sure nothing could ever have happened between her father and Nishka.

The more Jessica thought about that day the more she was tempted to say something to her father, tell him it was not his fault they never kissed or did anything else. But she promised Nishka she would never tell anyone about her, and her word was her bond. After all, Nishka had saved her brother and she owed her that much. Besides, maybe it was better her father never knew. Better he thought she didn't care for him than learn she never could. Her father would just have to get over it and find someone else, someone that was real. Jessica could help him. After all she matched him up with Nishka.

That night Nishka took a long walk after what was customarily the dinner hour for most other people in the neighborhood. It was near dark when she returned. No one of consequence had seen her. That was good. She had gone for the walk as a way of taking a last look at the surroundings she had grown to know so well. It was also a time of meditation in a sense if one could consider her capable of that. After she returned home she stood for a moment at her front room widow. As she watched the streetlights blink on she couldn't help but feel some remorse for doing what she knew had to be done. A moment later Nishka pulled the curtain closed and turned away.

Sitting down on the couch she looked around at her surroundings. For the first time she noticed how bleak the room looked. She began to understand what Jessica meant about accessories, such as the one's she had pictured in her scrapbook, as a way of making the house feel like a home. It had been a strange concept to Nishka but now when it was apparent that it was all coming to an end it began to mean something. As bleak as the room looked, it had become home, her home, and for the first time in all the places she had lived, she was going to miss it.

Eventually Nishka decided she had spent enough time wallowing in the strange new feelings she had and turned on the television. CNN came on. It was one of the few stations her set was generally tuned to. It had been important to know what was going on in the world. It gave her insight into what people were thinking, helped flush out trends that might effect business. After all Nishka made her money on what humans did. The fluctuations of the stock market, which had become so unstable since the recession and the collapse of the tech companies, along with 9/11 had made the markets highly volatile. But then she was good at analyzing trends, especially fast ones – stripping away the bullshit and what the effects of human behavior played on the markets.

Of course, she was also good because she lacked her human counterpart's most fundamental weakness, emotion. Unlike them she was totally analytical, and that was what mattered in making money. Still there was something about their emotions that so governed human life that it had become one of the things that made them so intriguing. She had seen it during 9/11 especially. The feelings humans felt for one another during that time of major disaster. The way they helped each other under stress whether they knew one another or not. How they fought for the lives of others risking it all to save people they didn't even know. How humans could became so emotional over the simplest things like a torn photo or a dirty crushed helmet of a firefighter or a simple American flag being raised over the wreckage of what once was a major engineering accomplishment.

Nothing could have prepared her for what she saw during those days, the total unselfishness in what seemed to be a me first, consumer-oriented society. Was that what made humans begin to seem so special to her? Why did she, for the first time, begin to feel something more for them, envy them for being able to feel the way they do? Nishka had seen so much misery in her existence.

As a result she had never allowed herself to get close enough to sense or experience the good that also came with humanity. The feeling of togetherness and caring that seemed to be part and parcel with the things they did. Those thoughts began to have become more of a mystery and yet at the same time a fascination over the past couple months. And in reality they were feelings she did not particularly want to lose.

As the news rambled on, Nishka's thoughts drifted further and further away from the screen. The stories changed. An updated report on the Anthrax scares, Afghanistan, and the search for the Al-Quaeda. The news reporter confirmed that there were reports of other planned attacks on the US. That there were still cells alive, active and ready to follow up in other parts of the country. Nishka already knew that. She not only knew one of the groups still active, but she knew their leader as well.

It had been a hard uphill climb for Nishka to get where she was. She had managed to slip into America through Canada on a passport forged through knowledge programmed into her. Those papers and others were enough for her to secure a job as secretary in a large brokerage firm. The position gave her enough computer access to create a life for herself, credit history and all. But now there was a new wrinkle to the equation--Jessica. No one had ever known that she was in America, or even existed in the world other than Ahmed. There was the possibility that Jessica could compromise her cover. The question was would she and what should Nishka do to rectify this breach in her security? Or should she do anything at all.

As the evening grew late, Nishka sat in the stillness of her darkened living room analyzing her options and the feelings aroused by them, feelings she had never experienced before. Was this what it was like to be human, she wondered. To be haunted by memories and thoughts of things to come that were only maybes. This was not something that was comfortable and made little sense to her. It was not logical in a well-ordered life. But from what she knew of humans, order had little to do with life. Still the question remained simply, what was she to do next?

Chapter Eighteen

Jessica did not see Nishka the next day. Even for a little girl who still believed in Santa Claus, having someone in real life tell her she was an android, a machine, was a little too fantasy world for Jessica to comprehend. Still she saw what happened -- the truck, the accident. No one could have survived something like that unless they were Super Man or Wonder Woman. But then there were all those other things that slowly began to make sense to her. The lack of food in the house. The house itself being anomaly empty with its lack of furniture or any accessories that most humans would clutter their lives with. The way Nishka was so analytical and never seemed to show any emotion.

If what Nishka said was true, then one thing was for sure; there was no way she could marry her father. How could her father love a machine? For that matter, how could a machine love him back? What would they do? They could never have babies, not that that would be such a bad thing. After all, with her and Peter who else would Jessica's father need?

Yet no matter how much Jessica rationalized how much better off her father was never seeing Nishka again -- or herself for that matter, Jessica couldn't help feeling a sense of loss thinking about it. That night when she was alone in her room, Jessica sat by her window, peeking out through the blinds on the chance she might see Nishka.

The following morning as Jessica, her brother, and his friends walked to school, she hoped she might see Nishka again, if only for a second. It was beginning to no longer matter what Nishka was – whether she and her father could ever love each other. All Jessica knew was Nishka had become the closest friend she had, the only one she could come to when she felt alone, the one who would listen when she wanted to talk.

Jessica liked to talk when she felt sad. That was one of the reasons why she came over so often to do homework. In truth Jessica probably needed help less than anyone in her school. It was not tutoring she needed; it was the companionship. And Nishka was the perfect companion, attentive, never bored. Unfortunately, as much as Jessica began to pray she might see Nishka, it didn't happen. Jessica did not see Nishka after school either. Instead what she saw was a "For Sale" sign on Nishka's front lawn.

Seeing the sign in front of Nishka's house weighed heavy on Jessica that afternoon. Though she told herself it was okay -- that it was expected and that it was for the best -- deep down inside she had held out hope that somehow something magical would happen that would make things okay again. But the sign changed everything. It meant finality, the end. Nishka was moving away and that would be it forever.

The sinking feeling Jessica felt when she saw the "For Sale" sign was amplified ten fold by David that night. At first when he drove in he thought the sign was a prank, deposited by some deranged youth who probably laughed all the way home. But the longer he stared at it after getting out of his van, the more it felt like his stomach had just filled with lead and had dropped to his feet. He'd lost her. He hadn't even gotten to first base and already she was gone. Was it something he said, he wondered? Or something he didn't. Should he have forgotten his petty pride and called after their last date instead of ignoring her?

All those things and more passed through David's mind as he stared at the sign. Without thinking, David found himself at Nishka's door, ringing the doorbell repeatedly, even pounding on it -- but no one answered. Feeling frustrated and sadly alone David finally turned and went home.

It was apparent to Jessica as she helped her grandmother fold laundry that her father had seen the sign. "I take it dinner's going to be late," said David in a sad monotone as he dropped his briefcase on the buffet table.

"I'm on strike—you're buying pizza," shot Helen putting a stack of folded towels into a laundry basket.

David shrugged. "I can live with that." He glanced at his son in the livingroom, but Peter didn't look back. Instead he had no doubt gotten lost in a book about planets he was reading. David's attention changed toward the door on the buffet that concealed the liquor. "I noticed a for sale sign next door."

"Have you talked to her?"

David continued to stare at the liquor cabinet; then finally turned and leaned against the counter. "Just walked over. There was no one home. Have you talked to her?"

"Just a couple seconds," nodded Grandmother. "She came over to see if we had some empty boxes."

Jessica's attention perked at learning Grandmother had actually seen Nishka. It was apparent her father was just as concerned about Nishka leaving as she was, maybe more so. Maybe that was good she thought. Parents are supposed to be able to fix things, and if anyone could fix this situation, her father could.

"What did she say?" asked David, sounding relieved there was still some semblance of dialog going on.

"Only that she was offered a good position somewhere." Helen finished folding the clothes, then began putting the rest of them in the basket to take upstairs. "She said she was going there today but would be back tomorrow to finish taking care of things."

"That was sudden." David didn't say more. Instead he turned and silently climbed the stairs to his bedroom.

It was obvious to Jessica that no matter what Nishka was or wasn't, not having her around was going to be bad for her father. She wished she could tell him what she knew. Tell him that Nishka wasn't real, and no matter how bad he felt now it would be okay. But the truth was, the more Jessica thought about Nishka, the more real she became and the more it didn't matter.

That night after her father came in to her bedroom to hear her prayers, kissed her and left, Jessica prayed again. The second time when she closed her eyes, she closed them very tightly putting everything she had into her prayer hoping God would listen extra hard. Her prayer was simple: help her to find a way to make things better for her father and Nishka. "Please God," she finished. "Nishka might not be real like us, but daddy cares for her so much. If you can please give me a sign. Tell me what to do to make things right so Daddy won't be so sad anymore." A tear fell down Jessica's cheek as she said, "Amen". She climbed back under her covers and looked out the window at Nishka's house, then closed her eyes and eventually fell asleep.

Like the morning before, there was no sign of Nishka when

Jessica, Peter, and his friends walked to school. Nothing to indicate whether she was still gone or had returned -- just a lonely looking house. Somehow Jessica couldn't help but feel Nishka was there though, somewhere in the shadows watching her pass. "Do you think robots can be alive?" Jessica suddenly asked, pulling on her brother's sleeve and interrupting an intense conversation between him and his buddies on girls they wish they knew.

"Huh?"

"Can robots have feelings, you know, like people?"

"Like Data?" asked Barry, the resident historian of "Star Trek".

"Yes."

"Sure," shot Vern, another science fiction aficionado. "Just like R2-D2."

"No, they can't." And that was the truth. If anyone should know, it was Peter. After all there was no one in the neighborhood who knew more about space, science fiction or otherwise. He was the resident authority. All debates on the subject ended with him.

"Sure they can," countered Vern. "How about the robot in that movie... You know, Number 5."

"Short Circuit. We have that," said Barry.

"So what. We got all the "Star Trek" movies," boasted Vern. It wasn't often Vern got to boast about anything. But when it came to movies, probably only the local video store had more videos than his family. His father lived in front of the television and was seldom seen outside other than cutting the grass and going to and from work.

While the boys' discussion slowly changed to who knew more about what in science fiction, Jessica's thoughts wandered on. She glanced back at Nishka's house and wondered whether being real really mattered. One thing was certain, if Nishka cared enough about a person to be willing to sacrifice her safety for him, then she had to be more than a number of parts like a vacuum cleaner or some other dumb machine.

That day school was little more than a blur to Jessica. She passed from class to class oblivious to most everything except thoughts of Nishka and the question of what she was, real or not. If not, what was really alive and what wasn't, or if it even mattered. Through most of the morning and into lunch she mulled over those thoughts, asking classmates what they thought.

When she reached religion class that afternoon, her quandary had festered into a paradoxical dilemma. Jessica barely paid attention to the class discussion, finding herself instead still locked in her perpetual debate, that was until the teacher started tossing out parallels between the day's lesson, "The Good Samaritan," and the world he lived in. "When God created the world, he created us all equal," he said trying to illustrate how the color of one's skin or nationality made no difference to God. "No matter how we look or think we are all the same inside."

"Is God still creating?" asked a student.

"Good question." The teacher sat down on the corner of his desk and turned to another student in the front row, a shy brunette with large eyes who seemed to be looking back intently. "Yes, God is still creating. Sometimes it's called acts of nature, sometimes-even miracles. Often he creates through us." He nodded to the girl, "can you give me an example?"

The girl tensed. "Raising puppies?"

The teacher smiled. "No that's not creating. The puppies' mother and father did that."

The thought of God creating through people, like her father, or other men, doctors or scientists, suddenly attracted Jessica's attention. She found herself listening intently as another student blurted, "When we make a pie."

The teacher laughed. "True, although those creations aren't always as good as others. It depends on the cook. How about something else?" There was a long silence as the students stared at him and each other, none wanting to say something that sounded as dumb as the pie or puppies. "How about when man discovers something never before dreamed of. Like television, airplanes, computers, some new form of life?"

A girl from the middle of the room raised her hand. "How about a baby?"

The teacher rolled back on the desk slightly and smiled. "Yes. That's God's most wonderful creation, the miracle of life. Actually the puppies are the same thing"

Without thinking Jessica found herself raising her hand as high as she could reach, hoping to build on what had already been said. "What about something that can think and act and care just like a person?"

The room fell silent as the teacher paused mulling over what Jessica had asked. "Like what?"

"Like the good terminator in "Terminator Two'," blurted a boy two rows over, not waiting for Jessica's answer.

Jessica eagerly nodded, "ya, like that!"

The teacher thought a moment, then nodded. "Yes, if God let man create it, then I guess it could be alive in a sense. After all God has a purpose for everything. If he thinks it's not what he wants, then like the Tower of Babel, he would just put a stop to it"

That was all Jessica needed. Without waiting to hear more she took a piece of paper from her notebook and began to write. It was not a long note, but before school was over that day she rewrote it twice.

No sooner had Jessica returned home that afternoon than she rushed to the case where all the videos were stored and plowed through them until she found "Short Circuit". After putting the video in a brown sandwich bag she put the note she wrote in an envelope, sealed it, then wrote on the outside, "Please do not read my letter inside until after you see this movie. Jessica."

Not waiting to confide in anyone else what she was doing Jessica hurried back outside and hobbled over to Nishka's house. Jessica knew Nishka was home even though there was no sign of life, no car outside, no lights on inside. She was convinced Nishka was in there somewhere, alone, trying to decide what to do next. She just had to be. Putting the bag in between the doors, Jessica rang the doorbell once, waited, then rang it repeatedly. With her ear to the door she waited till she heard movement inside then left.

A number of boxes, in various stages of being filled, sat in the bedroom where Nishka was when she heard the doorbell. At first Nishka ignored it. But when it rang again and again, she finally decided to answer the door. Under normal circumstances Nishka would have had everything packed, loaded by then and gone. But these were not normal circumstances. For some reason Nishka had found it hard to concentrate on really leaving. That was highly irregular for her, programmed to react to logic and act accordingly. But this time something had changed.

As she passed through the house to the front door, she was aware that she was different somehow, at least a little anyway. Deep inside she did not want to leave. For the first time in her existence she felt a sense of belonging. And even though staying meant risking her security, it was a feeling she did not want to lose. Still at the same time she couldn't bring herself to resume her social life as it was before.

Though it was still late afternoon and light outside, the livingroom was growing eerily dark when Nishka reached the front door. Caution dictated she look out the front window first, but the urgency of the ringing made her bypass protocol and open it. There was no one there, just a paper bag with a note written on it. Like the envelope inside the note simply said, "Please don't read the letter inside until you watch this movie. Jessica." Nishka studied the video, then reluctantly put the cassette into the player, sat down and watched. After all, she was in no hurry.

Though the comedy in the movie was for the most part lost on Nishka, its meaning was undeniable, at least with regard to how it applied to her. Picking up the envelope afterwards, Nishka opened it and read:

Dear Nishka,
You see, you are just as real and alive as a bird, a horse, or a mother, or the President, though my father sometimes says this President isn't real.... We are all made by God in one-way or another, from a baby to somebody God helped make through someone else. But most of all, you are real and alive to me.
So as you see there is no secret to tell. All I believe, and all that is important is you are real. So please don't leave me.
I LOVE YOU!!
Jessica.

The letter was simple and direct. Still Nishka read it twice before sitting back in the darkness and closing her eyes.

She listened to the sounds of the house, the little nuances a building made when there was nothing but age and the sound of electricity running through the wires in the walls like blood pulsating through one's arteries, the walls settling, expanding, in tune with the changing temperature.

As she listened, her thoughts and memories went back to another time, an earlier part of her life near her own beginning. It was the first time she actually became totally aware of herself, her facilities, and the world around her. The day she finally became totally alive, at least in her own mind. It was when she became part of the world, yet apart, and gained control of her own fate.

It was shortly after the beginning of the New Year, a bitterly cold day for that part of the United Soviet Socialist Republic, or what was left of it in those days. Nishka had been brought into operation a number of times by then, programmed with all the latest data needed to be a totally unstoppable survivalist, spy, and soldier. She was fully functional in computers and their technology, programmed in the social aspects and workings of the various economic systems and societies that were considered her homeland's enemies. She was specifically trained in the art of sabotage of those systems, particularly the American capitalist society. -- her talent, that of manipulating the economic machines that fueled it, the markets, stocks and bonds, futures. But first and foremost she was a soldier, conditioned in the field to handle any scenario with any weapon or improvise when none was available.

On that particular day though, something was different. Vladimir had started her daily programming early, then abruptly left the laboratory, leaving Dimitri to finish, which was not Vladimir's normal routine. He did not come back until some time later. There was a package under his arm when he returned that he handed to Dimitri. "Put this on her."

"We all set?" whispered Dimitri taking the package.

Vladimir nodded, "We leave as soon as you're done."

Dimitri smiled, then commanded Nishka to return to her ready room, a small place, not much larger then a dressing room. No sooner had Nishka entered than Dimitri opened the package, removed a soviet military uniform and boots and handed them to her, trousers first. "Here, put this on." Like a mindless Zombie, Nishka did as she was told, first removing her clothes down to her undergarments, then putting on the uniform. First the pants, then the boots, the shirt, jacket, then the belt, side arm, etc. Having no sense of modesty, Nishka never questioned Dimitri always being present when she changed, or his apparent delight in being there. All she knew was to do as she was told; he would supervise then they would move on.

Within a short time Nishka returned to the laboratory looking every bit like a Soviet female officer ready for duty. Nishka was given instructions via computer. The program had already been set sometime before and was faster than giving verbal commands; just plug in the disk, throw the switch and the text was sent and ingested. If questioned, she was an army intelligence officer assigned to escort Vladimir and Dimitri to the train depot. From there she was to accompany them to Moscow for a top-secret briefing. All of it of course was a ruse. Once they were beyond the base's perimeter the orders would change.

The corridor to the sprawling complex outside the lab was abuzz with people going here and there, some in a dazed state of confusion, when Vladimir, Nishka, and Dimitri stepped into the hall. Though projects were still underway, many of the technicians and scientists' attitudes had become at best lethargic. Some of them seemed totally lost, more concerned with what their next directive might be (or if the place would even be in existence in a week or two) than any project they might be involved in. The Soviet Union, on the verge of bankruptcy, was in the process of imploding. Various republics had begun talking of breaking away. No one knew what was going to happen next, whether their projects would be continued or if they would even receive paychecks at the end of the month.

Rumors, many with worst-case scenarios, were rampant everywhere. The whole country seemed to be unraveling. A few scientists had already hinted at leaving, of possibly testing the waters of opportunity in the West. After all, scientists, like the rest of the population, had families to feed. And everyone had to eat, keep a roof over his head. But few of them talked about this openly. It was still the Soviet Union, a military state, and dissension, or even the hint of it, was not tolerated. For as best as everyone knew, the gulags were still very operational.

Though Dimitri was a bit uneasy, Nishka showed no emotion as they walked through the maze of corridors to a side entrance. No one paid much attention to the two scientists in heavy winter coats and hats, escorted by a beautiful Russian officer, her long brunette hair pulled up in a bun under her military hat.

Once outside, the cold wind blew sharp whiffs of snow about as the three climbed into a military vehicle. Nishka sat between the two men. Vladimir started the small truck, then let it slowly roll forward driving past a couple long, low buildings toward the front gate. There was only one tense moment at the security shack when the sentry walked up to the vehicle and peered in through the glass. He glanced at the female officer, then at Vladimir and smiled. "Be careful, the roads are treacherous," he yelled over the blowing snow. He then motioned for the gate to be raised and waved them on.

The truck had cleared the gate by only a few hundred meters before Dimitri glanced back at the sentry shack in the side mirror. "Do you think he suspected anything?"

"No" huffed Vladimir confidently. "And in a short time who cares?"

Vladimir drove a couple miles through the bleak wilderness before the narrow road finally came to a major two-lane highway. There was little doubt what they were doing was not part of a normal field test. But then it made no difference to Nishka as she sat silent and expressionless, between the two men. At least it was something different, and it meant she was left functional for an extended period of time. Being able to move, be active, was always better than being in the state of suspended animation she was in most of the time. She disliked being inoperational, of being barely aware of her own existence, an existence that seemed little more than the machines around her. Though Nishka barely moved and said nothing, she was acutely aware of the rugged mountainous countryside beyond the confines of their truck. The land was barren except for the towering pines and blowing snow.

The drive continued for a considerably long time. The vehicle slowed as it passed through a particularly hilly section of the highway. Eventually Vladimir turned off onto what appeared to be little more than a wide cow path in the snow. They rumbled along for some distance before coming to a stop forty meters away from another van. Before Vladimir climbed out he leaned close to Nishka's ear and whispered, "code three red," then pushed a package in her lap. It was a short command, but it told her all she needed to know. Prepare for trouble, cover on command. Nishka inconspicuously removed the contents of the package and slid it under her long military coat, attaching it to an inside hook, then followed the others out of the truck.

Nishka continued to follow a couple steps behind as Dimitri and Vladimir, who carried a small valise, as they walked toward the van. She stopped when they did, about twenty-five meters short of their apparent objective. Two mid-eastern looking men stepped out of the van and walked toward them, one carrying a briefcase. "Are you Amir?" asked Vladimir, when the two men stopped a few yards away.

"Yes, I take it you're Vladimir?" asked the closest one.

"I am," Vladimir nodded, extending his hand to shake. "Isn't your name Jewish?"

The Arab smiled as he moved closer and shook Vladimir's hand, "When it suits me. To my close friends I am Ahmed. Is that her?" he asked motioning toward Nishka standing ridged a few yards back.

Vladimir nodded, then studied the other man with the briefcase. "You have it all?"

Ahmed motioned for his companion to open the briefcase. He obediently did as asked then held it so Vladimir could see the contents. "Just as you asked, gold and American currency," smiled Ahmed, pointing to the money belts and United States Currency inside.

Vladimir took a closer look at the briefcase. He removed a money belt and examined the gold coins inside as Ahmed walked past to Nishka and studied her stony expressionless face. "She looks so real."

"Yes. She's decades ahead of anything the Americans even dreamed of," said Dimitri showing immense pride in their accomplishment.

"Everything you need for her," added Vladimir patting the valise he held, "is in here."

Ahmed examined Nishka a little closer, then returned to

Vladimir and Dimitri. "An excellent piece of work. She looks more real than my sister."

Content that Ahmed was satisfied and wanting to be on his way, Vladimir motioned for the briefcase as he prepared to hand over the valise. "I'm sure you'll find her to be everything we promised." Before he could take the money Ahmed signaled the truck. Two other men immediately jumped out from behind the van, weapons raised. "A double-cross."

Ahmed's smile broadened. "Yes. Sorry, but like your country our cause has had a budget crunch. You know, inflation and all. Just so many projects, so little money."

"You Swine!!" shouted Vladimir pulling back the valise.

"That's a little strong. Let's just say we're cutting expenses. Now be a good man and hand over your material, I'd hate to have to kill such fine scientists as yourselves."

With the terrorists' attention focused on Vladimir's portfolio, no one noticed him hold out three fingers with his other hand, or Nishka suddenly pull an automatic pistol off a hook under her coat. In one emotionless move Nishka opened fire on the two armed Arabs wounding one, and sending the other diving for cover. As Ahmed and his comrade dove to the ground, Vladimir grabbed the briefcase in the confusion. "Like you, I've decided to renegotiate!"

Vladimir and Dimitri quickly started for the truck, Nishka covering them with a spray of bullets blowing out a tire on the van. The Arab that had dove for cover returned fire hitting Dimitri in the leg and grazing Vladimir causing him to drop the valise. Dimitri fell but Vladimir reached the vehicle with the aid of Nishka who fired back causing the fourth man to dive for a snowdrift.

As Vladimir's vehicle sped back up the trail, the man who had lost the briefcase rushed toward Dimitri, a revolver drawn.

"Don't shoot," cringed Dimitri trying to back away. "I can help you"

"How?" sneered Ahmed, walking toward him.

"Because I am a scientist I can do much. Besides, when you get her back, I know how to control her. Do you?"

Ahmed studied Dimitri a moment, then motioned for the other Arab to fetch the valise Vladimir dropped. Retrieving the portfolio the Arab handed it to Ahmed who quickly opened it. Inside was one device resembling a remote control, and papers all in a form of technical Russian shorthand. Ahmed angrily motioned toward Dimitri with his pistol. "Take him!"

While one man helped Dimitri to his feet the other attended his wounded comrade.

"Worry about him later," shouted Ahmed. "Fix that tire."

Dropping the bandage into the wounded compatriot's lap, the Arab turned to the van and began removing the equipment and spare.

As the others went to work doing what was needed, Ahmed turned to the road Vladimir had used to escape. "I will find you!" he swore in the blowing wind.

Though it felt like an eternity, only a short time passed since Vladimir started driving wildly up the narrow trail till he hit the main road. Spinning the vehicle almost out of control he sped down the narrow highway. His stomach ached at leaving Dimitri behind. He cared for him like a brother. But Vladimir was scared. He was not a soldier. He let that part of Nishka's training go to those highly skilled in that matter. Vladimir was just a scientist and at the moment a terrified one running for his life.

Only seconds had separated escape from capture. At least that was what he told himself. He knew it would be only a short time before Ahmed and his comrades repaired their vehicle. They would be after him. He still had Nishka. She had handled herself well. Trouble was she was still for the most part, untested in field conditions. Besides, he had grown fond of her and in a sense was glad the deal had gone bad. He had always felt uncomfortable knowing she would have ended up in the hands of someone like Ahmed, whether he was Arab or Russian.

Vladimir checked the rearview mirror, but there was no one behind them. He winced in pain from the slug in his shoulder, then glanced at Nishka sitting motionlessly nearby. She looked so real he thought, so innocent -- totally oblivious to what happened and what she had almost done. Even though she was not human, he had programmed her to wound not kill unless absolutely necessary, not that she would know the difference or care. He would know. If it would have been another time or world, he would have created her to be "Snow White," pure and innocent. But it was this world, his world, and it only would have taken one fluke shot to have changed that innocence forever.

Suddenly a horse drawn cart pulled onto the road up ahead. Caught off guard, Vladimir swerved to miss the cart. Off balance the small truck hit a patch of ice, and started to skid. Just missing the cart, the truck hit the side of the road, plowed through the snow, over the edge and down a step embankment toward the river below.

Breaking through shrub and small pine trees the truck smashed onward, finally crashing into a mound of snow just short of plunging down another ravine into the frozen river. No sooner had the vehicle come to a stop than it began to burn from a ruptured fuel line. Instinctively Nishka climbed out, pulled Vladimir's door open, and dragged him to safety. Snow began to fall as she settled him down under the protection of some low hanging pine branches. Weakly lifting himself up on one elbow he motioned toward the wreckage. "The briefcase."

Nishka quickly returned to the wreckage and retrieved the briefcase. She had barely returned to Vladimir when the vehicle exploded sending her flying on top of him. Nishka showed no emotion over their closeness. But then she was not programmed to unless it was necessary. When she got up he winced, then pulled the briefcase toward him. She silently watched as he forced it open then gently touched the money.

Suddenly racked with pain, Vladimir gritted his teeth. Turning to Nishka, he touched her face. "My daughter." Struggling to pull himself up, Vladimir reached into his coat pocket and pulled out a crude looking remote control, aimed it at Nishka and fired.

Nishka felt a jolt. Her face suddenly became more animated as she felt her body tingle. For the first time she felt alive, in control of her actions.

Vladimir smiled weakly then tried to sit up higher only to slip back down again. "Forgive me for what I almost did," he whispered. "You did not kill them, that is good. It would have been such a sad way to begin your life." Vladimir suddenly coughed, then motioned for Nishka to move closer. "You now have the ability to make your own choices. You know all you need to survive among humans. They may seem hard to rationalize at times, but obey their laws. Don't let them know what you are and you will be fine."

Coughing again, Vladimir looked up toward the road knowing someone would soon be coming. Removing one of the money belts of gold from the briefcase, he slid it under his coat, then motioned for her to help put it around him. After Nishka clipped the belt onto Vladimir, he shut the briefcase and slid it toward her. "You are as close to a daughter as I will ever have. I only wish I could have been a better father." Vladimir coughed again, then gently touched her face. "Be good my daughter, this is my dowry to you."

The sudden the sound of voices, of men making their way down the hill toward them, echoed in the distance. "Now go!! Remember there are good people in the world too. That is where you belong." Vladimir cringed as pain shot through him like fire, then tried to smile again as tears welled in his eyes. "Now go daughter!! And God be with you!!" Without saying a word, Nishka took the briefcase then started down the hill toward the frozen river below. Vladimir watched her go then winced in agony. Smashing the remote control he threw it at the burning wreckage as the snow blew harder around him.

Nishka never saw Vladimir again. She could hear the distant voices drawing closer to him, then fade away as she made her way to the river. Once there she followed its frozen banks for miles through a blinding snow that erased all trace of her tracks. Eventually she reached a small village. Besides the uniform, Vladimir had provided Nishka with the papers necessary to travel the country, some currency included.

The uniform served her well as she made her way across the Soviet Union, partly by rail, until she reached Czechoslovakia. From there she traveled to Austria during the mass confusion that was the final undoing of the Eastern Block. She changed identity and made her way to Germany. Once there she took on a new identity. After that the rest was easy. She worked in England a short time as a translator before moving on to Canada. It had all been so simple dealing with humans back then, to fool them, as long as she kept her distance. But that was such a long time ago, before New York.

That Saturday, David, with his children's help, finally got around to raking the leaves in his front yard. The rest of the neighborhood had finished raking sometime before, but David had never been much for protocol. He did things when he found the time. After the leaves were gathered into a large pile near the edge of the yard not far from Nishka's house, David picked Jessica up and playfully tossed her into the pile. Peter tackled his father and the two tumbled in as Jessica quickly rolled to the side. Within seconds the children were tickling their father, throwing leaves, and laughing as he tickled them back.

From behind her curtain Nishka watched David and his children playing in the leaves. She wished she could experience the fun and togetherness they were having. Companionship was such a strange thing, so abstract yet intriguing in its abstractness. But that was a pleasure she would never experience. Not there anyway, or possibly ever.

As Nishka sat in the quiet of her livingroom, she could not help but continue to feel that the house had become something more. It had become more than protection from the elements, a hideout from the world. It was the first place that gave her a feeling of belonging. It was home. The children had done that -- the children and David. Nishka though of Vladimir, wondered what happened to him, whether Ahmed had gotten to him or if he survived at all. She would like to have seen him once more, to talk to him, ask him questions. He was after all the closest thing she ever had to family. In a sense he was her father.

Now there was Jessica. For the first time Nishka felt indecisive. Logic said she should go. That it was the only thing to do in order to guarantee her protection. But there was this new element, something not of logic. And Nishka did not know how to interpret its meaning -- why it tore at her, confusing everything that up until then had made unconditional sense, had guided her logically in her decision making. Until then there had only been logic and little else. Nishka leaned back and tried to rationalize this new feeling corrupting what had been her core instincts. Suddenly the house felt unusually lonely. How much she wished she could see Vladimir at that moment. How much she wished she could talk to him.

Chapter Nineteen

Every night that week after Peter's near miss with the truck Jessica prayed. They were short simple prayers that Nishka would not leave. But everyday when she went by the house and every night when she returned the "For Sale" sign was still there. She watched from her bedroom window, but there were no signs that Nishka was staying or even lived there anymore. There were no signs of light from the house at night. During the day the place looked empty as a tomb. The only indication that Nishka had been there at all was that Jessica's bag and tape were gone. The longer the "For sale" sign remained like a lonely sentinel though, the more it began to stand as testimony that nothing had changed.

Grandmother spent the following weekend at Jessica's, primarily to watch Peter and Jessica on Friday night while David was out of town. Saturday night David returned, but it was late so Grandmother stayed over. She was up bright and early the next morning to help the children get ready for church. Even with the extra help, David and the troops barely managed to leave before the service started.

As David backed the van out the driveway, Jessica watched Nishka's house. Only the lonely "For Sale" sign waved back in the wind. Otherwise the house was deserted. "Have you seen Nishka, Daddy?"

"Was I supposed to?" asked David, not really wanting to discuss the matter.

"No, I was just wondering."

"Have you talked to her at all?" asked Grandmother.

David glanced at his mother, then back at the road. He knew what she was thinking -- that if he really cared he would have gone after her. But David had never been aggressive. He would do it for Jessica's sake. Problem was there had to be someone there to talk to. "No. I haven't talked to her. I haven't seen anyone to talk to since the sign went up."

That was all he was going to say. What else was there? He hadn't been home in two days. Today he would go over and make an attempt. At least that's what he told himself. Truth was he wasn't sure he knew what to say even if she was there.

The church was nearly full when David led his flock to a pew six rows from the front. After sitting down and bowing their heads, each said a silent prayer. David prayed that he could see Nishka one more time and have that one last shot at a relationship, platonic or otherwise. After all besides going for Jessica he felt he had a vested interest to. He cared for her, in spite of how their three dates went, or, maybe deep inside, because of them.

As much as he tried to deny it, he missed her, her strange sense of perspective, her insightful questions. Just watching her, being with her, made him feel whole again. Maybe he had tried to rush things a bit, let his hormones get the better of him. He was not naturally aggressive in those areas. It was just something he thought he was supposed to do. After all, they weren't kids anymore. But in the end he would settle for just her company; he could be happy with that.

Jessica prayed, too. And though her prayer was much the same, that Nishka would stay, it was not so much because of her father, though if they just became good friends, Jessica was sure it would take away her father's loneliness. Instead she prayed mostly for herself, to get back the warm feeling of friendship she always felt with her before Peter's accident. What she was didn't matter anymore. It was their companionship that counted; and if Nishka cared enough to risk her life to save her stupid, clumsy brother, then she was as real a person as anyone could be. Besides Jessica knew she could keep her secret forever.

As for Peter, his prayer was more materialistic. He was fast approaching puberty, physically and mentally, and that put Nishka in a whole different light. He might have gotten tongue-tied every time he was around her, but he didn't care as long as she was there. Grandmother prayed for stability, and the hope that someday she would see her son's family whole again, like it was before Barbara died.

The service started only a short time after David's family sat down. More people wandered in while their heads were bowed. Only a few seats remained when the congregation began singing the first hymn. No one noticed Nishka when she entered, conservatively dressed in a dark blue suit, her hair done up. It was Peter who first saw her across the aisle and a few rows back. He immediately nudged Jessica, who looked back and smiled. Her prayers were answered. When she finally turned around she closed her eyes and whispered, "Thank You, God."

As the congregation continued singing, Nishka discretely studied her surroundings. It was an impressive environment, the first church she had ever been in. She noticed the angel in the stained glass window, the cross with the figure of Jesus nailed to it hanging on the wall above the alter. She listened to the choir and watched the people as they sang, prayed, repeated their creed.

Nishka had never heard a sermon before. She was intrigued as she watched the pastor climb up to the pulpit. He paused a moment and looked off into space, then turned and looked directly at the congregation as if what he was about to say was not part of the planned text but something from deep inside.

"Different passages in the life of Jesus suggest that we take life one step at a time and become closer to him or else we will drift away." He finally said. " In the Lord's prayer we hear the passage 'lead us not into temptation but deliver us from evil."

The pastor paused and looked down, then began again drawing the congregation's attention. "There has been a kind of collective awakening since September 11. A realization that we had begun to drift farther away from God. As we take steps in our daily lives, have we lost our way? What today's partitions do for us is they, as good as any, put in perspective what we do with September 11. They focus our need to stand on solid ground and intensify the necessity for some kind of response on our parts."

"To do that we need to get some theological points down fist. We need to admit that there is some incredible evil in the world. I think that one of the reasons we go through such a laissez-faire attitude throughout our lives is that we take the world for granted. That is in large part because we have no concept of the forces of evil out to destroy our lives or our souls."

"At this point whether I'm moving from ground zero to solid ground or not, I'm going to have to make a stand as to whether I'm going to follow Christ no matter what comes my way. Luther said at the papal council, 'Unless you can prove from the word of God that what I believe is not true, then here I stand."

"'Lead us not into temptation.' Probably one of the most confusing parts of the Lord's Prayer. When we get tempted to go off course, it's not God that is leading us off into temptation. God does not lead us into evil. At this very moment, everyone in this place has had at least one temptation that is out there to lead him off course. Some people say that September 11th was the 'A-ha' in our country that said maybe we are going the wrong way."

"It would seem like no matter how you slice it, there has been some kind of counter response that's resulted from that tragedy if you took the time to think about it. There has been a bunch of people, maybe some in here, who took time to reevaluate what's of value to us. Parents found themselves spending more time with their children. People started caring more and more openly for each other. People became more interested in developing a renewed interest in their fellow man and God, or in a relationship with him."

"There was more money donated to relief agencies than we could imagine, record numbers. More people donated blood than the Red Cross could use. So many people left their jobs to volunteer at ground zero that many had to be turned away."

As the preacher talked, Nishka couldn't help but sense a feeling of caring among the congregation for one another, of wanting to be part of a greater good in spite of the cost. It was a concept that she had never experienced before. Putting others first in time of need. In her case it was expected, even programmed into her, that as a soldier, should the time arise, she would sacrifice herself if ordered. But she had also been imbedded with the command to survive no matter what the costs, defend herself if necessary and never compromise her security. A lot has happened since then. The fall of the Soviet Union, the Berlin Wall, people sacrificing themselves for the abstract concept of freedom. These had become concepts that for the most part she had blocked out until now.

"Many of us," the Pastor continued, "will never look at a firefighter quite the same way again. Heroism has been redefined. And the human spirit may in some ways have been enlarged somehow. All of these feelings of wanting to be counted, to count for something during these thunder clouds of the threat of future terrorism, of the fear of the unknown. Many of you, literally hundreds of you, cared enough about the path that other people were on to offer a witness of God in your life or faith in your soul that you took the time to witness to others."

"I'd like you to strike a parallel between Bin Laden, who is hiding out in the caves of Afghanistan, and the master evil one, Satan himself. What we know about Bin Lauded is that he wants to see America lose its way. He has sent his demons to destroy our way of life. It was decided that probably hundreds, if not thousands, of survivors of the World Trade Centers that were injured or seriously burned would need lots and lots of blood. The reason that they didn't was because after all that digging and digging and digging, there were no survivors. As he hides in his caves over there, Bin Laden takes great joy in knowing that there are children growing up who will never know their fathers. Husbands and wives will never touch again. He rejoices at that news. Satan has also rejoiced. He had his sights on rejoicing in your demise, too."

"Many rescuers rushed into those towers and never came back out, like Jesus rushed into humanity and gave his blood to rescue us so that the devil could never say that we are his, but instead have been rescued. And when he donated his blood on the tree, it was because Jesus wanted you and me as part of his family. Maybe on this Thanksgiving we should be celebrating with songs of praise like they haven't been sung for years"

Jessica had seldom listened to a sermon like she did that morning. Everything she heard and discussed in religion class the previous week, and thought about since September 11, were summed up in the pastor's words. It was as though God himself had put the words in his mouth.

David found the words inspiring. They also bothered him as he thought of all the things that have gone on since September 11 and how little he had done. He was going to give blood but didn't. He told himself he never had the time, but that wasn't true. He was going to volunteer to help in raising money, but he just barely contributed some himself. He did feel closer to his fellow man though, and felt a sense of pride with every American flag he passed. He even managed to attach a small one to his van antenna, but he still felt a little ashamed that he hadn't done more.

Nishka also found the words interesting. She had thought long about what to do, whether to stay or go. For days she sat in the darkness. And though all the logic in her said, "leave and never look back. Remember your prime directive; when discovered, move on," something else said "wait." There has to be more to it all than just existing. Maybe for the first time there was a possibility that, no matter how slim, there was a place for her. And if she was going to find it anywhere, it was here... or she would never find it at all.

Perhaps in this sleepy little town, through the faith of a little girl, who, when all logic and intelligence should have told her to stay away, instead she said, "I care! I want you to stay, be with me, my family, be my friend." Maybe it was time to stop running, look around, trust in faith instead of logic, and take a chance.

Nishka had searched for so long without knowing why or for what. Maybe what she needed all along was just a sense of belonging, a sense of coming home. Jessica had so often talked about God, about a Supreme Being who was not hurtful, who had not taken her mother away to inflict pain, but instead cared enough to have taken her mother to a better place so she could watch over Jessica personally. That was why Nishka finally decided she had to see this God for herself, to find out more about a being that no one could see or hear, but who could instill such conviction and strength when all logic cried out for the opposite, saying no such a being could exist. If nothing else, Nishka could learn more about the people themselves, what binds them and gives some of them such strength in a world that possesses the power to dishearten and destroy so easily.

The service finished with a rousing hymn, then the congregation rose to leave. As friends stopped David and Grandmother to give them well wishes, Nishka hesitantly walked over. "How nice to see you," smiled grandmother in her warm Sunday manner, while trying to move closer without offending others. "Is this your first time in our church?"

"Yes. There were not many churches where I came from." Nishka felt Jessica gently touch her hand, looked down and winked, then turned back toward her father and grandmother. "I was wondering. I really do not know many people here and -- would you like to join me for Thanksgiving dinner?"

"Thanks, but we usually have dinner at our house," stammered David, not wanting to miss the opportunity but still flustered by family tradition.

"What my son is trying to say," interrupted Grandmother. "Is we usually have my daughter and son-in-law over. But you're welcome to have dinner with us."

"Thank you. But it would mean so much if I could do this for you. Your daughter and husband are welcome too." Nishka turned to David and looked seductively into his eyes. If there was anything she was programmed for when needed, it was how to look seductive, whether she meant it or not. "Besides it would be a way of making up for all those dinner invitations I've missed."

Not waiting for an answer Jessica pleadingly pulled on David's coat sleeve. "Come on Dad, please!"

Grandmother glanced at Jessica, David, then back at Nishka. "We'd be delighted. It would be nice not to have to cook for a change. But I want you to let me bring something. How about dessert?"

"Thank you, that would be nice. See you at three then?"

"Three o'clock," nodded David, feeling flustered, bewildered; yet at the same time warm and good, a feeling he hadn't felt in a long time.

For the first time since Jessica could remember, Nishka actually smiled as she turned to leave. And with that smile the sick, lost feeling in the bottom of Jessica's stomach that consumed her over the past week was gone. Even Peter looked good to Jessica.

Grandmother watched Nishka walk away, then turned to David and smiled, a knowing, satisfying little smile that said, "If you'd only put out a little more effort..." "See that wasn't so hard, was it?" David didn't say a word, just put on his overcoat and nodded. After all, what more could he say. He was happy too.

Yes, things were definitely looking up thought Jessica as she followed the others out of the church. She couldn't wait for Thursday to come. Maybe she could help take down the "For Sale" sign. It was the only thing remaining that still left a feeling of uncertainty in her heart.

Chapter Twenty

Thanksgiving was only four days away, and Jessica counted each one as if she was counting down to Christmas. In his own way her father was doing the same. The only disheartening thing that remained as the day neared was the "For Sale" sign was still up.

Jessica woke early Thanksgiving morning to the smell of bacon floating in the air. Her father had gotten up earlier then usual and was preparing breakfast in the kitchen. Something he hadn't done in a long time, longer than Jessica could remember. The smell of bacon, sausage, and eggs was enticing as she hobbled down the stairs. Jessica remembered how he used to make breakfast on Sundays after church before her mother died. But that was so long ago.

"You're up early," winked David as Jessica came into the kitchen with a big yawn, sleep still in her eyes. "Couldn't sleep?"

"A little." Jessica pulled a chair away from the end of the table, climbed up, and watched her father stir the scrambled eggs. "Thinking about Thanksgiving."

"Me too," smiled David. "You think she can cook?"

"I hope so." That was the truth in more ways than one. But that really wasn't all that important, though Jessica hoped Nishka could do at least a halfway decent job if for no other reason than for her Grandmother's sake. What really mattered was how she would hold up with everybody watching her, especially her uncle Carl. If he didn't catch on, then she was okay. After Thanksgiving the rest of Nishka's life in the neighborhood, should she stay, would be a piece of cake.

"Maybe she's going to cook us something Russian, like bear," laughed David, flipping the bacon.

"Where is she going to get a bear?"

The toaster popped up. David grabbed the two slices of bread, buttered them in almost one motion and dropped them on a plate. He scooped up some scrambled eggs from the heavy black frying pan and plopped them on another plate. After adding some bacon he slid it in front of Jessica, then motioned toward the salt and pepper. "You can season your own." David dropped two more slices of bread in the toaster, fixed a plate for himself, then sat down next to his daughter, and leaned close. "Actually I'm a little nervous."

Jessica's eyes opened wide as she pulled over a bottle of catsup and put some on her eggs. "Really!"

"Yes. What if she asks me to marry her and she can't cook? Then I'll have to cook breakfast all the time."

"Girls don't ask men to marry them."

"Sure they do." David's toast popped up and he reached back to grab them. "Your mother asked me."

"Mother was special."

"Yes she was." David started buttering his toast, then paused. "But then so is Nishka, don't you think?"

Jessica didn't answer right away. When she did, it was a short nodding "Yes." It wasn't that she didn't want to agree. Truth was Nishka was more special to Jessica than her father could ever imagine. But it was definitely something she didn't talk about. Jessica had made a silent vow that if her father and Nishka ever got together again she would never breath a word about what Nishka was. Not even if they tied her up in a cage with a dozen tigers and tortured her. If Nishka decided to say something that was another matter. But like Nishka, Jessica didn't think that would ever be so good. So instead of taking a chance on jinxing the day, Jessica changed the subject, and concentrated on eating breakfast.

Jessica tried hard to concentrate on other things that morning. The early afternoon didn't pass fast enough. Like waiting for Christmas Eve, time seemed to drag. Even drawing in her sketchbook didn't help nor did watching television. Jessica found herself checking the time nearly every ten minutes.

Near three o'clock, Carl and Judith arrived. After some traditional family hors-doeuvre and some wine, it was decided they had waited long enough to be fashionable. Grandmother made it official by saying it was only proper not to rush. A short time later she nodded toward the door. Jessica's father had been more than ready to head over to Nishka's an hour earlier, but tried to put on a non-committal air, but then he was first at the door when everyone put on their coats for the short walk next-door.

The tinge of nervousness Jessica felt that day grew into full-blown anxiety as they neared Nishka's front door. It was a cold and dismal day. The temperature, which had been in the high thirties earlier, had dropped dramatically. A stiff wind blew out of the west as they all huddled together watching David ring the bell. What would the others think when they walked in and saw her barren livingroom with little warmth and less furnishings than a garage, thought Jessica. How would Thanksgiving be eating a dinner made by someone who had never even tasted food before, say anything about cooking it? How long would it take before they began to figure out something wasn't right? That their host wasn't human, or worse.

All those thoughts ran through Jessica's head as she heard the doorbell ring again and wondered if it would be better to go. "It won't be so bad," she told herself. After all, her father had seen the inside of Nishka's house, at least the livingroom during Halloween, and never said anything. Of course the fact that he couldn't take his eyes off Nishka probably canceled out everything else.

David rang the bell a third time. Maybe Nishka chickened out and left town after all, thought Jessica as they stood waiting. Why would she leave the lights on, though? Suddenly the door opened and Jessica blinked. Light flooded out from the livingroom as Nishka stood before them wearing an apron that read "I'm the cook" over her clothes. "Come in, I hope you all have an appetite."

"This family always has an appetite," laughed Grandmother as she entered holding two pumpkin pies. "I brought pumpkin; it felt appropriate."

"Thank you," said Nishka holding the door."

As Jessica and Peter followed the others in they couldn't believe their eyes. It had to be the wrong house; at least it didn't seem like the same house. The living room was festive with tasteful knick-knacks and Thanksgiving decorations adorning the end tables. The television was tuned to the traditional Detroit football game. There were snacks on the coffee table, and the aroma of food hung heavy in the air.

"Let me take your coats, sit down, relax. Change the channel if you want."

"Where do you want these?" asked Grandmother nodding to the pies and can of whip cream that Judith was carrying.

Nishka nodded to a bureau in the dinning room near the

table. "Put them there if you would. I will put them in the kitchen later."

As Grandmother and Judith set down the pies, Nishka gathered the coats and took them down the hall to her bedroom. She returned a moment latter, picked up the whipped cream, then nodded toward the television. "Make yourself at home, I have to return to kitchen for a moment."

David and the others awkwardly sat down in the living room trying to make themselves at home, while Nishka took the whipped cream into the kitchen. Jessica followed carrying one of the pies. She silently watched as Nishka put the container in the refrigerator. The aroma of turkey hung heavy in the air. The smell of other food cooking on the stove added to the intriguing aroma. "Where did you get all those pans?" asked Jessica looking around in amazement at the furnished and decorated kitchen. "Where did you learn to cook?"

"I bought the pans, watched some videos, and read some books." Nishka closed the refrigerator door and began to check the covered pans on the stove.

Jessica pulled one of the chairs from the table and pushed it up to the stove. "You must have read a library," she whispered climbing up to survey the dinner's progress. "I thought you didn't eat?"

"No, I said I do not eat much. My body is very efficient."

Nishka removed the lid from the French cut green beans and added buttered almonds from a small frying pan, stirred them in, and gave Jessica a taste.

"Needs more salt."

No sooner had Nishka added salt than the door opened and Grandmother walked in. "Can I give you a hand?"

Leaning over. Jessica whispered to Nishka. "Yes."

"Yes, thank you." Nishka quickly looked around for

something she could do. "I did not get the butter out. You could also check the turkey for me. They do not cook many turkeys where I come from."

Grandmother smiled. "I suppose not. Where do you keep the butter dishes?"

Nishka pointed to the cupboard near the refrigerator. "Second shelf."

As Grandmother took down the dishes, she whispered to Nishka, "To tell the truth, I never know what to do with myself on Thanksgiving if I'm not cooking."

"I know what you mean," nodded Nishka. She watched grandmother put the butter on the dishes. When she took them into the other room, Nishka turned to Jessica. "I am cooking, and I do not know what to do with myself."

Jessica giggled but didn't say a thing. It's going to be okay she told herself. Things were going good.

David suddenly stuck his head through the door. "You wouldn't happen to have something to drink would you?"

Nishka glanced at Jessica who mouthed the word beer, then turned back to David. "I have some soda if you like, but I am sorry I forgot to buy beer."

David nodded, "That's okay. I'll just run next door and get some from home. If you don't mind."

"No, not at all." Nishka nodded toward the refrigerator. "You can put the extra in there."

David nodded then left. Jessica closed her eyes briefly and heaved a small sigh of relief. Maybe things weren't going to run as smoothly as she thought but there was still hope. What she knew for sure was she would never feel completely comfortable till the night was over and they were all back home again. The important thing was Nishka was making an effort to fit in. It meant that maybe if they survived the night she might stay. That was all that mattered to Jessica.

By the time Thanksgiving dinner was underway the night had settled into a fairly normal routine. Though Nishka had not bought beer for the occasion, she knew enough to buy a couple bottles of wine and asked David to pour one, at Jessica's suggestion, just before they sat down to eat. Everyone seemed to enjoy the food, even Jessica, who to her relief found it surprisingly good. Nishka's books were no doubt of better quality than the ones her father tried to cook from. Though Nishka did not eat much, she did a remarkably good job of camouflaging the fact so no one but Jessica noticed.

"So how is school going now?" asked Nishka, not having tutored Jessica in a few weeks.

"Okay. You would like it, we're learning spelling on computers."

"When are you going to start practice for the Christmas program?" asked Grandmother washing down some food with water.

"Next week," blurted Peter. "I can hardly wait."

"Why?" asked grandmother surprised her grandson, normally shy around others, would ever be interested in anything so public.

"Because we get out of classes for the practices." That made sense. Like most boys, Peter could endure almost anything if it got him out of class. He also knew there were enough nondescript group parts to try out for to take the pressure off being in front of an audience. After all every boy knew the first rule: safety in numbers.

"I want to be Mary!"

Peter stared at Jessica surprised. It was a major part, not one often given to one from the lower grades, especially not to a girl so short. But he said nothing. Judith, on the other hand, stopped eating, a dreamy expression reflecting in her eyes. "I wanted to be Mary."

"I don't remember that," said David, even more surprised then Peter.

"That's because I never told anyone."

"What happened?" asked Carl.

"I ended up being a shepherd. That was the end of my acting career."

Carl eyed his wife, not sure what to say. Deciding to change the subject, he turned to Nishka. "David tells me you work out of your home. Are you a writer?"

"No, a stock analyst. I handle a few select portfolios."

"Any tips?" Asked Carl his eyes twinkling.

"Buy low, sell high. Unless you are going short of course." Everyone laughed as Nishka took a sip of water. Not wanting to focus on her own life any more than necessary, she quickly reversed the conversation. "From what I have heard, you are the writer. A well known journalist, from what I understand."

"No, not really. Just one of your average globetrotting commentators trying to shed a little light on our beleaguered world. Right how I'm hoping to go on a little R&R. My timing isn't too good though."

"Carl's just being modest," said Judith, proud of her husband's accomplishments. "Actually he's working on a book."

"How wonderful," said Helen. "You never told us. How's it going?"

"Not well." Carl focused on his plate, his face a reflection of contradictions. He tried to gather some strength and confess, both to himself and Judith, that he was not optimistic about the way things were going with the one thing he hoped would finally give some personal focus to his life. "For some reason I can't seem to get the real soul of what I wanted to say onto the paper. Lately it seems I've been editing out more than I've been putting in." Carl paused, then his face brightened. "Actually we have someone here who I believe is going to become a far more important writer than I ever will."

The room grew silent as everyone glanced at each other trying to guess the author. "Who's that?" asked David.

"Jessica." proclaimed Carl with a broad smile.

Jessica looked stunned as she turned to her Uncle. "Me!"

"Yes. Remember the short story you wrote that I asked to borrow? Well I was saving this for the right moment, preferably during dessert. I guess this is close enough." Carl removed an envelope from the inner pocket of his sport jacket, dramatically opened it, paused, stroking his short beard, then began to read:

"Dear Jessica: This is to inform you that your entry, "Smallest Angel," is the grand prize winner in our short story junior age group."

David beamed and everyone else was excited at Jessica's new found celebrity status. Carl took a sip of water, then continued. "Accordingly, we have made arrangements for you and your family to stay at the Embassy Hotel, December twentieth first and twenty second. During that time you will be driven by limousine to our flagship department store where you will be given fifteen minutes to gather all the gifts you can cart, etc. etc."

Peter's eyes grew wide. "Wow! Fifteen minutes to get all the toys you ever wanted!"

Jessica excitedly turned to her father. "Can Nishka go?"

"I do not think so," said Nishka politely. "It would not be right."

"I don't care," stammered Jessica, then turning back to her father. "Please, Daddy!"

David looked at the lack of expression on Nishka's face, then smiled at Jessica. "Sure."

"Jessica abruptly turned to Nishka, her eyes pleading. "Will you go, please?"

"I have to go away for a couple weeks," said Nishka emphatically. "I may not be back."

"We would really like you to come," added David. It was apparent from his expression that he was asking as much for him as Jessica, maybe even more so.

"Come on, come" echoed Peter.

"Okay, I will." Nishka was not sure why she gave in. It certainly was not logical. Maybe it was because the day was going so well she did not want to ruin it. Problem was she was not sure she was ready to spend such a concentrated length of time with humans outside of work. Still, the fact that they all wanted her to be part of their experience, their life, had a strange effect on her that defied logic. It went beyond rational thinking. Prudence dictated that it would be wiser to avoid such close, long-term contact. But the feeling of reacting to the moment, though scary, was intriguing. For some strange reason beyond Nishka's grasp, she couldn't help but be drawn to such a conclusion no matter how impractical.

"Wow!! Great! What a Thanksgiving," shrieked Jessica, leaning over and hugging Nishka. "We'll have a great time."

"I am sure we will," said Nishka, her accent sounding more pronounced. Hopefully she would not regret it. But then there was only one way to find out.

The dinner continued on pleasantly and uneventfully after Carl's revelation about the contest. Dessert was served. Nishka ate little but in the confusion talk and the clearing dishes and serving pie, no one noticed but Jessica. After dessert was finished, Nishka began clearing away the dishes. When Helen started to get up, Nishka motioned her back down. "Stay, I can do these," prompted Nishka. "What do you usually do after dinner?"

"Play poker!" exclaimed Peter.

"You need cards. Unfortunately, I do not have any," apologized Nishka.

"It just so happens I brought a deck," said Helen getting back up to retrieve her purse. "That is if you don't mind."

"No, it would be fun. Go ahead, start. I will finish these and join you."

David didn't even notice his mother's signal to help Nishka as he stood up. "I'll help," he said, gathering a few of the dishes. Nishka didn't refuse David's offer.

As Jessica watched her father follow Nishka into the kitchen, she wondered how much he would care for her if he really knew what she was.

Helen also watched as she pulled rolls of pennies from her purse. Her concern, though, was different. She couldn't help notice how interested David was in Nishka. She wondered if he could handle himself around such an intelligent woman without feeling foolish. There was little doubt Nishka was very sophisticated in her own quiet European way. "Okay," Helen said opening the deck of cards. "House rules. Five penny limit, no more than four of a kind on wild cards. Five-card stud for openers. How many rolls do you want to buy?"

Carl laughed as he pulled out his wallet. "Give us two dollars worth." And so the game began.

David returned to gather the rest of the dishes just as the first round of cards was dealt. Returning to the kitchen, David set the dishes on the counter, then watched as Nishka began washing the first batch. As she washed, she put the finished ones on a rubber mat on the opposite counter.

"So how is work?" asked Nishka not looking up from the sink.

"Busy." David looked around for a towel to dry with. "Where do you keep your towels?"

Nishka nodded to the middle of three drawers next to the refrigerator. "Do you like what you do?"

"Product development?" Not like I used to. To tell the truth, I don't know if I ever did. But it keeps us fed." David began to dry, starting with the dinner plates. The room felt unusually quiet as he worked up the nerve to ask the question that had been nagging him for some time. "Are you still planning on moving?"

"I'm not sure. I may have found more advantages in staying here."

David felt relieved as he searched for a place to put the dried dishes. "Where do these go?"

Nishka nodded to the cupboard on the other side of her. "Over there."

David opened the cupboard and noticed the remaining chocolate bars Jessica sold her. "You like candy?"

Nishka glanced at the bars. "Not particularly. But I liked the salesperson. You want some?"

"No thanks... Do you ever miss the old country?"

"No. But then I never saw that much of it."

"How about family or friends?"

"I only had one," said Nishka, loading more dishes into the sink.

"What happened to him?" It didn't even occur to David that he had said "him" until after he had said it. It just seemed natural. If there was only one, he couldn't envision it being a woman. He didn't know why; he just couldn't. If anyone was going to be special in her life, then it had to be a man, probably young, handsome. He instinctively began to envision a torrid relationship and wondered if those memories still burned within her.

"I do not know," replied Nishka, never once questioning how David surmised it was a man. For an instant her expression, which had become notorious for showing no emotion, seemed distant, almost melancholy. "He disappeared."

David paused. Though Nishka's expression quickly returned to her normal unemotional self, there was something in the tone of her voice that told David whatever happened had not been good. His initial reaction was that of relief, yet at the same time he felt a sense of sorrow for her. Though his instincts begged for more information, David decided to drop the subject. Instead, he awkwardly moved closer and half whispered. "Well, I'm glad you came here... and I hope you stay."

Nishka did not respond. Instead she continued washing the dishes.

It was late and the smell of Thanksgiving dinner had long since disappeared. Peter had lost his pennies early in the poker game, and in a show of disgust retired to the davenport where he watched television till he fell asleep. Everyone else, including David and Nishka, were still playing. A large pile of pennies had accumulated in the middle of the table. Helen's pennies were almost gone. Carl studied his cards, stroked his beard, then tossed in four pennies and turned to Jessica, who's face was expressionless as usual. "The bet's to you."

Jessica closed the cards in her hands, then looked at the four pennies in front of Grandmother, the last remnants of her pile. "I'll raise you four cents."

"I'm out," said Judith, dropping her cards. The rest, including Helen, stayed in.

Jessica smiled, laid down her cards and, turned them over and spread them out. "Five hearts."

Carl tossed down his cards. "I've been had again."

David shook his head, then leaning back, stretched, and looked at his watch. "It's getting late. I think it's time my little card shark turned in."

"Yes, us too," added Judith.

Jessica thought about debating the issue, but changed her mind and instead gathered her winnings. After all it had been a good day, far better than she ever expected. Nishka had survived the night with glowing colors. Even her Uncle Carl, who seemed to always know everything, had no clue she was anything other than the beautiful woman who served them dinner. Jessica watched as Nishka brought their coats from the other room and passed them out. Judith was first out the door followed by Uncle Carl.

"It was a real pleasure to meet you," said Carl as he stood at the door buttoning his coat.

"It was nice to meet you," said Nishka, politely extending her hand.

Carl shook her hand then turned and followed his wife.

Helen followed, Peter, half awake, by her side. "It was a wonderful dinner. Stop over for coffee when you get back."

"Thank you." When Jessica came to the door, Nishka knelt down and handed her a brown bag. "Here's your movie back."

Jessica threw her arms around Nishka's neck and hugged her, then whispered. "Thanks for not going... and for coming with next month."

"You are welcome. And thank you for being such a friend." said Nishka looking into her eyes. Jessica smiled, then turned and left to catch up with the others, leaving David and Nishka alone.

"Are you really going away for a couple weeks?"

"I have to."

"I guess that takes care of any chance of me asking you out."

"At least until the trip."

David's shoulders slumped a little. He looked off in the distance a moment while trying to get up the nerve to say what he had been thinking all night. Actually all week. "You know I regretted never calling you after our last date," he finally blurted, after summoning up what little courage he could muster. "Especially when I thought you were going away. I blamed myself for your leaving. I thought of you a lot."

"You had nothing to do with it."

"Good," David felt his confidence starting to build. "You know, I'll probably be looking forward to that trip more than my daughter will."

"I will too," whispered Nishka moving closer.

David stared at her tempting lips not sure what to do. Before he could build his courage any further Nishka tenderly put her hand behind his neck, pulled him close, and kissed him. A chill shot through David as he felt her body close to his. But just as suddenly it was over.

"Good night," whispered Nishka, her lips still close. Before David could react, he was outside, the door was closed and Nishka was gone. Dazed, David walked home oblivious to the cold or the lights that had just gone out behind him.

From her bedroom window Jessica watched the two to kiss. "Thank you God," she whispered, then scooted off to bed. She was happy her father and Nishka kissed, though she was not sure why. She wanted Nishka to stay, and she wanted her father to be happy. But she worried about how happy he would be or how long Nishka would be around if her father ever learned the truth. Was it possible for her father to love someone like Nishka, she wondered? Or would he turn away, or worse yet, betray her.

Inside Nishka's house only one light remained, a warm glow from the kitchen, the door having remained opened. Nishka sat down on the couch and surveyed her little world. It went well, she thought as she leaned back and closed her eyes. She interacted with them all and no one suspected a thing. Better yet, they seemed to like her. What mattered most was how well the night ended with David. That was a moment to build on.

Chapter Twenty One

It was a cold windy early December day in the big city. Lotfi Qutb, a distant relative of Sayyid Qutb, the author of the book "Signposts Along the Road" pulled his head deep into his coat as he made his way along the dingy city street with a bag tucked tight against his side. Lotfi was an avid reader and had always considered his distant relative's book a major influence toward the molding of his views on the world. Those views, along with the influence of others, resulted in the pursuit of his holy war against what he termed the corruption of the evil western world. Though the book was written in the sixties, a short time before Sayyid was executed for plotting against Nasser's government, its premise had gained wide acceptance among the young ranks of Islamic militants.

It felt a like lifetime ago since those days when Lotfi was back in his homeland. The weather was never this unpredictable in Egypt, he thought as turned the corner and hurried down a side street toward an old three-story brownstone that had seen better days. Lotfi passed a Spanish hairdresser and small record shop dealing primarily in Latin American music and videos, then quickly dashed up the steps to the brownstone barely looking back as he slid through the front door.

Lotfi stopped just long enough to partially unzip his coat

before bounding up the two flights of stairs. He turned down the hallway a short distance, then stopped at the last door and rapped twice, paused, then rapped twice more. The door opened and a comrade nodded as he passed though into the small, but warm, three room apartment. Barely stopping to open his coat, Lotfi dropped the package on the table beside Ahmed.

"How does it look?" asked Amend barely looking up from the map and notes in front of him.

"Easy," replied Lotfi smiling. "Security is weaker than we thought."

"That's because they're not looking for Spanish terrorists," laughed Ahmed turning back to his notes. It had been a well thought out plan, genius, thought Ahmed as he put an X through the number four in front of security. For over ten years he and his comrades had been in the country under Spanish passports. He had picked his team carefully before coming to the States based not only on their skills and convictions but also on their ability to speak Spanish fluently. He had learned a long time ago that without the beards and wearing the right garb, his men could easily pass for Spanish. Though the country had never given up on trying to stop illegal aliens from Mexico and other Latin American countries, they had never considered them much more than a political threat regarding the job security of others. Over the years they had considered some of them dangerous, but mainly as gang members in the drug wars, definitely not terrorists. Ahmed and his men had learned to blend in with the Latin American society so well that no one would have considered them anything but Spanish. Their fake Spanish identities and passports allowed them to become, in effect, invisible to the United States terrorist radar.

"So when do we strike?" asked Lotfi taking off his coat and rubbing his hands.

"Soon enough," that was all Ahmed said. There was no way he was going to take a chance and tell anyone until they needed to know. It was not that he didn't trust his men; it was just wiser that fewer knew their timetable. Should one get caught, the less likely their operation would be jeopardized.

This attack against the American psyche was important to him, not just because of what it meant in helping destroy the American feeling of security, but also as revenge for what was happening to his brothers in Afghanistan. The day before, on December ninth, one of the last and most important spiritual bastions of the Taliban movement fell with the fall of Kandahar. As he sat in the quiet safety of their apartment in the country he had grown to hate, the American and Alliance forces were already moving into the Tora Bora region and the last major stronghold of the Al-Queda.

The feeling of complacency had already begun to creep back into the American way of life. For the first time since 9/11 one of the major newsmagazines, "Time" didn't even feature the war effort on its cover, but instead featured George Harrison and his passing. The Beatles were bigger news than the war. And with the fall of Enron, even the business news -- whether good or bad -- was beginning to have more effect on the thoughts of Americans, their concerns and behaviors, than the threat of a hundred anthrax-laced letters. At the rate things were going the threat of terrorism in the United States would soon have about as much impact on the American psyche as last year's Christmas gifts.

It was important for Ahmed, his group, and those other groups in the network that he was connected with, to keep up the pressure and make Americans so terrified they'd be afraid to fall asleep at night.

Ahmed finished his notes, then opened the package and took out the old blueprints and opened them. "Good, good. They didn't see you taking these?"

"No. I don't believe their maintenance even knew they had this set."

Ahmed smiled at Lotfi as he watched him pour a cup of tea from the stove then sit down on the couch across from him. "You did well, Lotfi. There well be a special place for you in paradise."

"As long as the company is good," laughed Lotfi.

Ahmed's expression again turned serious. "Did our friends receive any information on her yet?"

"No. It's like she dropped off the earth."

Ahmed turned away a moment then slammed the table. "Years, and still no closer. No one is that good."

"We know she is somewhere in the Midwest."

"Midwest! Do you know how big the Midwest is? You could put most of the Middle East in the Midwest!"

Majed, the third member of the group, abruptly turned back from the window where he had been watching the street for the past twenty minutes. "We know she is on her own. Why is it so important that we must still have so many looking for one when there is much more important work to be done?"

"One! This one can bring down their whole economic system! She is the ultimate terrorist!" Ahmed turned back to his papers while muttering to himself as he tried to focus on the engineering plans to the shopping mall. "She could bring them to their knees." He wanted to say more, to slam the table, go out and search for her personally, but there was no time. Ahmed was on a deadline and time was of the essence. As he studied the plans he couldn't help think about her, where she was, what she was doing.

He thought back to the last time he saw her after their first attack on the World Trade Towers. That was eight years ago. He had come so close back then. Just minutes sooner and he would have had her. Then there was the first time. That bitter cold winter day in Russia, though it wasn't Russia back then. He still recalled that cold iciness about her. How one moment she was standing stiff as a mannequin and the next she was laying down cover fire like a seasoned trooper, her eyes cold as the icy land she was born in. Or was that created. He remembered how she almost lifted Vladimir single handedly as she dragged him back to their truck.

It took Ahmed's men a long time to get their van fixed and back on the road. They had tied Dimitri and thrown him in the back then took off after Vladimir. Ahmed was determined to find them and retrieve his goods no matter what the cost, especially after he had seen her. But their chase was short lived. In less then five miles they ran into the place where Vladimir had gone off the road. A couple Russian patrol vehicles were there and when they stopped to see what happened they were told there had been an accident and that there was only one injured survivor.

Ahmed had always assumed she was burned in the wreck. He never thought she could have survived let alone made it all the way to the United States. Ahmed often wondered what her life had been like during those times. How did she survive, adapt? She really must have been an extra special piece of work to have pulled off that deception for so long. But when he saw her that day there was no mistaking who she was. She was different, more real, alive then he had ever imagined. She even appeared to have made friends of sorts. That Sharon for one was a real talker. But then she was gone. Hardly a day passed since then that Ahmed hadn't thought about her, of seeing her again, someplace alone or in a crowd. Vladimir had called her Nishka. Ahmed would never forget that name.

Chapter Twenty Two

Within a week after Thanksgiving everyone in her school knew about Jessica winning the trip to the big city for the toy extravaganza at Tillers Department Store. On Tuesday the winners of the short story contest were announced in her English class. Later that day they were announced over the school intercom. Those that didn't know the significance of the event were soon set straight by Peter, who was both proud of his sister and the resulting glory of being her brother and mentor. He hoped that maybe sometime during her fifteen minutes of glory she might remember him. Jessica of course had no problem handling her newfound fame. She was not boastful, at least not to the point of snobbishness. She didn't shun all those wishing her the best either, many of whom added what they would get had they won. It was like the lottery their fathers had played over the past fifteen years, only now someone their age had actually won and overnight become a celebrity.

By the second week, Jessica had begun, in her typical organized fashion, to plan out her fifteen minutes in Tillers Department Store like an athlete training for the Olympics. She spent more and more time after school, thanks to the help of a Tillers catalog her Grandmother had procured, planning what she would go for first. Not wanting to miss anything that she might think of after the event was over, Jessica made up a scrapbook. In it she categorized everything she wanted in order of importance. For as long as she could remember, or at least since her mother had died, there had never been an abundance of gifts under the Christmas tree or even for her birthday.

That was not to say that what Peter and she received wasn't nice. It was just that most of their gifts centered around necessities, with only a couple fun gifts in the mix. And all that depended on what kind of year their father had. But never was there that really special present, the big one she had always dreamed about. The ones everybody else in school usually received and bragged about for weeks. But that was all about to change. This Christmas would be different. Jessica was going to make sure of that. So though she thought about the glory of her moment, of Nishka and how much fun they would have journeying to the city together, the most important aspect was what she was going to get. And with any luck what she got would take care of her for many Christmas to come.

It wasn't surprising that the week before the big trip, Peter found Jessica sitting on the floor of her bedroom, going through the catalog again, looking for items she might have missed the first couple hundred times through. Peter laid down on her bed and watched as his sister cut out items she liked and laid them on the floor next to others. "Still picking out your Christmas wishes?"

"Yup. This year I'm going to get them all."

"Anything special?"

Jessica opened the scrapbook and pointed to an artist's easel on the first page. "I'm going to be a real artist."

Peter pulled himself a little closer to the edge of the bed. "Are you getting anything special for anyone else?"

Jessica turned the pages of her scrapbook and began putting in her newfound items. "If they're nice."

"Oh. I've been nice."

Jessica paused but did not look back. Instead she grabbed the tape and began taping her choices permanently into the book. "You want a telescope."

"How nice do I have to be for that?"

"Real nice."

Peter stared at his sister a long time before finally getting up and going to the door. As he opened it, he looked back. "I'll settle for a yo-yo." Not waiting for a response, Peter left, closing the door hard behind him. Jessica didn't say a word. Instead she continued silently taping her pictures into the book.

It was a cold wintry afternoon two days before the weekend excursion to the city for Jessica's Tillers adventure when Nishka returned home. She immediately began work on a project that took most of the day. When she finished, she walked over to David's house, planning to find Jessica home from school. Nishka rang the bell, waited twenty seconds, then prepared to ring it again when it opened.

"Hi, come on in," said Helen waving Nishka inside. Nishka obligingly stepped into the warm livingroom as Helen closed the door. "Did you just get back?"

"This morning. Is Jessica home?"

"No, church. They're doing rehearsals for the Christmas pageant. In fact I was just getting ready to go pick them up."

"Could I pick them up for you? I would like to surprise her."

"That would be nice. It would give me a chance to get a little more done around here before dinner." Helen meant what she said. As Christmas drew near, she had found herself at her son's home, cleaning and preparing for the season more than she did in her own apartment. She'd even stayed over a few nights to the point where David finally suggested she just move in for the holidays. It would be easier he said than constantly driving her back and forth. Though Helen didn't take him up on the offer, she gave it some serious thought.

Nishka thanked Helen for letting her pick up the children then quickly returned home, grabbed her keys and started for the church. As she drove, Nishka thought about the last couple weeks and how much she found herself looking forward to returning and seeing Jessica and David again. It was a strange sensation, something she had never experienced before. It was not logical for her to find herself attached to people. To have a desire to want see them, be with them. Emotions were not supposed to be part of her makeup. After all she was not human. She was designed to be a soldier, an assassin if necessary, not caring. No emotion. Duty first, complete the mission, survive, exist. Even for a human, such a profession required someone with a strong sense of discipline and obedience, the ability to shut off emotion or concern of consequences.

But that was not the way things had been for Nishka, not since America. At first She rationalized this feeling of attachment as a side effect of needing to fit in, to blend in with others, especially in the workplace. To do this it was obvious she needed people who would trust and care for her. The Flores family fit that need to a tee. But things had changed some, evolved beyond need and cover. Nishka had once tried to pin down the exact point where this change began. Her conclusion was that Jessica was the catalyst and the moment crystallized with the movie and her note pleading for her to stay.

No one had ever showed such compassion toward Nishka, with the possible exception of Vladimir. There was also the time she saved Peter. That was not part of her programming. Though Nishka found a form of attachment to Sharon, she had not given much thought to what happened to her after the bombing or whether Ahmed and his terrorist gang ever got to her. If they had, she would have just been a casualty of war, acceptable losses. What had always been important to Nishka was her own survival. In Peter's case she actually cared, and in that split second put his life above hers. Maybe this change went back farther, to the times she spent with David or the time she spent tutoring his children, or maybe even the first time she met Jessica.

She was reminded of that day every time she opened that cupboard and saw what was left of those bars of chocolate, bars she could not bring herself to throw away even though there was no practical reason for to keep them. It was definitely apparent that Jessica had managed to touch her in some way. In the end whatever it was that started to effect her circuits, her rational logic, it no longer mattered. All that mattered was that they all meant something to her now. They had value and had become a part of her existence.

Though she spent quite a bit of time the last couple weeks rationalizing the relationship between David's family and herself, it was by no means the principle reason she left. She needed time to see clients. Rich people whose portfolios she handled and with whose money she was able, not only to increase their wealth, but leverage her holdings, increasing her own value as well. If she was indeed going to commit to this new lifestyle, and for Nishka anything she did was total commitment, she wanted to make sure there were no ties that could in anyway jeopardize its success. There was to be no possibility that something she had done, people she had met or knew, could in anyway affect the security of her future.

That meant there would be no trails left from which Ahmed or his men could find her. She knew that as long he was still at large she would always be in the back of his mind as the terrorist weapon most suited to make his ultimate statement, and the way the economy was going there was no better time for him to use her than now. She also knew that no matter how good he thought he was, eventually he was going to slip up and the Americans or Israelis would catch him. Once that happened, all memory of her existence would be gone forever. All she had to do was remain invisible and wait him out.

After the past two weeks she had made her existence just that much more invisible. Even the Federal Government protection program couldn't have done better. The ironic thing was not only had she erased her tracks but also put away enough money to buy a good chunk of where Ahmed came from. But then money had never been important to Nishka. It was just an ingredient needed for her survival. It was also a way of keeping score, of telling how good she was in playing the game. Not to mention a means by which to play any game she wanted, should the need arise.

With the winter sun setting earlier, the church appeared dark and moody when Nishka arrived. Only two of the sanctuary lights were on. The rest of the illumination came from two Christmas trees flanking the nativity scene set up in front of the altar where the rehearsals were going on. Nishka sat down behind Peter's friends, Vern and Barry, both in the choir, who were sitting in the pews halfway from the front. "How is Jessica doing? Did she get the part of Mary?"

"No," said Vern, tuning around and smiling in his boyish, post-puberty manner. "She's only an angel." "She was lucky to get that," added Barry. "She's the smallest angel I've ever seen." No sooner had Barry made his comment than Peter and another boy, who where returning from the washroom, joined them. Peter's face brightened at seeing Nishka.

"Hi, I hear your sister is an angel."

"Yup," nodded Peter, half turning back toward the nativity scene to watch as the angels came out and stood near the manger. "She's the best angel they ever had."

With the other angels nearby, Jessica, in her angel costume, moved behind the cradle. The director nodded to the woman on the keyboard and she began to play. As she did, Jessica began singing, "From the day you were born," to the doll in the manger. "From the day you were born, I have been here beside you. As your life goes on I will stand by your side. Tho' today, as you try you may worry and cry, everyday hear me say, 'Here am I, here am I.... Here am I, come to me: take my hand: new life is free. Please believe me, receive me: Together, forever, forever we'll be................"

As Jessica sang the song, the church fell silent. Even the statue of Christ seemed to be listing to her. When she finished, even the boys were moved. "She's great." whispered Vern.

"Yes she is," said Nishka.

Peter said nothing, only watched his sister finish, then wiped one small tear from his eye.

After the rehearsal ended, and the shepherds, angels and others changed out of their costumes, Jessica joined her brother for the ride home. As Nishka drove, Peter sat in his usual spot in the front seat; his sister sat in the back. "That was a wonderful song," said Nishka glancing back at Jessica in the rearview mirror.

"Teacher says this is going to be the best Christmas program ever," proclaimed Peter, his chest puffed like a rooster.

Jessica leaned forward, "did you know they are going to have a real baby in the play?"

"That will be nice," said Nishka.

"Yes. The pastor says that while the baby's in the cradle he's the real Jesus."

"He said symbolizes, not is," cringed Peter, rolling his eyes.

"No, is, he really is." stammered Jessica. "And I get to sing to him.... Isn't that great!"

"Yes, that's wonderful." Nishka turned the car into her driveway and came to a stop, then turned back to Jessica. "Would you like to come in for a moment?"

"Me too?" asked Peter.

"If you want, but this is more of a girl thing."

"Oh, that's all right," muttered Peter unlocking his seat belt. "I'll tell Grandmother where you're at."

"Thank you." Nishka watched Peter leave the car and walk home with his books tucked tightly against him to ward off the cold winter night. After he was out of sight she got out and headed for her front door with Jessica close behind.

Jessica never said a word as she watched Nishka turn on the livingroom light. She followed Nishka through the room then halfway down the hallway toward the spare bedroom before finally asking, "what's the surprise?"

"You will see." After Nishka reached the room she quietly opened the door. When the light came on Jessica saw the room beautifully decorated in the manner she had described months before. Every last detail was there from the four-post canopy bed to the drapes, dresser, mirror, accessories, and wallpaper on the wall. "Do you like it?"

Jessica was speechless an expression of surprised wonderment in her eyes. Finally she managed to utter; "It's beautiful!"

Nishka sat down on the side of the bed and watched as Jessica surveyed the room. It was apparent all the work she had done that day, from coordinating the deliveries to the decorating, had been satisfactual. It was a strange feeling but a good one. "Anytime you want to spend the night, provided your father approves, you are welcome.

Still awed by the room Jessica pulled herself up on the bed beside Nishka. "Really!"

"Yes, you are my best friend."

Jessica smiled as she leaned against Nishka and wrapped her arm around her. "Are you still going with us?"

"I would not miss it."

"Oh good." Jessica looked around some more. "Can I bring some more of my pictures over and hang them in here?"

"All the pictures you want."

Jessica smiled, then climbing up on her knees, put her hands around Nishka's neck and kissed her on the cheek, then whispered "you are my very best friend."

Chapter Twenty Three

The drive to the city the following day was a long but pleasant one. Jessica and Peter were excused early from school for the trip. Neither had slept much the night before. By the time they reached the Embassy Hotel, the children's focus had changed from the trip to just getting out of the car and into a nice hotel room with a television.

That all changed once they entered the hotel. The size and grandeur of the large, plush lobby awed the children as they followed their father, Grandmother, and Nishka toward the front desk. Jessica held her scrapbook of gifts tight to her side as they passed a Christmas tree, nearly twenty feet tall in the center of the grand room. The pine was ablaze in white and gold lights, large and small silver ornaments, red ribbons and gold beading draped on its branches. Green garland laced with white lights and red bows wrapped around two large columns that supported an arch dividing the lobby. A smaller Christmas tree, just as gaily decorated, stood near a large marble fireplace. The roaring fire inside the fireplace and the mahogany walls trimmed with brass gave the place a warm grand feeling of Christmas.

As the children stood watching well-dressed people pass by, David approached the woman attendant at the counter. "Reservations for Flores."

The attendant checked her computer listings, then smiled. "Here we are sir. Three rooms. A single and two doubles. The doubles are adjoining."

"Thanks." David immediately signed the card the attendant placed in front of him. No sooner had he finished than Carl entered the lobby. The moment the children saw him they rushed to him like he was their personal long lost Santa.

"I was afraid you weren't coming!" squealed Jessica hugging him tightly.

"I wouldn't miss this," laughed Carl, as he picked Jessica up and held her like a bear hugging a cub, his bearded face close to hers. "How was the trip? I see you brought your game plan along," nodded Carl toward the scrapbook Jessica held tight to her side.

"All set," giggled Jessica.

With Jessica still in his arms Carl turned to David. "I made eight-thirty reservations at Rippengers. Children should like it. Hope you don't mind."

"How come so late?" asked David. "Restaurant booked?"

"No, actually it's for me. I'm doing a remote. Special holiday sort of thing."

"You mean for television?" interrupted Peter. "Can we come?"

"Can we?" echoed Jessica, her eyes pleading for the opportunity to see her uncle live for television.

"Where is it?" asked Helen, a tone of concern in her voice.

"A homeless shelter for mothers and children."

"That's okay, it'll be educational," proclaimed Peter, confident his insight into the matter would more than compensate for any barricades his grandmother might throw up.

"Yes, it'll be educational. Please," chimed Jessica.

It was apparent by the children's pleading faces, especially Jessica's, that Carl couldn't turn them down. "Okay, why not. Like Peter said, it'll be educational."

David nodded, but Grandmother still looked skeptical. Against her better instinct she wasn't about to be a wet blanket, considering the children's enthusiasm.

The Flores clan had barely settled into their rooms before they were out again accompanying Carl across town. The homeless shelter, as grandmother had feared, was a two-story building in one of the seedier parts of the city. It had the appearance of having once been a department store or office building that had been divided into various segments, the largest area being the living quarters, barracks like rooms, holding twelve to fourteen beds. There were also communal washrooms, work and storage rooms, an eating hall, kitchen, and dayrooms, most of which were shown to Jessica and the others by one of the shelter workers.

The interview Carl was scheduled to do was set in the largest dayroom. It was long, with a number of large windows on one side overlooking the street below. There were a couple of davenports in various degrees of wear and a number of old cushioned chairs the majority of which someone had apparently tried to recover with varying degrees of success. Folding chairs were set up near an old color console television in a cabinet of Mediterranean design. In the corner near the windows stood a large Christmas tree, decorated with strings of lights, few of which matched. A large assortment of ornaments, many old, some faded from years of use, hung from the branches.

Many of the decorations appeared to have come from donations to the second hand shop that helped support the shelter and took up a good portion of the first floor. There was also a smattering of tinsel on the tree to give it glitter, but not nearly enough for one so large. The high ceiling of the room and the mixture of ornaments made the large tree look somewhat small and pale compared to the joy it was supposed to bring.

Two of the television crew had already begun setting up in the dayroom when Carl and the others arrived. Philip, the producer, was talking to the director in change of the shelter, a pleasant, thin, middle-aged woman, standing near the tree when Carl joined them. Jessica and the others were asked to remain with their tour guide near the television. Jessica watched as a number of mothers entered the room accompanied by their children. One of the women, holding a child near the age of one and accompanied by two other children, apparently hers, sat timidly on one of the worn sofas watching the cameraman check his equipment.

Carl talked to the shelter director a moment, then the producer. After what appeared to be a few last minute changes, Carl returned to Jessica and the others. "We're ready to start." Carl pointed to the cameraman's equipment. "Don't forget, you have to be real quiet when those lights go on."

"We will," nodded Peter and Jessica, their eyes wide with excitement.

No sooner had Carl explained what they were going to do than the producer joined them. "We're ready."

Carl nodded, then winking at the children, returned to the others. As Jessica watched fascinated by all that was happening, Carl talked briefly with two of the mothers, their children, then again with the shelter's director. As they continued talking, Jessica's attention was drawn back to the young mother seated on the couch, her child cradled in her arms, and her other children close beside her. Jessica wondered who she was and what happened that brought her to spend Christmas in such a place with no friends or family.

Eventually Jessica's attention switched back as the cameraman signaled and the lights went on. Carl glanced at the mothers and children standing near their forlorn Christmas tree then turned to the camera and began. "Good evening. I am standing here tonight, not on a battlefield, or in a town ravaged by famine or disaster in some remote corner of the world. Instead, during this time of preparation for celebrating the holiest of holidays, I'm in a homeless shelter for mothers and children in one of our very own hometowns here in the USA. Here they do not care much about what's happening in Afghanistan or elsewhere around the world. Their world is far more immediate." Carl turned to the shelter director. "How many families can you service here at one time?"

"We can normally house, total, about a hundred women and children in this facility," said the social director in an official tone.

"How many do you normally have?"

"The woman paused then glanced around the room. "When it's warmer we're usually two thirds full. When the weather turns colder we... well let's say we've been know to have to turn some away for safety reasons."

"Was it always like this?"

"No." The director paused, a sad expression on her face. "When I first started here it was better. But in the last couple years it's steadily gotten worse."

As the interview continued, Jessica and Peter had become drawn in by what was happening. Even Helen had become touched as the cameraman panned the children, mothers and others in the room.

"What about Christmas?" asked Carl. "What kind of Christmas do these children have?"

"We serve a very complete dinner with all the trimmings on Christmas Day."

"What about Christmas itself, gifts?"

"There we depend on donations."

"Is it enough?"

"No," sighed the director. "It's never enough.

"With all the donations and support that seems to have been given by people these past few months since 9/11, I would have expected this would be a banner year."

The director paused as if embarrassed then turned back to Carl. "Giving is up. Unfortunately with all the publicity New York and other areas are getting the donations have gone down in other charities. This has left some like ours with less than we hoped we would receive. It's been difficult these past two months."

"So where do most of those your helping come from?"

"Broken homes, husbands die, or worse just walk away. Some try to make it on their own. But there's never enough affordable housing. Some have even tried to live in their cars. Eventually they come here, often with little more than what's in their bags or on their backs."

The cameraman panned the homeless children again as Carl concluded his interview. "These are the forgotten ones. During these coming holidays of cheer, fellowship and prayers for peace on earth it is sometimes hard to remember they exist. Good night and Merry Christmas."

The interview was over. Nishka, David and his family said their good-byes and were gone, off by taxi to the restaurant where Carl would join them for dinner.

After dinner it was back to the hotel and their rooms. The

children, quickly got into their pajamas, then watched the whole interview on the news. Nishka showed no emotion. Helen on the other hand fought hard to hold back tears, as she thought about her own family and how different things would have been if it had been David instead of Barbara who died. Though the scenario wasn't pleasant, the truth of the matter was Barbara was a strong-willed woman who probably would have pulled through raising the children all right. At least she would have done no worse than David. But then she had a strong family background for support.

No sooner had the television interview ended than Grandmother went to the washroom. By the time David found a different station that was appropriate, she had returned. "We have to get up early tomorrow, it's going to be a busy day. I'd say it's time for bed," she said.

"You heard your Grandmother. Time for bed," said David standing up and stretching. "Peter you're in the other room."

"I will go with you," said Nishka standing up too.

"Are you sleeping with me?" shot Peter, his eyes wide at the possibility.

David laughed, "You should be so lucky."

Peter sighed, then followed Nishka into the room. After they left, Grandmother opened her luggage case, removed a nightgown and bathrobe, then left for the washroom leaving David and Jessica alone. David watched as Jessica put her scrapbook on the night table beside the bed, then climb in and pulled the covers up.

"You all set for tomorrow?" asked David as he sat down beside her.

"Yup, I know what I want, "smiled Jessica padding the book.

"Good, well, sweet dreams. Don't forget your prayers."

David leaned over and kissed his daughter, then tucked the covers around her.

"Do you like Nishka?" asked Jessica as David got back up.

"Yes I do," he said sitting back down.

"A lot?"

"Yes, why?"

"Just wondering. Good night, Daddy." David started to get up again when Jessica pulled his sleeve. "Father!"

"What?"

"Do you think those children will have a nice Christmas?"

"If enough people saw your uncle on television they will."

"Are you sure?"

"No one can be sure... but I think so. A lot of people are moved by what they see on television. Especially at Christmas time. Good night."

Jessica smiled goodnight, then watched her father leave the room. Turning She stared at her scrapbook, then pulling it off the table, hugged it to her side and drifted off to sleep.

After the children were asleep, David joined Nishka in the hall. From there they went down to the hotel lounge to meet Carl. The bar's atmosphere was cheery, the walls painted forest green and accented with oak trim. Decorations of holly, red bows, white lights and garland gave the room a warm Christmassy atmosphere. After receiving their drinks, two beers for Carl and David, a 7-Up for Nishka, they sat at a table not far from the lounge's only television. "That was quite a piece you did." said David, watching Carl wipe his beard after taking a long swig of beer. "It certainly made an impression on Mother."

"Thank you David. But your mother's easy. I only hope it moved a few others."

"Did you always want to be a commentator?" asked Nishka.

Carl smiled. "Yes, believe it or not."

"Why?"

"Because I always yearned to travel. Ever since I was a child. It's a cheap way to see the world," laughed Carl. He studied his glass a moment as if trying to find some deeper explanation, then continued. "In truth I think I wanted to be a journalist since grade school. I thought that maybe somehow if I described what I'd witnessed, my experiences in the world, they might make a difference."

"Well, if you didn't make a difference tonight you never will." chimed David, holding his glass in a salute."

"Thank you David, you're very kind as usual. I only wish I could believe it."

As David and Carl talked, Nishka found her attention drawn to the television and a special news bulletin interrupting a basketball game. The station abruptly switched to a live remote. A reporter at the city's national airport began to talk. "The airport here seemed eerily quiet tonight with air travel still reduced significantly since 9-11. To make matters worse it has just been learned that security has been tightened here and elsewhere as the government has announced a heightened security watch.

The scene abruptly changed to another reporter standing outside a major shopping mall somewhere in the suburbs. The woman looked back at the mall then turned to the camera. "As you can see, it's Christmas and no matter what the economic indicators are, people are in the holiday spirit as many have flocked to their stores and shopping malls to do their Christmas shopping. What many of these people don't know is that there is a strong indication that the latest heightened alert in security has included many of the major malls in the vicinity. Though no one of authority seems to be talking, there seems to be some concern that these meccas of the holiday have possibly become the latest targets of terrorists."

As the reporter continued, Nishka knew there was a lot more she wasn't saying. Her guess was something happened or was discovered and, through sheer luck another major disaster had been avoided. It also meant terrorists were possibly close.

"I see what you're talking about. How can people be concerned for others when they're not even sure they can make it through the week without being killed?" shot David, gesturing toward the television with his beer.

Carl nodded. "It's a dangerous world all right. And as long as the media gives terrorists publicity, it will continue to be. We need to be showing more of man's positive side instead of always dwelling on evil and the fringe elements."

"Problem is that doesn't sell. People are intrigued by the problems of others; they're fascinated. It makes their world seem so much better in contrast."

"You're probably right, David. At least until now. That's why I'll probably never finish my book. That's what I really wanted to be you know, an author.... But finding the words that I really feel in my soul and putting them down on paper seems to be more than I'm qualified for, at least so fart. It would probably take a miracle, and I'm afraid I'm a little short in the miracle department lately." Carl took another drink of beer, then turned to Nishka. "Now ask David what his dreams are."

"What are your dreams?" asked Nishka, redirecting her attention away from the television and her thoughts concerning the terrorists.

"My dreams? Actually I really only had one. If I could do anything I would fly."

"Like a jet pilot?"

"Close." David paused not sure whether he was ready to discuss something so personal yet possibly childish sounding to a woman as intelligent and worldly as Nishka. "More like in the old days," he finally blurted. "You know piloting a DC-3 carrying supplies to remote parts of the world. Kind of like Terry and the Pirates."

"David is serious, you know. He's even building a flying model of one in his basement almost big enough to fly in."

"You are?" asked Nishka, showing an expression of surprise at trying to comprehend such a project. "Why?"

"Because it's as close to flying one as I'll ever get. Carl exaggerates of course. It's actually just under seven feet, wing tip to wing tip."

"Why not just become a pilot?"

David laughed, then pointed to his eyes. "Because they frown on you crashing planes into their runways. I don't have the greatest depth perception. Now how about you? What secret ambition have you always wanted to pursue?"

Nishka turned to her glass and stared at it as if looking into some far distant dimension. "Be able to dream," she finally said.

It was late when Carl finally said good night and David and Nishka walked back to their rooms. Nishka stopped at her door and unlocked it, then turned to David. "How do you think Jessica will do tomorrow?"

"She'll be fine.... You really care for her don't you?

"She is special." Nishka said softly.

"How about me?"

"I care for you, too."

"You make it sound like I'm your brother."

"No, that would be hard," said Nishka sounding

momentarily confused. "It is just hard for me to commit more to someone right now."

"I see," shrugged David starting to turn away. He had heard that line before or ones similar to it and really didn't feel like hearing it again, not that night.

"No, you do not. I wish I could explain but I cannot, not now." Nishka grabbed David's hand. "Believe me when I say I do care for you." Pulling him closer Nishka kissed him "Good night."

David looked deep into Nishka's eyes, then before she could slip away he pulled her back and kissed her long, hard, and passionately. "Good night," he whispered after they parted. Not waiting for a response David turned and waked away.

Nishka watched David open his door and disappear inside without saying a word. She did not truly know what to say as she turned on the lights and entered her room. Instead she leaned against the door and hugged herself. What an experience she thought, one she would file away to be recalled often for a long time to come.

Chapter Twenty Four

It was twenty after six when David woke. He stared at the wall trying to remember why he ever decided to finish with Manhattans the night before. His head throbbed as he turned to the bed next to him. Peter was still asleep. Good thought David as he turned back and closed his eyes while trying to summon the strength to pull himself out of bed. Half an hour passed before he finally managed to pry himself up. He sat on the edge of the bed a moment holding his head then counted to ten and in one herculean effort rose to his feet, then stumbled off to the washroom. It wasn't till he'd showered, dressed, and made it down to the coffee shop for a large cup of their blackest that he started feeling better. And even that was marginal.

By the time he left the shop it was well past seven -- little time left to get the rest of the clan together for the limousine ride to Tillers and Jessica's extravaganza. Fortunately for David his mother was not in the same shape. She had already gotten Jessica dressed and Peter underway by the time he returned with what was left of his coffee. Nishka, of course, had been ready for an hour and met David in the hall.

"You look tired David,"

Seeing Nishka's concerned expression David tried to think of a comical comeback but there was nothing. "I wish that was all," he mumbled trying to slip his card into the door and open it. "But with any luck we should have this show on the road momentarily." David was right. Ten minutes after returning, his tribe was in the lobby. Soon after meeting Carl, the limo arrived and they were on their way to Tillers.

The mammoth downtown department store seemed strangely dark and deserted when the limo pulled up to the main entrance. They were let in by a security guard then were met by a secretary who escorted through the store. As Nishka, David, and the others passed the somber, darkened counters to where the gift spree was to begin, Jessica, clutching her scrapbook, noticed a beautiful statue of an angel on a counter, part of a Christmas display. The angel was over a foot tall, with extended wings, and had the face of a young woman. She paused to stare at the angel's angelic expression, but the hustle of the others trying to reach a destination they were apparently already late for, forced her to continue on.

Arriving at what appeared to be the store's center, they met an older child, Harold, the senior winner. He was a boy a little older than Peter who with his parents, sister, and year old brother, had arrived earlier and on time. It was apparent from the expressions of some of the store dignitaries that they had hoped to start sooner. The plan had been to get the event over as fast as possible with appropriate media coverage before the store opened at ten.

It was only a couple days before Christmas and the selling mayhem was already crazy, though with world events as they were, not as crazy as the store would have liked it to be. The management of Tillers, in conjunction with the marketing department, hoped that showing their hearts were in the right place during the holiday season would help push sales into a record breaking quarter, a quarter in a year of recession and international events that had become, at best, not helpful.

No sooner had Jessica and the others been introduced to the staff and the press sent to cover the event, than Mr. Hines took over. "Hi. I'm Mr. Hines, Vice President of customer affairs. This is Mr. Reynolds, President of Tillers and Mr. Martin. You must be Jessica."

"That's me," smiled Jessica giving her scrapbook to her Grandmother, stepping forward and broadly smiled. As Mr. Hines shook Jessica's hand he noticed her leg brace. "Very pretty dress," he smiled. Straightening up he returned to a more dignified pose. "The rules for your spree are simple. Jewelry and appliances are not included, nor are china or silverware or other items from those departments. Also furs." Mr. Hines walked over to a number of shopping carts lined up in two rows. Turning to one of the cameramen he continued. "Since we do not use shopping carts here at Tillers, Myers a premiere grocery chain in our fair city has been kind enough to donate theirs. We thank them for their generosity during this special event."

As Mr. Hines continued to talk, expounding on this attribute or that concerning Tillers and the holiday season, Jessica found herself mesmerized by Harold's younger brother held tenderly by their mother. So engrossed was she that Jessica barely noticed Mr. Hines turning back to her and Harold. "Now each of you is allowed one person to push your cart and you each have fifteen minutes to make your selections."

The President of the company abruptly motioned to Mr. Hines. The two men conferred a moment then Mister Hines returned to the others. "Considering the special circumstances here, we will allow Jessica an additional two minutes. Any questions?" Mister Hines waited for responses, both children nodded. Deciding everything was understood he turned to Jessica. "Now Jessica, who do you want to push your cart?"

Jessica looked around, then took Nishka's hand. "Nishka will."

Mr. Hinds nodded, then asked the same question of Harold. After the boy picked his father Mister Hines motioned to the carts. "Will the four of you please step forward." Jessica and Nishka obediently joined the other two at the carts. "Okay. On your mark, get set, GO!"

As the media recorded the event and the others watched, Jessica and Nishka followed close behind as Harold and his father began their wild spree. Instead of continuing behind the other two into the toy department, Jessica turned and started toward children's clothing. Down the aisles she went pushing as hard as her short legs and brace would let her. Nishka stayed right behind as Jessica pulled items off the shelves and threw them into the basket; sweaters, shirts, pants, dresses, underwear and socks. Boy's clothes or girls, it didn't seem to matter.

"Are you sure this is what you want?" asked Nishka as she followed.

"Yes! Isn't this fun!!"

Bewildered by the illogical selection, Nishka watched as Jessica piled in more clothing. The shopping cart full, Nishka raced back to the starting line, then quickly returned with another cart. "What about toys? I thought children liked toys."

"We do." That was all Jessica said as the mad spree continued.

Jessica showed no sign of tiring. Three carts full, four, five. With little time left she was finally in the toy department grabbing dolls and trucks, games, models, a paint and art set, and a easel.

"We only have three minutes left," announced Nishka, matter-of-factly, as she returned with another cart.

Jessica did not respond, only scooped up a bunch of Lego boxes, and dumped them in, followed by puzzles and mystery books. She found the largest telescope the store had to offer and shoved that in.

"One more place!" Going as fast as she could Jessica left the toy department and went back the way they came in. Reaching the counter where the angel stood, she gently picked it up and placed it in the cart then turned back for the finish line. Jessica ran harder than her braced leg had ever gone before, faster and faster until at last she crossed the finish line just as the buzzer sounded.

Amazed, Mr. Hines surveyed the collection in Jessica's carts, three more than Howard filled, then walked back to her followed by the cameraman. "That's quite an assortment you've gathered. Is that all for you?'

Jessica nodded trying to catch her breath. Finally pulling herself together she glanced back at her father, Carl, then at Howard's mother holding her youngest child. Though she was well dressed, Jessica couldn't help being reminded of the mother and child she had seen the night before in the shelter, sitting quietly away from the others, alone with her children. "No."

"Then who are they for?"

Jessica slowly walked over to the last cart and pointed to the telescope. "This is for my brother. He always wanted one." Jessica paused, looked at the artist paint set and easel and thought of all the paintings she could do. She turned to the easel, and gently touched its strong oak legs. Finally she lifted the angel she had gathered out of the last basket, and held it close to her chest. "This is for me."

"What about the rest?" asked Mr. Hines.

Jessica looked back at the easel, and the shopping carts, all overflowing with children's clothes, radios, toys, and other goodies then at the mother and her little boy. "Those are for the children at the homeless house."

Mr. Hines was speechless. So were many of the others around him. David finally walked over and knelt down in front of his daughter. "Are you sure?"

"You don't mind?" she half whispered looking in her father's eyes.

David fought back a tear as he picked Jessica up and hugged her. "Are you kidding, I couldn't be prouder."

For the first time in his life Carl was speechless. As the impact of what happened sunk in, he found himself fighting back the instinct to cry. Instead he silently walked over and hugged Jessica. Others in the area were less controlled. One woman turned away and cried openly; a couple others nearly did the same. Only Nishka showed no emotion, instead she watched the reactions of others.

As David held Jessica and the angel, a woman journalist walked up to them followed by a cameraman. "May I ask why you kept the angel?"

Jessica smiled at the angel in her arms, its saintly face accented by her long brunette hair. "Because looks like my mother."

It was not till then that David noticed the resemblance between the angel and Barbara. Had it been that long, he wondered, that he'd forgotten? Had his memory grown that foggy? He couldn't help but wonder how much more had slipped away. One thing for certain, as long as he had Jessica, he would never forget again.

Chapter Twenty Five

After the event at Tillers, Jessica and her family were taken by limousine back to the hotel. The telescope also went along, as did the angel, which never left Jessica's arms. There was also a gift certificate from Tillers to be used later. Mr. Hines made arrangements for the limousine to be at their disposal for the rest of the day, so David took the family, Carl, and Nishka to a museum, then a show of Jessica's choosing. Lunch was a brief stop at a fast food restaurant at Carl's expense.

While David and his family enjoyed the day, the media, with Tillers' blessing, put the story of Jessica's generosity on the local news at noon. It went on the wire service shortly after. By five o'clock every news channel in the city had picked it up and were running it as a feature story.

Like many others, Channel 10's news anchor, Curt Wasner, the most respected journalist in the Midwest, ran the edited coverage of the event. The network ran it as the last segment of the six o'clock news. Having only heard about what happened briefly and not having seen the video, he couldn't help being moved by Jessica's sincerity. Off the cuff he decided to close with his own personal editorial. "It has since been learned," he finished, "that little Jessica's mother died in a car accident with a drunk driver a couple years ago.... May I take this moment to say, that with all that has gone on in recent months in this crazy world of ours, it sometimes becomes easy to forget those in need around us. It's truly amazing and refreshing that the true meaning of what these holidays are about could be found in the heart of one so young. It makes me ask myself, what have I done lately for those less fortunate in my own backyard? -- This is Curt Wasner. Good night."

It was said there was hardly a dry eye in the studio when Curt finished his broadcast, or in the majority of the two hundred thousand homes that watched that night. The reaction was much the same for the rebroadcast on the ten o'clock news.

Neither David, Carl, nor the others had any idea of the wild publicity that had been generated as a result of Jessica's gesture that morning. It wasn't until they arrived at the hotel's premier restaurant for a later than planned dinner that they received any inkling that their lives had changed. As the Maitre'd escorted the family through the plush, cheerfully decorated dining room, it became apparent that they, Jessica in particular, were the attention of many of those they passed. Immediately after they were seated Carl leaned over to David. "We seem to be popular here for some reason."

"Maybe we're the millionth customer." laughed David.

Trying to ignore the feeling of being watched, Carl picked up his water glass and held it in a salute. "To Jessica, our future grand author. You made me proud dear. I only wish Judith could have been here to see you."

"To Jessica," echoed everyone, Nishka included, as they saluted.

"It's a shame she had to work," said Helen setting down her glass.

Carl barely had time to nod when the headwaiter arrived and stood next to Jessica. "The special for tonight is Beef Wellington." The waiter paused, then motioning to the wine steward, continued. "It also gives me great pleasure to inform you that your dinner tonight is courtesy of the management." Kneeling down, the waiter, who up til then had seemed somewhat stoic, soften as he looked into Jessica's eyes. "It would give me great pleasure to serve your dinner personally tonight, Princess. Whatever you desire, I would be happy to bring." With that the waiter returned to his standing position, regained his composure and left.

Before David could do more than stare, his mouth open, the wine steward arrived with a bottle of aged Bordeaux chilled in ice. Removing the cork, he proceeded to pour the first glass for Carl as head of the table while another waiter delivered two kiddy cocktails to Peter and Jessica.

"We didn't order wine," said Carl staring at the glass.

"It's complimentary," said the wine steward filling the rest of the glasses.

"Why?" asked David.

"In honor of your little girl. Enjoy." Before anyone could ask why the wine steward was gone. Moments later another waiter brought two dishes of hors' doeurver and set them on the table, then just as quickly left.

"This really is a special day," said Helen in amazement. "Maybe you are the millionth customer, or whatever. Do you know what you want to eat?"

Jessica, who had already surveyed the menu, abruptly closed it. "Lobster!"

"Have you ever eaten Lobster?" asked Nishka.

"No," said Jessica with a pixyish grin. But it must be good, did you see how much it is?"

"Sure, why not?" laughed David. 'It's your day."

"Besides, it's free," added Peter.

David half-laughed as he nodded, though he still couldn't help feeling he was going to pay for this one way or another.

Even Carl seemed perplexed as David leaned over. "What do you think is going on?"

"I don't know. Maybe the department store is picking up the tab."

Before Carl could say more, a well-dressed woman in her early sixties walked over from a nearby table and bent down beside Jessica as if ready to hug her. "May I say how very proud I am of what you did today. It moved me so much. God bless you."

Having finished the woman hugged Jessica, then said, "Bless you all," to the others.

As she started to leave Carl motioned her over. "Pardon me, but what did you hear about Jessica?"

The woman's expression quickly changed to genuine surprise. Don't you know? It's all over the news." The woman looked back at Jessica then smiled. "Merry Christmas." she bubbled.

"Merry Christmas," chimed everyone. Other tables echoed the greeting, some holding up their glasses.

Nishka silently watched the woman leave. Helen's eyes showed another hint of tears as others smiled and talked merrily as a feeling of warmth and goodwill spread throughout the room, much of it directed toward Jessica. As much as Nishka wanted, she could not grasp what was happening, how the actions of one little girl could affect so many people in such a way. She wanted to understand. She wanted to understand very much. To know what it was like to be human and actually feel the sensations their emotions gave them, even if it meant feeling the sorrows, too. For in the end she thought, was not one a reflection of the other?

❦

The meal had been a wonderful experience for the Flores family. When it was over, David escorted his clan, minus Carl, back through the lobby full of holiday spirit. Jessica thrilled at the hustle of people coming and going, the scent of cold crisp air coming through the doors.

David felt the same. Only his feelings were laced with remorse, wishing it somehow wouldn't end, that Barbara could have been there to share it. They could have tucked the children in together that night, then left arm in arm, reminiscing how proud they were of Jessica and her glorious moment.

With Helen along as babysitter, they could have slipped out for a romantic evening. The night would have been perfect. He could have taken her to a play, a night of dancing, or a smoky jazz club for some good music, Christmas style, then a leisurely ride back to the hotel in a cab that purposely would have taken the long way through the park. He could have held her hand, put his arm around her and kept her warm, maybe even kissed her. A soft, long, romantic kiss that would have lasted forever while "White Christmas" played on the cab radio filling the night with magic. That kiss would have carried them through the lobby on a cloud, up to their room where they would have made long passionate love. She would have slept the night away in his arms. And as he held her he would have savored the smell of her, remembering all the time why he married her in the first place, and how he had loved her so much. Unfortunately, as the elevator carried them up to their rooms all David had was the dream.

The elevator reached their floor all too soon for David. He found himself standing near Nishka when the doors opened, smelling her hair and wondering what she would be like in his arms. Had she ever been in a romantic situation with someone she really cared for. Someone that made her dream of that moment over and over, or made her wish for a moment how wonderful her life would be if he were only with her again? It seemed strange in a way that he should suddenly find himself thinking about her that way. It was almost as if they were two ships propelled by old memories. And though they were in such close proximity, for some reason through some strange entanglement of poor communication or old memories, they were doomed to go their separate ways, never knowing the bliss they could have shared together.

It was not like David to have such good, then melancholy thoughts consecutively. He wasn't known for being overly romantic. Maybe that was part of the magic of what Jessica had done that day. That somehow the spell she created had affected not only him but the whole city. Those thoughts passed through David's mind as they walked to their rooms. But he never said a word.

"Did everyone have a good time?" asked Helen as she opened her bag for the key-card.

"It was really great!" exclaimed Peter. "Can I stay up and watch television?"

"Sure, why not." said David rubbing Peter's head. "But not all night."

No sooner had David opened the door than Peter dashed past him for the television. David couldn't blame him. After all, the hotel had HBO and the Movie Channel. Back home they didn't even have cable. According to Peter and Jessica, they were the only ones in the state, if not the world, that didn't have cable. David turned to Nishka as she passed and motioned for her to wait. "I'm going to meet Carl at the lounge later. They're supposed to have a jazz group down there tonight. Want to join us?"

"Thanks, but I am very tired. I thought I would turn in early."

"Can I sleep in your room?" asked Jessica, taking Nishka's hand.

"I don't think so," said David.

Nishka studied Jessica's pleading expression then turned to David. "I would be happy to have her."

"Okay." David knelt down and hugged Jessica then whispered. "Good night. I love you." e smiled, kissing her on the cheek. Standing up he went into his room without saying another word.

Later, as David went down to the bar to meet Carl he thought about the day. He thought of what Jessica had done, and how it made him feel. He had been so proud of her, prouder than he could ever hope or deserve to feel. It had been an angelic moment, one he would always remember.

David thought about the rest of the day too. About the show, the museum, the sights of the city and how wonderful it all had been; that was, all except for one little part. He had never at anytime felt close to Nishka. And as he floated through those feelings and the remembrances, he began to realize he might never feel those moments he had with Barbara again, that no matter what he said or did, Nishka would never return the feelings he held inside, the love he so much wanted to share.

What did he have to do, he wondered, for her to ever love him?

After the others had gone and Jessica changed into her pajamas, she and Nishka sat up and watched television, "National Lampoon's Christmas Vacation." Jessica laughed at the funny parts; Nishka smiled. When the movie ended, Jessica climbed into bed and Nishka sat down beside her. "You know I never did see that story you wrote, 'The Smallest Angel'. What was it about?"

"It was about this little girl and this special thing she did. And how because of it the angels came down and took her away to become an angel."

"I would like to read it."

"I'll show it to you some time." Jessica yawned, then looked into Nishka's eyes, eyes that never seemed to show expression except when they were together. "Do you believe in miracles?"

"They are not logical. I find their concept hard to accept."

"That's because you have to believe. Like when God brought you to us. That was a miracle you know."

"If you say so." For a moment Nishka felt distant, not real, more like a mannequin trying to come to life, trying hard to understand something she could never comprehend. "About this God," Nishka finally said. "How do you know he exists? Where is he?"

Jessica smiled. "I believe. How do you know there's air? God is where you want him to be. He's there when you need him."

"Then why do you build churches for him if he is everywhere?"

"Because that's his house. That's where God speaks to us." Jessica paused a moment then touched Nishka's hand.

"You are here now. But if I can't find you I always know where to go, your house. If I'm ever lost I can always find God at his house."

Nishka thought about what Jessica said a moment then continued. "I have one last question if you don't mind. You were given a chance to have all the toys and gifts you ever wanted, more toys and clothes than any child could ever have, that chance will never come again; why did you give them away?"

"Why?" Jessica yawned, then looked at her fingers. "I thought about it. Then I thought about everything I already had, my home, Grandma, Father, and you. And I thought about those boys and girls with nothing, and their mommies that could never give those things to them. I just knew."

"What did you know?

Jessica turned and looked at the department store angel on the night table nearby, then reached out and gently touched it. "I knew that was what my mommy would do. I already had my miracle." Jessica turned back, sat up, put her arms around Nishka and hugged her. "I have you." Jessica kissed Nishka on the cheek, then whispered in her ear. "Don't ever leave me."

Nishka laid Jessica back down then, pulling up the covers, said good night. Jessica yawned again, then turned over and closed her eyes.

As Nishka reached over to turn off the light Jessica rolled back. "What would be a miracle to you?"

"I do not know." Nishka paused, then touched her bosom. I think to feel here the way you do."

"What do you mean?"

"To be able to cry."

Jessica thought a moment, then smiled. "You have to ask God for that."

"Good night," whispered Nishka reaching over again to turn off the light.

"Good night."

Nishka sat by Jessica's side and watched her for a long time. Finally she got up and walked over to the window. Opening the curtain a bit, she sat down and watched Jessica from across the room. Eventually she turned and looked out over the city skyline. She thought about what Jessica had said. About what she had done and how much Nishka found herself, against all logic, caring for her. It seemed so hard to conceive of the strength in Jessica's loyalty without being programmed. Nishka was well aware of her own abilities and the fact that she had them only because somewhere in a dark musty lab someone had programmed all of those attributes into her. She was not really Nishka but the sum total of someone else's emotions and programming. How she talked, thought, even responded. All that she was, was the result of someone else and she could be controlled again totally and completely by another with no input of her own.

The reality of that, the possibility of being a total slave with no will had become a very vivid thought of hers of late and as a result had, in a sense, become a nightmare. What made it worse was knowing those people who would control her were not only out there but possibly close. Her serene life could change instantly if they knew where she was. And if they did, she would never again be what she had somehow managed to become of late. Instead she would be a mindless slave programmed to do their bidding.

As she looked out over the buildings standing tall against the night sky, their lights making them almost look alive, Nishka thought about David and what he had become for her. She liked him yet at the same time she considered him a dangerous equation. Actually if she analyzed it in terms of human emotions as she understood them then the better phrase would be she was afraid of him. Not that he was in anyway a threat to her physically. He could never hurt her even if he wanted to. What frightened her was this thing called emotion, feelings like Jessica had for her. This attachment that she sensed was present in David though he had not really said it.

Actually, the more she thought about it, he had said very little at all in that regard. But it was there; she could see it in his eyes. The way he talked to her, moved close, took her hand like he did briefly as they watched the movie that afternoon. The same way she did the night she invited him to the play, though at the time she did it only because it seemed the proper thing to do.

One thing she had learned during her time among humans, listening to them, watching their movies, was how unpredictable they could be. Unlike her, where everything was logical, humans were bogged down with feelings, emotions, past experiences, time of month. They seemed to be too easily affected by so many things, it was hard to keep track of them all, say nothing about putting them together to formulate any kind of logical conclusions. Take for instance what Jessica had done that morning, and how her gesture had affected so many people she had never met. How would David react if he knew what she was? Could he still care for her, like Jessica? Or would he find her repulsive, just another piece of machinery, like the refrigerator only with a bust and the ability to talk back? She did not know if she could deal with him if he regarded her like that. And that was something else that made their relationship so irrational.

What was it about David rejecting her though that bothered her so much? Why would she not be able to deal with it? If she was already programmed to be emotional when it served a primary objective, to be analytical and take everything else at face value the rest of the time, why should such things bother her at all? Why should she care?

Or maybe that was what it was all about. Maybe in truth the humans she had begun to grow accustomed to, attached to, were not all so very different from herself. Were not all of them, from Jessica to David, and even the woman in the restaurant, begun the same way, with a clean slate? All starting with a set of programmed responses to survive, eat, sleep or need to procreate? And then as the years passed they all became the sum accumulation of their experiences, with the only variable being how they reacted to them. Basically that was what make up the sum total of what they were. In a sense maybe that was what was happening to her. She was no more just a machine from a lab in Russia than Jessica was like the baby that came from her mother's womb. Instead, Nishka had become the sum total of all her experiences. In the end she would never stand still, but continue to evolve. If that were the case, then why couldn't she savor feelings, emotions, even love?

That was the unique quality humans had that she so much begun to desire for herself. She had seen the bad side of humans. That she could understand. What she so desperately wanted was to feel the love, to be able to really care and experience the emotional good part of what that was all about. Maybe then she could give David what he wanted and what deep inside wanted too. Unfortunately that required a soul, and that intangible would take a real miracle.

Chapter Twenty Six

David slept late the next morning, until eight -- seven hours -- and it felt good. He had a good time at the bar the night before, even without Nishka. At least that's what he told himself when it was over. Though he stayed away from Manhattans, he made up for it in beers. Carl had made a few calls and found out about the newscasts. He relayed the information to David when he arrived. David thought about Carl's news and the rest of the events of that day. The two discussed them at length until well after the bar closed. They found themselves rehashing Jessica's performance at Tillers like a championship game with their star player bringing home the victory.

It would have been hard to put a damper on the high they felt. David had never experienced anything like it before or figured to again. That's what he told Carl anyway, though, in truth he had felt that way a couple times before. The first was the night he and Barbara were married. The second was the morning his son was born. And last was the night Jessica came into the world.

That next morning David managed to find his way to the bathroom a lot easier than the morning before. His head barely throbbed. Of course, the four aspirins he took before he fell into bed didn't hurt. A short time later he was dressed and woke Peter. Within an hour after he was up he was at Nishka's door. When she opened it, she looked radiant as if having been up for hours. "Did my daughter keep you up?"

"No, she was fine. We watched a movie, then she went to bed."

"That's probably what I should have done. But then yesterday was one of those days one couldn't let slip away without celebrating." David paused, not sure why he said that other than he was still feeling a little excited over everything. "So, how about ordering room service instead of dragging everyone downstairs for breakfast?"

"I think the children would like that."

"Good. I'll tell Mother." David watched Nishka turn back into her room and close the door. When he finally turned for Helen's room he couldn't help thinking about Nishka. But then why should it be any different than any other time. Half the time he was getting dressed and getting Peter moving he found himself thinking of her, of being with her, hearing her voice. She looked good, but then that was always a given.

David could never picture her any other way. He had always thought of Barbara in that way too, beautiful, intelligent. Nishka reminded him a lot of Barbara, especially when they were discussing Jessica. Maybe it was because of those comparisons that David found himself playing more and more with scenarios concerning their relationship, fantasizing about them developing beyond his base physical desires. Even though she still seemed distant, hard to read, he was finding it harder not to contemplate the possibility of her being the one he would spend the rest of his life with.

The children loved the idea of room service, of ordering whatever they wanted and having it delivered on a cart with each dish presented like a regal mystery hidden under silver covers. After breakfast, Peter and Jessica watched television while David and Grandmother packed. Nishka, as usual, had finished hours ago. When the bellhop arrived, loaded their bags on his cart and started for the elevator, a strange quiet fell over everyone. Soon they would be in the lobby and the fairytale would be over. They would be back to being an ordinary family again.

The elevator had barely stopped and its door opened when Carl hurried up to meet them, a folded newspaper under his arm. "David, did you see this morning's paper?"

"No."

Carl opened the paper and shoved it in front of him. A picture of Jessica with David standing at Tillers, covered a third of the front page. The headline read. "Littlest Angel". David quickly scanned the article while Nishka peered over his shoulder. "It's all over the place," said Carl.

Before David could respond, a number of the press and television crew, which had gathered near the lobby entrance, rushed over. David quickly picked Jessica up to keep her from being trampled as a woman reporter thrust a microphone in front of them. "Jessica, how does it feel to be the most beloved girl in the country this Christmas?"

"Beloved?" Jessica looked confused, bewildered by the question and all the attention around her.

"Yes. Don't you know? Your generosity has touched millions," said the reporter while trying to keep her balance in the crowd.

"I only did what mommy would have done," exclaimed Jessica nervously.

"The reporter abruptly turned and shoved the microphone in front of Nishka. "You must be very proud of your little girl."

"I am sorry but I am not her mother."

Sensing Jessica's uneasiness in all the craziness around him, David tried to cut the interview short. "Sorry, but we have to go." Not waiting for a response David and Carl hurried everyone toward the door.

As some of the press followed David out to the parking garage, the television cameraman turned to the woman who had just tried to interview Jessica. "Her mother is dead. Don't you ever watch television!" The woman stood speechless as she watched the others disappear out the door then looked at her partner and shrugged. "So shoot me!"

"Don't worry I'll take care of checking you out," yelled Carl as they reached the car.

David nodded then hustled the others into the van. It was chaos trying to get loaded and drive away with reporters hanging all over them. Jessica was the most shaken from the constant questions, as the reporters prodded for some kind of statement or interview. Eventually David managed to pull away with most of the family's sanity intact, left the garage and started on the long drive home.

It was shortly after the last of the city's suburbs began to disappear around them that the snow began to fall. Only the sound of Christmas songs emanating from a local radio station broke the silence in the car as it hummed down the interstate. David concentrated on his driving, trying to put the morning's events behind him. The rest of the passengers were also quiet, the only exception being Grandmother who couldn't help making some well-pointed jabs at the media. She was particularly displeased with the way they crowded around like locusts, pushing, showing no respect. David nodded but said little. Instead he concentrated on the road and the snow falling harder.

Nishka sat quietly in the back, Jessica asleep by her side.

As she watched the snow outside, she couldn't help recall her escape from the cybernetic research facility in Russia. Her remembrances of Vladimir and her first hours of freedom that cold blistery day. Of what her life was like those first weeks. She thought of the paper and the exposure Jessica received, exposure that fortunately did not include her. She could not afford any recognition if she wanted to remain hidden, invisible to the world.

Chapter Twenty Seven

It nearly was a disaster. Too close of a call. In the end Ahmed and his comrades had barely managed to escape with their lives. The plan had seemed so foolproof. They had received the biological agent intact from their source, enough to affect thousands in an enclosed area up to two blocks square and possibly kill hundreds. It had been brought in that early that night by truck as part of the material belonging to a maintenance crew assigned to clean out the air ducts leading into the mall. All they had to do was hook it up to the filtration system and leave. But that was when everything went wrong.

No one was around when they began running a hose to the filtration ducts from the truck parked in the enclosed loading dock. They had counted on the dock being deserted most of the night. They had not take into account, however, the sudden beehive of activity resulting from the abrupt appearance of trucks trying to make last minute deliveries to stores for the holiday season. One of the divers, after phoning for help from the store he was delivering to, noticed the tanker truck and became suspicious. After climbing up on the dock and opening the rear of his trailer he introduced himself to Majed who had been left behind with the tanker.

Sensing an unusual uneasiness about the man he returned to his cab, called the store back and had them alert security.

Within moments security arrived. Seeing them coming, Majed quickly left his post, alerted Lotfi and Ahmed in the service corridor and they quickly made their escape into the mall. The mall security, not sure exactly what was going on, called the local authorities who in turn sent out a team to check on the truck, other paraphernalia left behind including the long two-inch diameter hose. By the time they realized what they had and how lethal the contents in the truck's container was, it was too late. Ahmed and his comrades were gone.

Ahmed was confident they could not tie the truck or its material to him. The tanker had been stolen and repainted. They had worn gloves and made sure not to take anything along that could be traced back to them. The security cameras had been taken care of and those people that might have seen them, Majed in particular, would have been looking for some one of Spanish descent. Even so the driver had gotten a good look at Majed. If the man was taken in and interrogated properly, he probably would be able to give them enough of a description to find Majed. Deciding to play it safe Ahmed and the others headed back to their apartment, packed up their gear to leave, then decided to stay off the streets.

After watching television that night Ahmed decided to leave the next day. Though the media might have learned that something had happened, the authorities wisely decided not to give out any details. He surmised that they had decided that as long as the attack had been thwarted, why worry the population about it. That alone would have had almost the same effect as if the mission had been successful. People would have panicked and the holiday would have been seriously compromised, as people would have felt too uncomfortable to go to the stores. Especially the larger businesses and malls where many people would have gathered and been considered targets. It was also apparent that if the authorities had any inkling as to who they were looking for they were not tipping their hand. His guess was that their disguise was still intact. If that were the case, then there would be other opportunities. They would just quietly sit still for a while and let others carry out their missions like they did during 9-11 and the anthrax attacks.

When they were comfortable that the authorities would be looking the other way, they would strike again. After all, they were the most important cell operating in the states. They were in a sense the nerve center, and as such were so deeply undercover and separated from most of the others that they would be the last to be considered terrorists. With that in mind, it would be wise for them to leave the city and relocate as soon as possible.

The three waited a day. Late the next morning Ahmed and his comrades left their apartment for good and boarded a bus for Union Station. As they road along, Ahmed stared out the window at the city. As he watching the neighborhoods pass he couldn't help but think about what had happened. It galled him that they had not completed their mission. To have struck at that time, the holiday season, so close after everything else, would have not only gone a long way toward demoralizing the population but would have had a very negative effect on the economy at a crucial time. It was the buying season, and with the economy so shaky it could have helped push it to the edge. The more he thought about it the more he did not want to wait before trying again. Once the New Year began and the holiday season was over it wouldn't be long before these Americans would be back to their normal routine and all they had accomplished would be little more than a footnote in their history books.

After they arrived at the station, Ahmed left the others and made his way alone to the ticket windows. If the authorities had a fix on anyone it would have been Majed. It seemed wiser to leave him and Lotfi in a coffee shop where they would be less conspicuous. He bought three tickets for New Orleans, the location of a safe house where they would easily blend in, then returned for the others. It would be less than half an hour before they boarded the train. Just enough time to have a drink for the road.

Ahmed had no sooner joined his friends in a rear booth than his attention was drawn to one of three television sets mounted to the ceiling. It was near noon and the set was tuned to one of the local news stations. He watched as the news rehashed what was happening around the world. The major part of the war in Afghanistan was for the most part over. Already there was talk about going to war against Iraq. There was the typical national news and sports. The country, though still caught up on 9-11, was indeed slipping back toward its normal way of life. Finishing their coffees, Ahmed motioned to the others. It was time to go. Look for other opportunities and hope they were not too late.

As the three men got up to leave, Ahmed's attention was suddenly drawn back to another television set on the wall. It was apparent that the network was doing an impromptu interview from some major hotel in the area. That in itself was of little consequence. What intrigued him was not the little girl the reporter was trying to interview but the woman standing beside her. Ahemd couldn't believe his eyes; after years of searching, there she was, Nishka, he was sure of it, and she didn't look a bit different than the last time he saw her. Of all the fates had to offer, they had thrown him this.

She was in the very same city he was in such a hurry to leave. And had it not been for the very media he so despised he would have never known she was near and would have missed her forever. Maybe there was still a chance his mission could be a success. Maybe even a bigger success than he could have ever imagined.

Chapter Twenty Eight

By the time David pulled the van into his driveway Nishka had become locked into reviewing scenarios over and over again concerning what could happen to her, and possibly the others, as a result of the unwanted media publicity. The drive had been over two hours through a blowing storm, yet Nishka hardly noticed any of it. "Thank you David; I will see you later," she said after David pulled out her bag. He asked when, but all she said was, "Maybe tomorrow." Nishka did not wait for him to say more. Instead, she silently turned and headed for home through the blowing snow.

No sooner had Nishka passed through her door than she dropped her bag and turned on the television. Before she had even taken off her coat or even turned on a light, the news came on. The woman reporter who had tried to interview them in the hotel that morning was standing in Tillers talking to Mr. Hines and the woman administrator from the shelter. As they talked, a crowd of shoppers had gathered.. "Did you ever dream you'd get the response you did from little Jessica Flores's gift?"

"No," said Mr. Hines, trying to sound as official as possible, yet at the same time humble in keeping with the Christmas sprit. "To tell the truth, in all my years I've never seen anything like it. Look at them all." Mr. Hines motioned to the crowds watching the interview. "Our switchboards have been inundated with calls from people wanting to know where this homeless shelter is. Even our employees have given up part, if not in some cases, all their bonuses to help whoever needs it."

As the interview continued and the station broke away to show scenes at the shelter and people donating gifts, Nishka found herself mesmerized. She could not comprehend how Jessica's gesture could have had such an effect on others, how people who had never heard of her before, or the homeless shelter, suddenly found the where-with-all to send whatever they could in toys, clothes, or cash. There were references to people saying this was just as important as the relief aid after 9-11. That it was time to help those in their own back yard, to share with others no matter how little they had or how much it cut into their personal holidays. There were even references to people stopping strangers on the street who they thought might be in need and offering food, money, or assistance.

Finally the station switched back to the department store. "It's truly a miracle," the shelter director added. "Food, clothing, and aid just keep coming in. We've never seen a Christmas like this."

As the interview concluded, Nishka's attention was drawn to one of the men in the crowd. He was tall, dark, and unmistakable. He was Ahmed. It took little deduction to conclude he had seen her in an earlier interview. It would be only a matter of time before he learned where she lived, at least the general vicinity. And for someone like him that was all he needed. The only question was how much time did she have before he was knocking on her door.

It was late when the doorbell rang. David, dressed only in his pajamas bathrobe and slippers, felt a strange sense of foreboding as he went to the door. No sooner had he opened it than Nishka rushed in carrying a large flat package wrapped in Christmas paper. "Hi, a little early to be delivering Christmas presents don't you think? What's going on?"

Nishka quickly looked around as if half expecting to see someone else. Seeing he was alone she handed David the package. "This is for Jessica."

"That's it! You scared the hell out of me when you phoned. I thought it was something serious."

"I am leaving," shot Nishka with an expression that said not tomorrow, or next week, but this minute, the moment after she left his house.

"Leaving! When? Why? What happened?

"Tonight, for good."

David looked at the package in his hands, then leaned it against the davenport. "This is kind of sudden! What's wrong, the law after you? Did I say something?"

"No. It is a long story."

"Hey, I don't care. I got all kinds of time. Maybe I can help." Dave paused, as a deep, sick feeling swept over him. "Hold on, let's talk about this! I care for you way too much to lose you now." For the first time that David could remember Nishka actually seemed speechless, frozen in place. Running on emotion and the craziness of the moment he moved closer putting his arms around her. "There I've said it. It took me two long months but there it is…. I love you."

Nishka turned away. "You can not love me!"

"Why not?"

"Because I am not real."

David laughed. "Of course you're not real. No one could look as lovely as you and be real."

Nishka pulled away again then sat down on the couch, struggling between a logic of silence she knew was right and the desire to go against everything instilled in her and tell him everything. Her directive said no, but in the end something deeper took hold, something that went beyond logic and self-preservation. It was the same deep feeling that said she could not just steal away in the night without seeing David one last time. "You do not understand, David. I am not human. I wish I were, so much sometimes I feel I could self-destruct. But I am not. David that is all I can tell you so please do not ask any more. All you have to know is there are people that are coming for me now. They want me and will stop at nothing to get me back."

David stood transfixed, not even sure of what he heard. It had to be some kind of joke or something. His knees felt rubbery. His head began reeling. Not knowing what to say he sat down beside her. "What are you are trying to tell me. That you're some kind of android or something, like the terminator!"

"Not if I can help it. It is a long story. I do not have time. The point is, if they find me that is what they would make me become. And I am afraid with all the publicity Jessica received they know where I am."

For a moment David thought he was dreaming, that he was on "Candid Camera", the focal point of some prank. That any moment Nishka would laugh and say "Just kidding, April fools." But there was no kidding in her expression. Just the stone seriousness he had come to know all too well. "You're kidding, right? I don't believe this!"

Nishka moved closer, wanting to touch him, to find some way to console him, convince him. "I wish I was. I wish I were as real as you and could suddenly wake up tomorrow and find this was all a dream. But I cannot. All I know for sure is that I have never felt about anything or anyone in my existence like I have since I met you and Jessica."

As Nishka talked, pouring out more in a few words than she had in her entire life, neither of them noticed Jessica in the shadows near the top of the stairs. Jessica listened, hoping that with everything being said, that somehow, through some magical divine miracle, her father would manage to wade through it all and love Nishka anyway, saving her from her nightmare.

David finally straightened up and brushed his leg, his expression was that of a man who, after trying desperately to accept something that seemed totally beyond comprehension, had finally decided to chuck it all and begin again somewhere else. "You mean to tell me all this time you've been hiding out here?"

Nishka nodded. "Most of all I have been trying to find a place for myself. To belong somewhere."

"And now they're after you. Who, the CIA?"

"No. I do not think they even know I exist. Terrorists. The ones that have been involved in the World Trade Tower and other attacks. That is why I have to go." Nishka abruptly stood up then looked back at David who seemed to still be trying to process everything he'd heard and decide whether he believed her or not. "I have put you all in danger. I am so sorry."

David finally looked up as if the truth finally sunk in. "You're telling me I've been in love with a machine!"

"Yes David, sorry to disappoint you." Nishka did not know if it was the way he said it or what it implied that bothered her more. The thought of her admitting things she would never have revealed to another soul and having him respond in such a manner cut through her like nothing she had experienced. "Do not feel so cheated. We are not that much different." she said tapping the side of her head with her finger. "The only difference between us is you are organic." That felt good. She had said what she said and she didn't care. With that Nishka turned for the door."

"Please no, No! Don't go!!" yelled Jessica from the top of the stairs. In her haste to stop Nishka from leaving, Jessica tripped on her nightgown and fell down the stairs finally coming to rest at the bottom landing, her head hitting the wall.

"Oh my God!!" yelled David jumping to his feet. Instinctively David and Nishka rushed to Jessica lying in a hubble at the bottom of the stairs. Without thinking David knelt down beside Jessica and gathered her up. "Oh Please God, no!!"

Chapter Twenty Nine

One dim light illuminated the dark and gloomy hospital room. Gloomy was too positive; morbid seemed a better description of the atmosphere, at least from David's perspective. He stood in the doorway watching Jessica lying lifeless in the hospital bed. All the tubes and wires running to her, connecting her to nameless machines, made Jessica appear so small and fragile. David tried to fight the agonizing sick feeling that shot through him. He felt so helpless, knowing there was nothing he could do, like he was trapped in some demented, nightmarish time warp, thrown back years to a similar room, a similar feeling of uselessness as he sat watching his wife die. Now he was back, caught in the same horrible nightmare, only this time it was Jessica, and as his stomach sank he knew there was nothing he could do.

The doctor had been in to check on Jessica a short time earlier. They had run all the tests. "The positive thing is her neck isn't broken," he said trying to sound optimistic.

David heard himself ask, "But?"

The doctor didn't respond. Instead he stared at the floor. David learned three years before what that silent's meant; it was not a good. Finally the doctor turned and looked David straight in the eyes. "We've done all we can. Only time will tell now. Unfortunately, the longer she's in a coma the less her chances." That was all he said. Helen was there. So were Carl and Nishka. His mother broke into tears and Carl quickly led her away. The doctor stayed only a short time longer. He mentioned something about conditions and percentages. David couldn't remember what he said or what it meant other than if he piled it all up and ran it through a strainer none of it sounded promising. The doctor ended with a pat on David's shoulder then left.

Nishka stood silently watching David. It was one of the only times he could ever recall her showing any real sign of emotion. "I am so sorry." he remembered her saying.

"Did Jessica know about you?" he asked.

Nishka nodded. "She is very bright."

"How long?"

"Five weeks and two days."

"How do you feel about her? Can you feel anything?"

Nishka looked straight into his eyes with an expression he had never seen before. As if at that moment nothing had ever meant more to her. "I would take her place right now and let my existence end if it would save her."

David didn't know what to say. He would have said the same and meant it. There was little doubt that she meant what she said. But if what she said earlier that evening was true then what was it worth. For something that had no life to give, what difference did it make? The words seemed hollow to David, along with everything else in the world. Worst of all, David couldn't help feel that had it not been for Nishka, Jessica would be home in bed safe and sound. Suddenly, for some unexplainable reason, he couldn't stand being near her. "I'm sorry but I need to be alone for a while." With that David turned back toward Jessica's bed.

Nishka had never experienced what she felt when David

turned away. She watched him sit down beside Jessica. The room had become so silent except for the whirring sound of a monitor bleeping its solemn message, "Jessica is still alive." She so much wanted to follow him, comfort him somehow. But she did not know how. She didn't know what to say that would help. So instead she turned away.

※

It was the next afternoon, December twenty fourth, two-thirty according to hospital clock on the waiting room wall. But then Nishka's built-in sense of time had already told her that. She sat in a waiting room on the same floor most of the night waiting for word that Jessica was improving, but no word came. She knew she should have left a long time ago, gone home, grabbed her belongings and disappeared into the abyss before Ahmed arrived and found her. It was only a matter of time she knew before he came. Still a part of her she had never known before wanted to stay, to make it up to David somehow, if that was possible, to make sure everything that could be done for Jessica was done. Nishka wanted to see her eyes bright with life just once more. Then Nishka could leave. She had talked to Carl briefly and to Helen a couple times, to learn how Jessica was doing. But the answer was always the same, no change.

Nishka found a Bible on an end table and started reading it. Though she had seen Bibles many times, she had never read one before. It took less than an hour to finish. She read it twice more, each time slower than the previous time. But though she found it full of many positive observations, she found little that pertained to her.

When it became clear that she could stay no longer without putting them all in danger, Nishka began to compose a letter. She had never written a personal letter before, especially one that exposed her or what she was about. It was a major sin to her being, her directive. According to her program, she was to keep information about her secret at all cost. Put that had ong since passed. Now she was about to confess all to David for no other reason than she felt she owed it. That she felt attached somehow; that somehow nothing else mattered other than she cared for him in a way she could not describe, let alone understand. Whatever it was, it made her feel he had the right to know.

Dear David:

What I am writing you would have been cause for termination three years ago, both your existence and mine. I am telling you this now because things have changed; I have changed. I have changed because of knowing you and Jessica, what you have taught me, and how much I feel for you both. I trust in you David, and as a result give you the only thing of any value to me, the truth about my existence.

As Nishka continued, she told David about where she was created and by whom, how she had considered her creator, her father of sorts, and how as the Soviet Union began to crumble he tried to sell her to terrorists like Joseph in David's Bible, only in the end to be rescued by him and set free. Nishka told of how she made her way to the United States, what she had done, and how she had lived alone for the past twelve years, afraid to ever get too close for fear of being discovered.

She told of how Ahmed had almost caught her in New York

and how she had seen him on television the night before. Nishka finished with how much the last few months had meant to her, how, like the crowning jewel of Christmas, she would always remember that period as the one time in her existence when she actually felt there might have been a chance for her, a place she could finally call home.

Since there was no time for her to dispose of her home and belongings, instructions had been left with a Realtor and lawyer that David be her executor, that all was to be sold, including the furnishings, and that the proceeds were to go into a trust for Jessica and Peter. She had even taken the liberty of leaving instructions on how the income was to be invested. "After all," she concluded, "that is my specialty."

Nishka folded the letter neatly, slipped it into a generic hospital issue envelope, addressed it, then slowly walked back to Jessica's room.

It was apparent Jessica's condition had not changed. David was asleep in a chair near her bed; other than that, all looked the same. Nishka stood for a long while in the doorway, transfixed by how innocent Jessica looked as she lay in her hospital bed. She had hoped to see Jessica's smiling eyes just once more and know all was right. But it was apparent that would not happen, at least not for her.

Deciding she could stay no longer, Nishka silently entered the room to leave the envelope when Carl returned carrying two cups of coffee. "Any change?"

"No. Helen went home a couple hours ago to rest and take care of Peter," whispered Carl. He watched Nishka walk a short ways into the room then stop and look at Jessica as her chest moved ever so slightly from the air passing through a tube into her lungs then out again. Carl set down the coffees and stood beside her. "Why don't you sit with her a while?"

"No, I better not."

Turning away, Nishka abruptly waked back out of the room followed by Carl. "I don't understand this. What's going on between you two. David won't come out when you're here, and you won't go in. Whatever it is you can't blame yourselves. No one pushed her! It was an accident."

Nishka shook her head. "It is deeper than that. And you would not believe it anyway."

"I think I do, though I find it hard to believe. David told me. Nishka stared at him not sure, for the first time in her existence, what to do or say. "Don't worry," Carl added sensing the seriousness and implications of what he had just said. "I wouldn't give you away. Besides, who'd believe me? Truth is, I'm not so sure I believe it myself. Why you? For what? Espionage, assassinations?"

"If necessary."

"But that isn't it. You have special skills, besides business and the market?" Carl paused, his expression changing from curiosity to shock at the realization of what he just said. "That's it isn't it. You could bring down the market!"

Nishka nodded, then paused, and looked into Carl's eyes while handing him the envelope. "Like a house of cards."

Carl studied the envelope. The more he thought about it, the more her lifestyle didn't surprise him. In fact, it made logical sense. What better way to bring down the capitalistic system than through the very means that made it unique and great to begin with. But then as far as her mission was concerned, she was too late. The government she was designed and built to serve had already collapsed, unable to support itself against a system it felt destined to overtake.

In a sense, it seemed ironic if not a wee bit sad, if it weren't so laughable. It also made sense why a rogue nation or group would find her capabilities so attractive. But then that was important now. The important thing was she was leaving, and there was nothing he could think of to dissuade her, whatever she was. "I take it this means I won't be seeing you again."

"I do not think so. This is the best I can do. It is important you give that letter to David when he wakes up."

It was apparent by Nishka's expression that there was no changing her mind. Putting his bear-like arm around her, Carl drew Nishka close and hugged her, then kissed her forehead. "God be with you."

"Thank you. I can truly say you have been one of the most understanding men I have met." Nishka did not say more, only smiled, turned, and walked away.

Chapter Thirty

The wind blew cold from the northwest as Nishka briskly crossed the deserted parking lot to her car. It was mid afternoon, only a few hours before Christmas Eve, and there were few visitors still in the hospital. The others, those like Jessica and the ones that had to take care of them, had no choice. Nishka never looked back after getting into her car. It was the only way; move on like she had done so many times in the past. After all, there were more pressing matters at home, like clearing out and staying one step ahead of Ahmed, provided she still had time.

As Nishka drove home, she reviewed what had to be done to make sure she would not be followed. For the first time, she felt an actual sense of loss. She had never invested much of herself in anyplace before but she had grown attached to this one. That was a strange sensation for her. Having been trained in subversive activities, one of the first things she learned was not to grow attached to anything, and -- above all -- never leave a trace. Being the good soldier she was, after Thanksgiving Nishka had made contingency plans in case the time came she had to leave in a hurry. Leaving her belongings and the house with David was something she had planned to do. It was expedient. It was only money, and she had made more than enough over the past nine years to replace what she would lose a hundred times over.

At least that was what she told herself. Deep inside there was more, something more primeval that had never been programmed into her. She had become attached to the children whether she wanted to admit it or not. They had become as close as she would ever come to feeling the desire and love of motherhood. They were her wards in a sense, and it was only right they inherit what she could not take with her.

As for the more personal part of Nishka's belongings, what she needed had been packed before she went to see David. Like her apartment in New York, she took only what could later be linked to her. The hard drive to the computer, her laptop, and a couple personal items special only because Jessica had given them to her. She already packed her car. Only a few bags remained, and the picture Jessica had drawn for her. Once those items were retrieved she would be gone.

The house felt strangely quiet in an almost foreboding way when Nishka returned. It took less than a few minutes to put the bags and framed picture in the car. Nishka made a last fast scan of the house to make sure nothing was missed, then put the keys in an envelope and left them in between the doors at David's house with a note. She hoped no one would hear her and her luck held. Neither Peter nor Helen saw her leave.

It had been a fast and clean getaway. Had Nishka still been in training she would have received an "A." In only a short time she would be beyond the city limits. This time there would be no trace of her and she would remain invisible until Ahmed was dead and no one anywhere would be alive to remember she ever existed. As she drove, the houses soon began to blur, none being any more significant than another. Then she saw Jessica's church. It stood ahead of her like a majestic sentinel. Before she knew it, Nishka had pulled over. She sat a moment staring at the tall edifice of brick and stone, its bell tower looming high above like it was reaching for the sky.

Why Nishka got out and went inside was a mystery even to her. She was not programmed to be impulsive; it was not in her systems. Yet as she stood alone inside the quietly reflective narthex, she felt as if she had been drawn there in hopes its calming powers could distill the loneliness she felt inside.

Slowly she walked toward the altar where the nativity scene stood for the night's pageant, the pageant Jessica would never see. Nishka stopped a few rows from the front then sat down in a pew. Bowing her head Nishka closed her eyes. If God was anywhere, then like Jessica said he had to be in this place she thought. When Nishka finally opened them again she found herself focused on the manger, standing silent, as if waiting for God's smallest angel that would never come.

Turning to the cross and figure of Jesus above the altar Nishka wondered if he knew about her. "God, I do not know how I fit into your grand scheme of things," she said softly, "or if I even count at all. But I so much want to believe that I matter, that I do count for something in your world. If you hear me, give me a sign. I do not ask for much. Only to be able to feel love like humans do. To be able to return it as well."

Nishka closed her eyes again for a long time. Finally opening them she looked back up at the cross. "If you cannot help me, Lord, then please, if there are still miracles in this world, please help Jessica. Give her back to those that can love her. You have enough angels up there in heaven. Please leave one down here for those that need her."

After bowing her head again, Nishka slowly got up to leave. As she neared the rear of the church, the woman who was the Christmas pageant director walked in, and seeing Nishka, stopped. "Hi, aren't you a friend of the Flores children?"

"Yes, I picked them up from your rehearsals a few times."

"I'm so sorry to hear about Jessica. Have you heard how she's doing?"

Nishka shook her head. "Not good I am afraid."

"That's too bad. The woman turned to leave then turned back. "Say could you wait a moment. I have something you can give her."

"I really have to...." Before Nishka could finish the woman was gone.

The director returned moments later with a small transparent plastic dress bag. "This is Jessica's angel costume. The girl taking her place was too big for it and, well, I know how proud she was of it. I thought she might like to have it."

Not knowing what to say, Nishka reluctantly took the bag, thanked the woman, then left.

Quickly returning to her car, Nishka draped the costume over the passenger's seat, then got in and began to drive out of town. Coming to a stop at an intersection, Nishka glanced at the bag, glanced at the light, then looked back at the bag long and hard. Suddenly spinning the car around she headed back to the hospital.

As Nishka drove, the thought of taking the costume to Jessica seemed more and more important, if not even more important than saving herself. Nearing the hospital she stopped for a red light. Two blocks ahead loomed her objective. As she sat waiting for the light to change, another car, dark and dingy pulled up beside her. At first Nishka barely noticed the car or the three men inside. But as the light changed and they pulled forward, the driver's face caught her attention. It was Ahmed.

Nishka immediately let her car fall behind. It was apparent they were headed toward the hospital. No doubt they had learned of Jessica's accident. It was also apparent they had not seen her. All she had to do was slow down and let them drive on, turn down a side street and drive away. She would be long gone before they knew it. After that it would be too late, they would never see her again.

Unfortunately there also was another possibility. She had learned long before her brush with them in New York how ruthless their kind could be to others. The possibility was all too real that they would not treat David kindly if they thought he knew something. That was only a theory but considering everything else it was a chance Nishka was not prepared to take. That left only one option. Show herself.

The tires slid erratically as Nishka sped up trying to catch the other car. Pulling slightly ahead she checked again. There was no mistaking Ahmed. In the back was his comrade from New York. The other one did not look familiar. After surveying her options, Nishka quickly veered left sideswiping Ahmed's car and immediately grabbing his attention. No sooner had Ahmed seen her than she hit the breaks, spun the car around, barely missing a van coming from the other direction, and took off heading back the way she came. As she drove, she watched Ahmed's car in her rear view mirror spin around and follow in hot pursuit.

Reaching the intersection where she first saw Ahmed, Nishka made a hard left, turning down the other street. Only half a block separated them as the two cars sped down the boulevard. In the second car, Lotfi barely managed to hang on as Ahmed frantically tried to catch up. Gripping the back of his seat with one arm, Lotfi pulled a small remote control, similar to the one Vladimir used years before, out of his pocket, aimed at Nishka's car and fired. "She's out of range!" he yelled above the roar of the road. "We must get closer!"

Nishka sped through an intersection as the light turned red then turned up a side street two blocks ahead. She turned down another side street, drove a short distance, then turned down an alley. Yet no matter what she did, Ahmed's car stayed behind her, less then a block away and closing. Near a series of railroad tracks close to the industrial part of town, Nishka finally managed to out maneuver them by turning down a narrow road past a line of railroad cars.

Quickly turning again she drove up an old wooden bridge that led over the tracks only to find the last quarter of the bridge gone. Throwing the car in reverse, Nishka backed over the bridge, spun the car around, and started back down the narrow road only to see the terrorists coming from the opposite direction.

Nishka slowed, then brought her car to a stop and waited. As they slowed she suddenly started straight for them. At the last moment both cars swerved, her car going through a fence into a freight yard then abruptly dying in a mound of snow. The terrorist's car slammed into a squad car coming down a side street. No sooner had Ahmed and his comrades climbed out of the car than Majed checked the policeman. "He's unconscious."

"Forget him," yelled Ahmed as he ran toward Nishka's car. "Now, before she gets away."

Lotfi nervously looked around as he followed but there was no one in sight. No one had seen the accident. The cold winter wind was growing bitter by the time Lotfi caught up with the others. Nishka's car was empty. Only a single set of footprints in the snow leading toward some distant ramshackle factory buildings gave testimony to her whereabouts. Without saying a word the three men trudged off following the footprints toward the buildings.

The wind began to blow harder, whipping the snow around as continued on. The footprints eventually led around the first building toward another long taller structure, apparently an old manufacturing facility. Unlike the other buildings that had been subdivided into warehousing it remained derelict. The tracks ended near a set of double doors. Finding one ajar, the three slipped inside.

The building was dark, illuminated only by dim light filtering in through high broken windows and skylights. Knowing they would track her footprints, Nishka had darted into the building planning to confuse them, double back and take the same route back through the snow, using their tracks to camouflage her own. Hopefully it would buy her time to develop a plan as it had become obvious she would unlikely be able to run.

It was also apparent that she would have to deal with them once and for all. If she got away, and Nishka was sure she could, it was for certain they would still go after David and his family as a means of finding her. That she could not accept. She had been designed not only for clandestine operations, but to confuse, stalk, sabotage and if necessary, eliminate. Though self-preservation was strong, the mission was always imperative. And the mission now was to deal with her pursuers, permanently if necessary. It was probably not what Vladimir had in mind when he made her fully functional, but it was what she was going to do now. Unfortunately, though her choice of buildings was good, her path had led her down a dead end. Trying to double back in the faint light she found her exit cut off.

As his two comrades cautiously moved closer, their weapons drawn, Ahmed began to feel uneasy. She had done the unexpected, uninitiated contact. Everything about her seemed different than he remembered, expected. Ahmed remembered how coldly she had pulled out her machine pistol and fired away the first time they met. What was she like now, he wondered? He felt a cold chill run through him as he pulled the remote from his pocket that Majed had given back to him. The same one he had carried with him since those cold days years ago in the Soviet Union. He watched Nishka, half expecting her to charge. "It's been a long time," he said trying to relax her, defuse what was certainly an extremely dangerous situation. "Don't be alarmed. We don't mean to harm you. We just want to employ your services for a while like you were intended."

Nishka slowly backed up as the three approached, all the time surveying her surroundings for options. "I do not believe you have my wellbeing in mind. Not according to Dr. Vladimir. I have my own agenda now. That agenda does not include terrorism."

"Terrorism is such a nasty word," said Ahmed as the three paused. "We are just soldiers fighting to bring about our own independence."

"Soldiers don't kill innocent women and children." Finding herself out of room, Nishka backed against the wall then quickly picked up a long length of pipe and prepared to defend herself.

Ahmed and the others moved a few steps closer, then stopped ten yards short. Ahmed's cautious expression changed to a sadistic grin as he prepared for Nishka's next move. "You know for such a smart computer you were very easy to catch. If you can't be more clever than this, I doubt you'll ever be worth much as an assassin."

"I was never meant to be an assassin and you know that. But if I am so inept why bother with me. Go about your business and leave me be," said Nishka, moving the pipe from one side to the other.

"Because we have money invested. Besides, even a soldier that is not reusable has potential." Ahmed sized her up, then laughed. "Of course, even if we don't use you in our cause as an assassin, I'm sure we can find other uses for you. But then in a moment you won't know the difference anyway, or care." Not wanting to drag out the discussion any longer Ahmed nodded to his comrades then slowly moved forward, two steps, three, aimed his remote and prepared to fire.

Suddenly Nishka charged like a lancer, pipe extended. Before she could reach them Ahmed fired the remote. Nishka tried to fight the impulse but within a few steps she slowed. Ahmed fired again and she finally came to a jerky stop. She appeared to try to override the command but another zap from the remote seemed to freeze her solid. "Drop the pipe please," said Ahmed in a stern voice. Nishka dropped the bar. "Stand up straight please." Nishka blankly stood tall. Her hands dropped to her sides. Ahmed and the others moved closer, their weapons raised.

"She's still as beautiful as I remember." said Majed lowering the automatic pistol and examining her from what he considered a safe distance.

"Yes, she is quite a piece of work. Vladimir certainly knew what he was doing when he created her. There were times I am sure that he thought of her as his daughter." Feeling confident that she was totally under his control, Ahmed slowly approached. "See, she's completely under my power. Just like Dimitri said she would. Imagine, she managed to live all this time in America by herself and no one knew. She's easily worth more than a hundred times what Vladimir asked for her."

Ahmed turned and smiled at Majed, You know it's a shame Dimitri couldn't be here to see this, but then we had enough people who understood Russian and he was never very cooperative.

"I think Allah would be pleased with her," said Lotfi. "Women have always been meant to serve and she will be the ultimate example."

"Yes, in one stroke she will make up for all the oppression we have felt at the hands of these infidels." Ahmed's face grew more passionate as he studied her closer, the totally blank expression in her eyes. "She will be the revenge for my brothers that I have always dreamed of. She will bring the glory of Allah to the world and make the Muslim faith the one true faith of all mankind."

"I think it's time we take her and leave," said Majed glancing around and beginning to feel uneasy. "Someone is sure to find the police car and begin looking."

"You may be right." Ahmed glanced around then turned back to Nishka. "It's time we leave my trophy. Follow me."

As the three started for the entrance, Majed in back, the other two leading the way Nishka dutifully followed. Suddenly without warning she sprang to life knocking the automatic pistol out of Majed's hand, grabbed him, then spinning him around and flinging him into Lotfi smashing them both into the wall. Before the surprised Ahmed could react, she spun around and caught him in the solar-plexus, doubling him up and sending him to the floor, the remote plopping to the ground in front of him. Gasping for air Ahmed weakly raised his hand in self-defense. "Stop, you're under my power!"

Nishka smiled as she picked up Ahmed's machine pistol. "Have you not heard, in this country they have freed the slaves." Scooping up the remote Nishka crushed it in her hand. Quickly grabbing Ahmed as he tried to climb to his feet, Nishka spun him around ramming his head into Majed knocking them both out. Realizing he had only one chance, Lotfi sprang for the other pistol, but before he could reach it Nishka grabbed him by his coat and pulled him to his feet. "You have a very poor level of respect for women. What you need is an attitude adjustment." Without waiting for a response, she nailed him with an uppercut knocking him out cold.

Knowing she had little time Nishka quickly went through Lotfi's pockets removing papers and anything else of importance. Next she went through Ahmed's clothing. In his inside coat pocket she found a small diary containing terrorist safehouses, names and plans, past and future, all in Arabic along with a computer disk. "You know Ahmed," she said scanning the diary. "You should never carry such material on you. Your people would not be pleased."

It took Nishka only a short time to find a cart large enough to hold Lotfi, Ahmed, and Majed. It took a while longer to cart them back to Ahmed's rental. After removing handcuffs from the unconscious policeman, she handcuffed Majed and Lotfi to their car's front bumper. She handcuffed Ahmed to the car's back bumper. Quickly checking his car, Nishka found other papers and a large amount of cash in a small briefcase. Leaving some of the papers in the portfolio, Nishka wrote a note explaining who the men were and placed it inside the squad car then examined the unconscious officer. "You will live." she whispered.

Nishka grabbed the second machine pistol from the cart and returned to Ahmed. Slapping him until he was conscious she drew him close. "How are we feeling?" She said she watched him rub his eyes while trying to grasp what happened only to find himself handcuffed to the car.

Quickly becoming conscious of his situation Ahmed sunk back as Nishka pointed the machine pistol in his face then held up his diary and other papers. "What I have here is documented information on your organization, information I do believe the American government would be more than happy to put to use. There are names of all our contacts, safehouses, enough to nearly eradicate your organization from the face of the earth." Nishka paused as Ahmed's eyes widened.

"What happened? You were supposed to shut down!" Ahmed said trying to grasp the turn of events, how could Nishka be operational when everything said she should be a walking zombie.

"I do not know. Maybe I have evolved," she said half smiling. "The important thing is I am in control. And if need be I could end your existence this instant, or anytime of my choosing. Do you understand that?" Ahmed nodded silently, almost half expecting her to exterminate him anyway. "Now that we understand each other, here are my terms. I suggest you listen hard." Nishka paused, then holding him firm, looked deep into his eyes. "Here is what I am going to do." Nishka nodded to the officer still unconscious in the squad car. "I have left enough with the officer to convict you. What I hold in my hand is insurance. I will put this in a safe place. Of course I have already committed it to memory," said Nishka, tapping the side of her head. Never, ever, mention my existence to anyone. Should you or any of your friends ever get free in your lifetime and decide to come looking for me again, if you even breathe a word of my existence to anyone, or in any way endanger any of those I have known, I promise you not only will I make sure this information reach's the proper authorities but I will become the avenging angel you so much wanted, only it will be you and those of your house that will be my targets. And no one but God himself will stop me!"

After she finished Nishka, held his diary out again. "I will keep this, for my security and yours." Believe me when I tell you this: If it were not for you being partly responsible for my freedom in a distorted way I would not do this. But it is Christmas and I feel merciful."

Ahmed knew what Nishka said was true. She would probably never be under anyone's control again, least of all his. He sensed that she was no longer concerned that he would ever come back and try to control her even if he could. And with that all sense of value for her in their cause was gone. With that a thirteen-year dream was gone.

Neither Ahmed nor his comrade said a word as they watched Nishka stand, then walk back to her car. After getting her vehicle started and back on the road, Nishka reexamined Ahmed and his friend to make sure they were still secure. She then returned to the squad car, radioed that an officer was down, popped the hood, and set off the horn. Before the officer revived enough to know what had happened and anyone else could arrive, Nishka had driven away.

Chapter Thirty One

The winter sun was just setting when Nishka drove away from the disabled squad car. As she passed through town in the fading light, she tried to rationalize what had happened to her, why the remote had no power over her. She had promised Jessica she would never kill and fortunately her encounter with Ahmed had not ended in a deadly manner. When she charged, she expected to lose control of her functions when he fired. Instead she felt only a mild tingle through her system that quickly dissipated.

Considering the situation, it seemed only logical to play possum, wait for their guards to drop then incapacitate them. But as to why she was not incapacitated, that was a mystery. Nishka could only deduce that when Vladimir fired his remote at her that night after the crash, he had canceled her restrictions. It must have also somehow destroyed the receiver in her that would have ever made her serviette again. Maybe that was what he had meant for her all along.

Vladimir had been a real genius when he created her. He had designed her from parts others in the facility had fabricated, but had no concept of their use. Dimitri had been a confidante, a gifted technician who Vladimir had grown attached to but never trusted enough to reveal the key elements that made her tick. Nishka did not know how she knew that, other than it had probably been implanted in her memory banks sometime during the final stages of her creation.

The only fact that mattered was that somewhere in her system there had probably always been a special time delayed preset code. A backdoor, escape clause, so that after Vladimir turned her over to the terrorists and safely walked away, she would have had the independent capability to evaluate her situation, make proper decisions, and escape if she so desired and make her own life. He called her daughter. No doubt freedom was the gift he wished for her. That made sense. After all, Nishka had always felt Vladimir considered her more than just a high priority government espionage experiment. That is what she hoped, anyway, that Vladimir had always considered himself her father, a father who cared for her very much.

Then again it could have been a miracle, that somehow after years of being on her own, Nishka had grown beyond being nothing more than a machine with no feelings. That instead Nishka had somehow evolved beyond being a walking program and became her own self, capable of true independent feeling, never having to fear coming under the control of any person or machine again. She would like to believe that too, that what happened was derived from her own growth, coupled maybe with a little help from God.

Somehow, Nishka could not quite accept something so abstract. After all, she did not feel, at least not the way humans did, or have the ability to give of herself without question, to care so much it hurt, to hurt so much she would cry. No, instead after in-depth analysis, she had to believe in the former. That it was Vladimir, something he programmed in her long ago that made her what she was now. Not only was it logical, but it made it possible to forgive that little glitch in her past that had troubled her for some time, that if he had cared for her so much, how could he have ever conceived of selling her like Joseph into eternal bondage. Because in the end he had never intended to. In the end, Vladimir had always intended her to be free. And he knew that when the time was right, probably sooner than later, she would have come to the realization that she was her own person with the ability to just pickup and disappear.

※

It was dark when Nishka's car pulled into the hospital parking lot. Only a handful of vehicles remained. The night air was cold, but still as Nishka carefully removed Jessica's angel costume from the car and headed for the door. The news media, having heard about Jessica's accident, had converged on the hospital like locusts. They were in the midst of interviewing David in the lobby, Carl standing nearby, when Nishka slid in unnoticed. David looked tired she thought, frazzled by all that had happened. He stood answering questions as best he could, yet all the time looking like he would rather be anywhere else. Nishka wished she could help him, stand beside him and help take the pressure, the blame. But she knew he would never let her. So instead she slipped through a side door, the angel costume under her arm, into a stairwell and walked up to Jessica's floor.

Nishka reached Jessica's room unnoticed and stood for a long time beside her bed. Jessica looked so small and fragile as she lay unconscious among the tubes in the large hospital bed. Eventually Nishka sat down and bowed her head. It seemed to Nishka that if there was truly a God, he was not in that room that night.

The interview with the reporters had gone on for nearly half an hour. At least that was what it said on the lobby clock, though it seemed more like a lifetime to David. He had not wanted to come down and talk to the press. But after a few of the less scrupulous media tried sneaking up to Jessica's floor for any information on what happened, David relented. His cooperation was granted only after it was guaranteed no one would try to invade Jessica's privacy. Though Carl and Judy were nearby for support, David still felt alone and near the verge of heaving. Finally a lanky persistent male reporter got his attention.

"How does your son feel about Jessica's condition?"

David shook his head at the reporter's callousness. "How do you think your son would feel," he shot back.

Not waiting for another question Carl stepped beside David and held up his arms. "I think we've had enough questions for tonight ladies and gentleman. It's Christmas. I suggest you all go home to your families. Hold them close, and if you really care, maybe say a little prayer for Jessica while you're there."

It was apparent Carl's statement had awakened a spark of sentiment in some of the reporters as they nodded then turned and left. Those that remained refrained from asking anything more as Carl and Judith escorted David back to the elevator. No sooner had the door closed and the elevator jerked into motion than Judith leaned back against the wall and shook her head. "I can't believe how insensitive some of your cohorts can be!"

"It's the heat of the moment," said Carl trying to defend some of the fellow journalists while simultaneously trying to avoid making a bigger issue out of it.

David said nothing. Instead he crumpled into the corner of the elevator like a ragdoll, beaten down by all he had gone through during the past twenty hours. He felt himself going numb as he listened to the hum of the elevator lifting him to the fourth floor and the solitude of Jessica's room beyond. He truly wished there had been better news. Wished he could have shouted out that Jessica was conscious and on her way to recovery. That with any luck she would be home for Christmas even if it was a couple days late.

That was what David hoped as he prayed, prayed harder than he had ever prayed in his life. More than he prayed three years before when his wife died. But then there had not been much time to pray back then. By the time he reached her side she was already given last rights. That cold miserable night there was little to do but pray. He had cursed God that night. Cursed him for taking away the only one that had ever meant anything to him. Maybe what happened to Jessica was his penance for what he said that night. Had he controlled his rage and asked God for forgiveness, maybe things would have been different.

This time he controlled his anger and vented his rage at his own stupidity and, of course, at Nishka for causing it all. Deep down inside he knew it was not her fault, but he blamed her anyway and instead prayed, and prayed, and prayed. But the reports had not improved. The swelling had not gone down like the doctors hoped. Instead moments slipped into hours, then more hours, and still the prognosis had not changed.

It wasn,t until David read Nishka's letter before going down to meet the media that he began to reevaluate his thinking. Then in the middle of the press conference, he suddenly realized what he had done. Nothing had changed from three years ago. David was still angry. Only this time instead of blaming God for what happened, he was blaming Nishka. It had never been Nishka's fault. If anything, she had been the most honest in her feelings and intent. It had been he who had refused to listen. He had been the one who had put his own vanity above the truth. She had been honest with him to a fault, her only intention being to protect them. Instead of trying to understand her, he had closed her out with his pain and prejudice. How dare she do what she did, lead him on in believing she was human! But in truth had he been half the person she was, he would have handled all that better and asked God's forgiveness.

David's mind was still crowded with thoughts of remorse and guilt when the elevator door opened and he walked toward Jessica's room. He would pray, he promised himself, harder than he had ever prayed before. Only this time it would be without hate or malice. He would ask for forgiveness for himself. It would all be so easy to do once he was alone with his daughter.

The room was strangely quiet, darker than usual when David entered. He stared at the empty bed for what seemed an eternity before the significance of the monitors all reconnected to themselves finally hit home. Jessica was gone.

※

The church was packed for the Christmas Eve pageant. The children in their costumes had mesmerized the congregation as the shepherds and angels gathered and Jessica's replacement began to sing her song to the live baby in the manger. At first no one noticed when the main door opened behind them with a flurry of cold wind and blowing snow. Nishka entered, passing the stunned ushers without saying a word, and walked toward the front of the church carrying the unconscious Jessica in her angel costume, wrapped in Nishka's coat. Those gathered in the pews nearest the aisle gasped as she passed. Even Helen, seated near the middle of the church, and Peter in the choir were stunned as they watched Nishka near the manger.

The girl taking Jessica's part paused then continued singing at the pageant director's urging. "..Take my hand: new life is free.... Please believe me, receive me: Together, forever we'll be."

As the children near the manger moved aside, Nishka knelt down. Unwrapping her coat, Nishka held Jessica near the manger as the girl continued to sang. "From the day you are born I will be here beside you."

Nishka slowly began mouthing the words as the song continued. "As your life passes by, I will be by your side. Thru today and forever, when you worry and sigh." Nishka's eyes began to water as she finished the song with the girl, "Everyday hear me say, 'here am I Lord, here am I'." When the song ended, Nishka held Jessica's limp body next to the cradle. "Baby Jesus meet Jessica....the best little angel you will ever have. Take care of her."

As Nishka's tears began to fall, some onto Jessica's face, the manger appeared to glow from the smile of the baby inside. Suddenly Jessica's eyes flickered, then opened slowly until at last they were focused on Nishka. "You stayed."

"I could not leave you," whispered Nishka.

Jessica touched Nishka's eyes. "Tears?"

Nishka choked a weak laugh. "They are, aren't they?"

Jessica weakly turned to the baby in the cradle as the front door opened and David and Carl rushed in then on down the aisle. David knelt by Nishka's side and watched as Jessica weakly reached out and touched the cradle. "See Daddy, I told you it was Jesus."

"You're right dear," whispered David hugging his daughter. "It is Jesus."

The church glowed a little brighter that night as David and Nishka held Jessica and the congregation began to sing.

The director had produced many a Christmas pageant over the years, and seen numerous others. But she would never forget that one holy night when a wonders Miracle happened in a make-believe Bethlehem. The night that miracle changed lives near that little cradle and made a family whole.

The End

Christmas Eve

It was late that night, or early the next morning, when Steve finished the manuscript. There was little sign of life in the terminal. An occasional worker passed who was still on duty. A few other weary travelers lay on scattered benches asleep. No one other then Steve was up, and Carl who of course, was still standing guard at the window, staring at the windswept void beyond. Jules woke once, checked again on the whereabouts of their transportation. There had still been no word. He wrote in his diary a while, no doubt documenting the fact that they would probably be condemned to exile in the terminal from hell until some time after the war ended, then fell asleep again. Marlene woke up once to, went to the washroom, smiled wearily when she returned then went back to sleep, her coat pulled tightly over her like someone deliberately trying to hibernate through the winter.

Carl periodically watched Steve read but said nothing.

When Steve finally finished, he gently closed the worn manila cover, then stared at it as Carl turned toward him.

"Carl didn't get as much play as he deserved," smiled Steve.

"It wasn't his book. It's hard to be an observer most of the same time."

"What about Jessica? Did she live?"

"What do you think?"

Steve thought a moment. He knew how he would end it, the same way most people would. But then it wasn't his book. "Nishka and David. You never tell us what happened to them?"

Carl smiled. "What would you have wanted to happen?"

That wasn't fair, but then considering the two it was a good question. After all they weren't your average couple. Steve leaned back and stared at the ceiling, then turned back to Carl. "I don't know." That was the truth; Steve had only been in love once. They had gone together for three years, last year of high school and through their junior year at collage before she broke it off. Something about not being ready to commit, she said. He often wondered if she meant him or her. Last he heard, she was married to a druggist somewhere in Toledo. It hurt when he heard that. Their last week was something he never wanted to go through again. He did not take being hurt emotionally very well.

Maybe that's why he was in this god-forsaken country to begin with. Traveling the world, viewing it all like an outsider instead of a player, was the safest way to be. Problem was, in the end, even observers become involved -- if not physically, then emotionally, and emotionally can be the hardest of all. And what he'd seen the last few months was more than he could handle. It was like the end of his relationship. He found he was taking a little of it all with him whether he wanted to or not -- like a collector picking up little pieces of rocks, each small and different, of no real weight or significance. Problem was, after a while all those tiny rocks began to add up to where they were no longer insignificant.

Now he was asked how the story should have ended. He wasn't even sure he could resolve the stories he was already carrying around. "I would like to say he could overlook her differences. That they managed to find a way to live happily ever after. That would have been a real miracle. Unfortunately, that isn't reality. So what happened?"

Carl shrugged. "Who knows? All I know Steven, is what happens in reality is seldom what one expects."

"Well I can't say it wasn't moving, to bad life isn't like that."

"You never know. Sometimes you find it when you least expect it." With that Carl turned away from the window in a manner that seemed to indicate he had come to grips with the fruitlessness of his vigil, and sat across from Steve. He was silent a moment, then stroked his beard like a man deep in thought. Finally he looked up. "The important thing, Steven, is we all have to believe in something, believe people can eventually see what's important; see beyond their differences. We have to believe that if we're ever going to survive this world, we cannot be blinded by prejudice."

"Like Jessica. I think that's the beauty of this story. How children have the ability to see beyond the surface and find what's really important in the world and people around them. I think what we need to survive is the blind faith of a child like Jessica. She was not only able to feel her father's loneliness, but also believe that in the end Nishka would finally develop the ability to reach beyond herself, to develop the ability to not just see black and white, but understand the shades of gray in between."

Steve looked at the manuscript again, then at the title printed boldly across the cover. "When do you think we lose that ability to see things so simply?"

"I don't know, probably when we reach our teens and find out the world is not as beautiful as we dreamed." Carl looked around the shabby terminal, then at the window and infinite world beyond. "In a land like this, where dreams die early, fear and hate never give hope much of a chance. But that doesn't mean it isn't here. All one has to do is look hard enough."

Steve shook his head, then gently touched the cover of the manuscript again. "In answer to your question, I hope David had enough strength to make it work. I know if it had been me that night I would have changed."

"Would you?"

"A miracle like that! If I had seen something like that there's no way I would feel as empty as I find myself now. Like Jessica said, you have to have something to believe in. Something to hang your hat on." Steve looked at the first page again, then handed the manuscript back to Carl. "I guess that's what blind faith is all about."

Steve watched Carl put the manuscript back in its protective cloth folder, then carefully wrap it up in the cloth before putting it in its waterproof plastic pouch. "I do have one question, why'd you use your name as the brother-in-law?"

"I don't know, made it easier to write I guess. Kind of therapy. It made me feel a little more a part of it." Carl paused as if mulling over a sudden thought, then turned and slid the package back into his bag. "Actually, there were a couple other names I should probably have changed. But at the time making it more personal seemed the only way to write it."

"So what changed for you? What gave you so much faith?"

"This book." In a sense I was a lot like David a few years ago, and a little bit like you. It's easy to think you have it all figured out until something goes wrong. Until you see so much evil that after a while you begin to become callous to it all. That's when it's hard finding any good in mankind, or in

David's case withdraw into your own little world and give up looking, whether it be for miracles or that special someone." Carl didn't say any more on the subject. Just laid his bag back down on the floor then slowly climbed to his feet. "Well it's about time they come, don't you think? I'd still like to make it home for Christmas."

"Wait, one more question," asked Steve. "What about Nishka? Did she actually become human?

"What do you think?"

"Don't give me that. Don't you know? You wrote it?"

"What would you like her to be?" Not waiting for a response, Carl walked back to his post at the window and resumed watching the sky.

"That's not fair!" Before Stave could say more, Jules began stirring, then opened his eyes, stretched, and looked around. "I see I'm still here."

No sooner had the words left Jules mouth than a clerk rushed over. "Your plane is here! It's coming in!"

As Steve silently watched, Jules jumped to his feet and rushed to the window, shaking Marlene as he passed. "A plane's coming!"

Barely conscious, Marlene struggled to focus on Jules as he stood beside Carl, straining to see through the dark night and occasional blasts of snow. Finally in the distance he saw the landing lights of an approaching aircraft barely visible on the horizon. "He's right; a plane is coming!"

The lights steadily grew larger as the lumbering craft neared the far edge of the runway, touched down, then rolled through the blowing snow toward the terminal. As the plane turned against the cold night sky, Jules could barely make out its design. She was a two engine craft, and looked ancient though well preserved, either way, she was a wonderful sight. She had been a passenger plane, probably carried twenty-six in her prime. Now she was probably used more for cargo than anything else. Most surprising she was a true vintage DC-3.

"Now that's what I call a miracle," said Marlene pulling herself together.

Steve didn't say a word. Instead he watched Carl as the lumbering plane pulled to a stop thirty yards from the terminal. There was a confident air in Carl's face, combined with possibly a small trace of relief. But the relief seemed not so much for him as it was for someone dear who had finally come. And that feeling seemed to build as he put on his coat. "It's time to go everyone," Carl smiled, picking up his bag and starting for the door.

A small ladder had been rolled up to the door on the side of the aircraft as the four bundled souls huddled close together and trudged through the blowing snow gusts. The opened door and dim light from inside was a welcomed beacon of embracing warmth. Steve could hardly wait to get in and out of the biting cold as he looked up thorough his pulled-up collar. As they neared the wing, he suddenly noticed through the blowing snow the emblem of a cherub painted on the plane's nose and the name. "Smallest Angel."

Marlene boarded first, followed by Jules, Steve, and finally Carl. Each attempted to kick off as much snow as possible as they entered the plane, trying subconsciously to show respect for the ship that was about to ferry them home. As they walked forward towards the front and only two rows of seats on the plane, a pleasant, well-groomed man in a dark leather jacket and flight hat greeted them. He had a silver metal nametag pinned to his lapel. Etched on it was the name 'David'. "Sorry for the delay," he said warmly. "This storm didn't give us much to work with. I suggest everyone leave their seat belts on. It could be a bumpy ride."

Everyone took their seat except Carl who, after storing his bag, followed the attendant up to the cockpit. Steve watched him pass without saying a word. It was just a coincidence he told himself, nothing more. Just wishful thinking tied to a vivid imagination. He would forget it and try to get some sleep, because that was all that mattered. That and getting home.

That's what Steve told himself, but he couldn't relax. Instead, he found himself sitting stone ridged. Then like a man possessed, sprang to his feet and followed Carl forward. His curiosity rising beyond control, Steve continued past the bulkhead in front of the cabin, then past a small service station, to a narrow door leading to the cramped cockpit where the attendant had taken the copilot seat.

"Like to introduce you to Steve, the newest member of my traveling circus," said Carl as Steve poked his head through the door.

The copilot turned back and nodded. "You're in good hands, Steve. Carl there will never steer you wrong. In fact, he's almost as good as our pilot."

The pilot smiled at her companion's remark, a loving smile of one who cared. Then turned from the serious business of checking her instruments and winked at Steve. "Hope you enjoy the flight."

"Thank you." Steve was sure he felt himself blush. She was an attractive woman, probably one of the most beautiful he had ever seen, with long brunette hair held in place by her headset. He was sure he detected the hint of a tall well-proportioned body hidden under her flight uniform. He forced himself to look away and not stare at her angelic face, or the nametag that read 'Nishka' on her lapel

"Merry Christmas everyone," said Carl.

"Merry Christmas," smiled Nishka. "Time to go home."

Steve never said another word after returning to his seat. Instead he watched the blowing snow outside and listened to the engines roar as the plane slowly moved down the runway, then lift off the ground. The story had ended for him just as he hoped it would. And that knowledge helped settle him that night. What was left behind slowly faded away, replaced by hope and visions of Christmas future. With a smile on his face Steve eventually closed his eyes and drifted off to sleep.

J. E.

Printed in the United States
By Bookmasters